BROTHERS

Kirk Weddell

DEDICATION

To;

my wonderful wife Mary for your unconditional love
and support; Mark Shields and Christopher Taylor for
your insightful comments on the screenplay and all
of your help with the novel; Ian Sillett for keeping my
creative flame alight; Philip Athans for your guiding
hand; Dick & Rosa Lonergan, Sara Smillie, Jim &
Carey Hammond and Louise Shoult for your keen
eyes and diligent notes; Mum & Dad for inspiring me
to dream; my brothers Craig and Scott for our journey
thus far and for all the adventures still to come; my
Irish friends and your enchanting culture that inspired
me to write this story; and to puppy Coco for keeping
my feet warm under my desk.

I hope that I can give back all that I have been given.

ABOUT THE AUTHOR

 Kirk is an award-winning British writer and filmmaker who currently resides in London. He graduated with a BSc (Hons) on the first Neuroscience degree course taught in the U.K. His study of the mind instilled his love of psychology and character that inspires him to write. He was shortlisted for the prestigious Academy Nicholl Fellowship for his science fiction screenplay *Alone* and won Grand Prize at the Writers Store Screenplay Replay Contest for his *Brothers* screenplay, which is the foundation of this book, his debut novel. When he is not writing, Kirk likes to be either up in the air, on the sea, or strumming his guitar.

You can visit him at:

www.kirkweddell.com or www.brothersnovel.com

Published by Clink Street Publishing 2019

Copyright Kirk Weddell © 2019

First edition.

The author asserts the moral right under the Copyright, Designs and Patents Act 1988 to be identified as the author of this work.

ISBN:
978-1-913136-48-2 - paperback
978-1-913136-49-9 - ebook

DISCLAIMER

This is a work of fiction. Names, characters, places, and incidents are the products of the author's imagination or are used fictitiously. Any resemblance to actual events, locales, or persons, living or dead, is entirely coincidental.

PROLOGUE

Don Pedro de Mendoza, the war-weary Captain of El Gran Grin, roared out a loud, crude sailor's oath when the deck dropped from under his feet and slapped the lid from his hand. The heavy laden chest slid, leaving more furrows in the already torn plank floor of his quarters. The twenty-eight-gun galleon tossed him off his feet, and he ended up half sitting, half lying, on his sea and rain-soaked bunk.

The chest slammed into the wall, rattling a lantern that had long-since blown out. Don Pedro gritted his teeth and sucked in a hissing breath. His entire body tensed—then the ship lurched again, forward this time. Don Pedro took as deep a breath as he could, sucking in enough rain and salt spray to make him choke. He pushed himself off his bunk and, with the practiced gait of a veteran seaman, danced his way across his cabin to the chest, which obliged by sliding neatly toward him.

The lid had slammed closed, and Don Pedro checked one set of iron hinges with his bruised, almost-numb right hand and the other with a quick glance. If they bent any more, locking it would be a waste of time.

"*¡Capitán!*" a man called from the doorway—Don Pedro hadn't heard the door open, or at least hadn't been able to pick that sound out from the racket of his ship being ripped to splinters on the jagged rocks.

"*¡Fuera!*" Don Pedro roared back, pressing down with all his considerable weight on the lid of the chest. He blinked up at the seaman who stared back at him, eyes wide, blood pouring from under his hairline to mix with the rain and paint his face a livid orange in the flickering illumination of the nearly constant lightning.

"*¡Las rocas!*" the sailor shrieked back.

Don Pedro lunged at him, riding the heave of the deck under his feet to crash hard into the man. He took up the sailor's torn and drenched tunic in his fists and bellowed into his face, "*¡Vete, perro estúpido!*"

He pushed the sailor back out of the door. For a moment Don Pedro thought the sailor had slapped him across the face, but then his mouth filled with a rain-drenched cloth. He grabbed at it as he half-fell, half-stepped back into his cabin. The door slammed in front of him, striking the toe of his thick leather boot and sending a knife of pain up his leg. He swore again and tumbled back, and the lightning illuminated the cloth—a tattered quarter of the pennant of the Squadron of Biscay.

Tossing the flag aside, he fell to his knees and cast out on both sides for anything to grab onto. The ship lurched again, and he huffed out a breath but managed to stay on his knees at least. Lightning flashed bright and close, and he could finally see the ruin his cabin had become—heirlooms lost, charts soaked and torn, glass and splintered wood everywhere. The cabin leaned hard to the port side. Thunder crashed above him, so loud his ears began to ring.

The chest slid past him, following the thunder with the grinding sound of its iron bindings once again tearing through the decking. The chest caught something Don Pedro couldn't see, and then it tumbled over.

"¡No!" he shouted, but the chest tipped to one side, then plowed the rest of the way into the wall.

Lightning flashed again, revealing the blazing reflection of a mountain of gold coins—a king's ransom, a treasure no man could ever turn his back on, a fortune worth a hundred galleons of Spain—all to pay for safe passage home in case of capture. Ransom money for a ship and crew not yet held hostage. It was more gold than Don Pedro had ever dreamed existed in any one place, let alone that he'd ever be trusted with its safe passage.

Safe passage …

Don Pedro surged to his feet and took two long steps, then fell onto the chest. The ship rocked under him again and there came a splintering crash—wood ripping itself apart. *"El mástil,"* he whispered to himself. He couldn't hear the words over the sound of the mast coming away, but the feel of the words on his lips made his flesh crawl. *"Dios,"* he cried, *"¡Dios me ayude!"*

And he pushed the lid closed. A few of the coins slid away as the ship rocked again, not coming back to center but listing ever more to port with each deafening crash. The gale whistled, so he couldn't hear the coins bounce away, couldn't hear the sound of the lid finally coming closed. He'd saved most of them—lost only a few.

And how many men? he thought.

Don Pedro shook that thought out of his head, spray whipping from his dense gray beard. He caught sight of himself in the mirror his wife had given him— just a glimpse as it rolled past to shatter against the wall. He looked older—older even than he felt. The lines in his face were deep, the bags under his eyes deeper still.

Holding the lid closed with his whole body weight, Don Pedro tore the ornate gold key from the chain around his neck. Holding tight to the bow, beautifully, lovingly shaped into a crown-and-anchor. He made three attempts to stab it into the keyhole of the big black iron lock while his ship broke apart. He could hear it being torn to shreds, and he screamed in harmony with it.

The deck dropped from under him, and the chest slid away. Don Pedro turned the key to lock the chest, then yanked it from the hole as he fell back and his head slammed against … something. His bunk? The ship listed harder to port. He held on to the side of his bunk with his left hand to keep from sliding. The portside bulkhead came away then, revealing the storm-tossed sea only a few feet beneath him.

Lightning arced across the sky, and he could see land.

"*Dios me ayude,*" he said, squinting into the rain, his words drowned out by the roar of thunder.

He put the heavy gold key to his lips and kissed it, and the deck fell out from under him. The cold sea surged in, and to Don Pedro de Mendoza it felt as though the whole of the ocean had fallen atop him. He grabbed for something, anything to keep him from the water and the rocks. His fingers found cold steel—he couldn't see what it was—but before he could register that perhaps he'd saved himself, whatever he held came free of whatever held it and he was falling. The air was driven from his lungs, and he closed his eyes so he couldn't see himself taken from his ship, from his command, from his treasure, to die on the cruel rocks of a foreign shore.

CHAPTER 1

The water ran brown, bits of hard-packed dirt and flakes of rock swirling away from his hands.

Owen tried once more with the soap, and a little more dirt came off. He rinsed his hands again, satisfied with good enough, and turned off the tap. He couldn't get the towel to budge on the first try—he'd set his heavy pick down on it. When he finally got it free, he ended up adding a little more dirt to his hands. Thunder rumbled in the distance—miles away—and Owen glanced at his watch. He took a deep breath, cleared his throat, and rubbed his face with the towel. More little bits of dry dirt, bits of pebbles, and the odd twig of thin, desiccated root came loose from his thick gray beard. He knew he was rubbing as much dirt into the deep lines of his face and the bags under his eyes as he left on the old towel, but he rubbed it in just the same.

He turned to the living room—which was really just another part of the same room with no wall to separate it from the kitchen—and took a deep breath, letting it out with a puff of his cheeks. He wanted to get out of his grimy, light blue, collared short-sleeved shirt—spend more than a few seconds cleaning up, maybe—but there was more work to be done. There was always more work to be done.

The living room was furnished by someone who took the word "furnished" at its most literal. There was a leather armchair that was surely older than Owen himself, a low bookcase cluttered with books and unopened mail ... very little else. The lighting was dim, so the distant lightning was difficult to ignore, flickering in the dirty windows. Owen lumbered his burly frame across the room, tossing the towel onto the bookcase to cover the stack of unopened mail.

He shivered a bit in the drafty room—it was never warm in there, no matter the time of year. At the end of the room was the lantern tower, barely three-dozen feet across. He ambled slowly—tired, sore, stiff—to the foot of the stairs that spiraled up along the wall. Lightning flashed again, and it took almost until he got to the top of the stairs for the still-distant rumble of thunder to make itself known.

The drive shaft of his lighthouse beacon ran down the center of the tower, clad in black-painted steel. The paint was beginning to chip. Owen would have to see to that. Below, the custom-built motor that was installed after the original clockwork mechanism was removed rumbled away. Owen stopped at the top of the stairs. He breathed hard, almost panting, though it wasn't too high up—not too many stairs, just too many hours of hard labor.

Too many years.

He cleared his throat with a growling resolution that made his chest puff out a bit as he stepped into the lantern room at the top. It was a little tighter up there but the paneled windows made it feel open, endless. A glass door gave way to a balcony that went all the way around—the black paint on the steel railing even more chipped and starting to show signs of rust again. Rain beat down on it, streaking the windows.

Another flash of lightning, and Owen saw it arc from the low, gray-black clouds to the northeast. It must have struck somewhere between Corraun and Glassillaun. He didn't bother looking down, over the edge of the cliff upon which his lighthouse perched. Below were rocks that might have been the fangs of a dragon—a monster with a hunger for ships.

In the middle of the room, the lantern lamp itself sat encased in a lensed glass dome. With his light safely turned off, Owen opened a hatch in the housing of the lens mechanism and squinted into the works. He went round to the little workbench and grabbed up a clean rag and an oil can.

The windows rattled from a gust of wind, and Owen stopped, listening to the *bean sí*—or banshee's—shriek he knew would follow. However many times he'd heard it, still it gave him pause. His chest tightened, and he rubbed the back of one rough hand across his furrowed brow.

The shrill call of the wind died down, and Owen went back to crouch in front of the lantern works. Just a drop of oil here, a few more there, then he wiped the excess away with the rag. He squinted again—a drop too much there—and dabbed it away with a clean corner of the rag.

Lightning again, and thunder following closer on its heels. He stayed there, crouched in front of the mechanism, satisfied that it was in good working order but feeling no need to stand too soon. He had a minute. He could feel his lighthouse around him. He felt its pulse, its breathing, as though it were a living thing. He knew precisely when to turn the lantern on and when it was safe to turn it off. And he hadn't missed that precise moment in … He had never missed it. It was his job not to miss it.

His calves started to tingle as he closed the hatch, and he dragged himself to his feet with a hand on the black-painted steel frame of the lantern, just then feeling even older than his sixty-five years.

It passed soon enough, and Owen replaced the oil can and rag, then grabbed hold of a steel lever. It was like something out of an old steam train or some antique piece of construction equipment. He squeezed it closed, pushed it down, and let go. It clacked into place, and the floor vibrated a little. With a groan to humble the *bean sí*'s screaming wail, the motor engaged and the lens began to turn. Then another big cast-iron switch thrown to turn the lamp on and the lantern burst into life. Owen knew better than to look directly at it, so he turned to the windows and looked out west over the North Atlantic. The water was gray in the fading light, and wind-tossed breakers threw themselves at the rocks a few hundred feet below. Had a great sea dragon reared up out of the frigid water at that moment, Owen wouldn't have been surprised. The sea was an ancient gray, so vast and old …

He felt the heat of his light as it washed over his back, and he gently closed his eyes as it reflected in the glass in front of him. The lantern left a red glow through his eyelids, steady and true, and it was as if Owen could see his own heart beating. He could see his light's heart beat, anyway, and that made him smile.

The rain seemed to die down a bit, and Owen nodded to himself, then made his way, a careful step at a time, back down the gently curving stairs to the lighthouse keeper's residence. He held the drive shaft housing, not the railing, as he went, and timed his steps with the thrum of the motor, a last check to make sure it was running smoothly and at the proper speed.

Owen stopped at the front door. It rattled a little from the wind, and Owen grimaced. A hinge had come loose. As he crouched down to investigate, he noticed a letter had been slipped through his door.

Was that all the day's post? Just the one?

With a grunt Owen bent to scoop the letter up and went to toss it on the pile with the rest of them, when something made him stop—four identical stamps with the American flag? His thick navy-blue fleece jacket with worn leather elbow pads was sprawled over the back of the leather armchair. He took his reading glasses from the right pocket, which was the baggier of the two, and put them on.

They were American stamps, all right, with their flag and the single word "FOREVER." The letter was addressed to him:

> Mr. Owen Kerrigan
> The Lighthouse
> Clare Island
> Ireland

Someone had stamped it "AIRMAIL."

Owen licked his lips, and they felt as rough as sandpaper against the tip of his tongue. His mouth was dry, and his hands shook. Still, he turned the small envelope over and read:

> Ciara Kerrigan
> 114 Spruce Avenue
> Boston, MA 02129 USA

He stared down at the address until his eyes began to blur.

Then he cleared his throat, put away his reading glasses, and took a few steps to the bookcase. The towel had slipped off, taking some of the mail down with it, and Owen bent just a little, moving to pick up the letters, but instead he reached for the towel and threw it over his shoulder.

On the top shelf, between a copy of *The Armada* and a dog-eared *Granuaile*, was his lighthouse's lone photograph. It was framed in tarnished silver, setting off the faded old black-and-white image of two boys, one—the older, better groomed of the two wore glasses and had his arm around the shoulders of the other, who looked like he'd been playing in the dirt. They wore identical sweaters. Owen remembered that his was blue and the other one green, but in the photograph they were only dark gray.

He blinked at the photograph for a few seconds, then picked it up. He held the frame closer, but the image blurred. He didn't want to put his reading glasses back on. He knew what the photograph looked like anyway.

He put the frame back down, a little too hard, and stifled a small gasp.

But the glass didn't break. There it stood, in its tarnished silver frame, none the worse for wear.

The door rattled on its hinges behind him and he

could just barely hear the thin, ethereal wail of the wind. He stuffed the letter into his baggy fleece pocket. The storm was coming in. The wind picking up. The rain coming back harder.

He brushed off as much of the dirt and dust from his clothes as would give way, then slid his arms into his fleece and resisted the temptation to look back at the photograph as he zipped it up and opened the door to the falling night and the pounding rain.

• • •

Owen could hear the music long before he opened the door to the Clare Island Community Center.

He was already brushing off the rain from his fleece as he stepped in, barely registering the interior of the place. He'd been there so many times, he knew every inch of every corner of it, from the little stage barely big enough to hold the three-piece band—a few of the local boys with their guitar, violin, and accordion— to the cramped booths set up along the walls. He remembered when they'd put the big televisions in and hadn't liked it.

Darragh was at the bar, and he and Owen exchanged a quick nod. Owen stood just inside the door as the rain dripped off his fleece to pool on the cheap linoleum floor. So many coats had hung there after so many rainstorms over so many years; the floor should have worn away by now, like a canyon dug out of the bedrock over millennia.

His fleece was a little damp, but despite its age it still provided a reasonable barrier to the elements. It would soon dry out, so he decided to keep it on rather than hang it with the other coats.

Then he sat on the same stool he always sat on and gave Darragh another nod. He was a strapping kid—man, Owen quickly reminded himself. Darragh had to be thirty, but to Owen he would always just be one of the local kids … and one of the few who hadn't hared off to Dublin, London, New York, Boston, or … just about anywhere else but lonely Clare Island.

There was a football match on the big, too-bright flat screen hung behind the bar, but Owen paid it no mind.

Owen reached into his fleece pocket and pulled out the letter just as Darragh set a glass of whiskey down in front of him.

"The lotto tracked you down for your winnings, have they, Mr. Kerrigan?" Darragh quipped with a cheeky smirk.

Owen stopped him short with a little grunt, a grimace and a shake of his head; he obviously wasn't in the mood for wisecracks. Darragh shrugged and wandered off down the bar, grabbing a remote control on his way. He started flipping through the television channels. Blinding bursts of static alternated with the muted images of another football match, rugby, some kind of monster movie … and Owen looked away.

The letter, still unopened, felt heavy in his hand, though it might not have contained more than a single sheet of paper. He slid a thumbnail under the edge of the flap, then decided he needed a drink first. He set the letter down on the bar, face up so only his own address looked at him—a little less accusatory than the other—then he took up the shot of whiskey and almost spilled it when the door burst open, startling him.

Mary O'Reilly came in, arm in arm with another woman. Owen, though he only meant to give them a quick scowl and then go back to his drink, noticed the resemblance. This woman could have been Mary's sister.

They were both soaked to the skin and laughing—cackling really. Owen turned his attention back to the letter and set his glass back down on the bar without having taken a sip.

"I can't believe you're here," Mary shrieked, her manner too girlish for a woman in her fifties. Owen furrowed his brow and worked at ignoring them both, though he couldn't help but find her uncharacteristically manic. "Come on, you have to meet everyone."

Not everyone, Owen thought, and just like that they were behind him, both of them, hovering over him. He could feel the rain-drenched warmth of them.

Darragh came over, stopping right in front of

Owen before Mary even started to say, "Darragh, you have to meet my lovely cousin Ellen. She's come back from California after … too many years? She's going to write a book."

"Pleased to meet you," Darragh replied, and Owen couldn't help but think maybe his accent had suddenly gotten thicker. He wasn't a kid anymore, but he was still young enough to lay it on for the American girls—even if this one had only been temporarily American. "Got fed up with all that sun, did ya?"

As loud as the music was, Owen couldn't avoid the conversation happening right around him. Without hardly standing up all the way, he shuffled along a few stools farther from Mary and her cousin. If anything, the music got softer, and their voices louder.

"You've got plenty of sun here," Ellen O'Malley said to Darragh, smiling with teeth that were whiter than any teeth Owen had ever seen. How did they manage that in California? "It's just behind all those black clouds."

Owen sighed to himself and reached over toward them, realizing he'd forgotten the letter and his whiskey. He slid the drink and the envelope closer to him, and Mary watched his every move as though she'd bet on him in a horse race. He steadfastly refused to meet her eyes.

"Oh!" Darragh said with a smile. "An optimist, then. That's all we need on this island. What can I get you, my love?"

Ellen smiled back and said, "Well, I've been dreaming of a nice glass of stout …"

"A glass of the black stuff it is, my love," Darragh replied. "Mary?"

At some point the little band had set off on a mashed-up medley of traditional Irish jigs. Mary, ignoring the bartender, started rolling her hips and laughed like a girl a quarter her age. Owen picked up his drink again as the boys sang, and over it Mary called out to her cousin, "Dance with me!"

Ellen shook her head, her face flushing—not an unattractive shade of red under her soft ginger locks. Mary grabbed her cousin's hand. Although Mary had married an O'Reilly, she was O'Malley blood just like Ellen, and seeing them side by side, it was plain to see.

Darragh put a glass of stout down in front of them both.

Then Mary spun her cousin around and right into Owen's side. Warm whiskey went all over the place, and Owen stood up faster than he'd stood up in some years and grated out under the music, "For feck's sake!"

Before he could go any farther, he looked up and found himself staring into Ellen's cool blue eyes, then to her straight auburn hair curling a bit just where it lay across her shoulders, which drew his eyes to her defined cheekbones and finally her big, red lips. She was a beautiful woman. She could have been fifty but looked late thirties, so Owen figured he'd split the difference at somewhere in between …

"I'm sorry," she said, and Owen could see in her eyes that she meant it, and he realized he'd probably been staring at her a little too long and so looked away, brushing the whiskey off the front of his trousers.

"I prefer my drinks in my glass or my mouth!" he grumbled.

Before he'd finished speaking, Ellen was already saying, "Please let me buy you another."

"Don't bother," Owen said by reflex action. Then he managed to soften his voice just a little at least. "It's done now."

He cleared his throat and stepped back away from her, almost tipping over the stool. She reached out for him, and he flinched back again and almost tripped. But he managed to stay on his feet, grabbed the shot glass but forgot the envelope, and turned for the nearest table. The place wasn't very big, and there was almost no one else there, so that table wasn't too far away. He slid into a chair with his back to the two women. Even with the band still playing he could hear Mary making excuses for him.

"That's Owen Kerrigan," she said, her voice louder than she likely realized, trying to be heard above the music, "our joyful lighthouse keeper. You'll be lucky to get more than a couple of words out of him."

Owen wondered if that was supposed to be funny.

"Clare still has a lighthouse keeper?" Ellen asked. Owen liked the sound of her voice.

"Come on," Mary said. "You have to meet everyone."

Owen lifted the shot glass to his lips and realized it was empty.

"Just a minute," Ellen said to her cousin.

A woman's hand—long fingers, nails done just so, only the beginnings of age spots—set the envelope on the table in front of Owen, and he felt the blood drain from his face. Her hands seemed so small, and so clean, next to his scuffed and calloused and grimy paws. "I'm sorry about that," Ellen said.

Owen glanced up at her for just a second, saw the corner of her mouth curled into a little smile. He saw nothing there that said she was teasing him, so he dragged his eyes back down to the tabletop. He grabbed the unopened letter, damp with spilled whiskey, and stuffed it into his saggy pocket.

"I'm Ellen, by the way," the woman said.

Owen didn't look up but said, "Ellen ..." the name sounded good on his tongue. He'd always liked that name. Owen cleared his throat and said, "I have to be going. I can't leave my light for long."

"Well, let me redeem myself by buying you a drink next time," she said.

The medley came to an end, and Mary whooped and clapped—the only response the three boys got that night.

Owen stood, shuffling around the table to keep it between himself and Ellen. She sat on the chair across from the one he'd just vacated, and Owen was able to get back to the bar in a couple of steps. He tipped his chin to Darragh, who met him at the bar with a smile. "I owe ya for the—" Owen started to say.

But Darragh cut him off with a wave of his hand.

"Thought you might need rescuing," Mary said from the table behind him.

Owen heard the chair scrape back and then Ellen's reply, "You'll be the one who needs rescuing when I've finished with you. Come on, let's see what you've got."

The cousins started dancing again as the band fired up their next song.

Owen gave Darragh a nod and shuffled off to the door. "Goodnight, Owen," the bartender said.

Owen offered a companionable wave, and as he turned he caught sight of the two women dancing, Mary singing along with the song, as though neither had a care in the world. How many years did she say her cousin had been away?

Owen opened the door, and the rain slashed into him as he stepped out and shut the door behind him.

He went a few steps into the gravel car park and rubbed at his wet, unkempt beard. He took the letter out of his pocket. As if God himself thought the envelope was wet enough, the rain died down to a trickle. Owen stared down at it … in the dark, without

21

his reading glasses … but still his thumb found the edge of the flap, and he knew how easy it would be to slide his thumbnail under it and …

"Damn it all," he whispered. His hand tensed a little, but he couldn't screw the letter up and throw it away any more than he could open it. "Not yet." *But if it got any wetter it wouldn't be worth opening anyway*, he thought, and rummaged around in his pockets. He pulled out a crumpled see-through plastic pouch that looked like it was intended to hold coins and stuffed the letter inside it, then tucked the flap in to seal it up.

He glanced up and squinted into the dying rain. Casting his eyes to the southeast down toward Grace O'Malley's castle keep on the harbor, some way out to sea was a ship's light—the ferry *Granuaile* up from Roonagh Quay. Owen watched it make its slow way up to the pier as he clenched the letter clad in its plastic pouch.

Then he shoved it back into his baggy fleece pocket before his hand went to his beard again. He needed to get back to work …

CHAPTER 2

The now distant lightning flashed irregularly, but his lighthouse beam swept the island in perfect time. Owen watched it all the way back from the pub, and when he finally got home, he was satisfied that it was working properly.

He took only a few seconds once he stepped in to shed the rain from his fleece and make sure he wasn't tracking in mud. He kept a flashlight in the same spot on the same little table so he didn't have to bother looking for it. He just grabbed it as he passed.

His legs felt heavy, his knees stiff, as he struggled up the spiral staircase. He yawned, blinked, rubbed his eyes with the back of the hand that held the flashlight—and he noticed a smudge on the handrail. He must have had a little oil on his sleeve and brushed along it when he came down earlier.

He stopped with one foot on a higher step than the other and took a handkerchief from his pocket and scrubbed away the little smudge.

Then he went the rest of the way up to the lantern

room, one stiff, exhausted step at a time. Clicking on the flashlight and rubbing his eyes again, he illuminated the weathervane. It wasn't too difficult to remember that the wind was coming from the north-northwest … he'd watched the storm track that direction all night. And sure enough, the weathervane told the same tale, with a gust of twenty knots rattling the windows.

He checked visibility using a big black rock almost straight due north from his lighthouse cliff, then a turn to the south-southeast and the old castle keep illuminated by the lights of the quayside—which tonight he couldn't see. And then a careful look at one of the towering triangular rocks near the cliff to measure the tide.

Carefully avoiding the bright rotating lighthouse lamp, he read the temperature by shining his flashlight out of the window to the big old thermometer mounted on the outside steel frame of the lantern tower—and found it was just what he'd guessed from the feel of the air on the walk back from the pub. And built into the same sturdy steel frame as the thermometer, the barometer—pressure starting to rise as the storm passed.

Owen whispered the readings to himself so he'd remember them as he turned and made his way back down the spiral stairs.

He left the flashlight precisely where he'd found it in the living room and went into the kitchen, where he was sure he could hear his joints creaking as he sat down at the table, crowded a bit by the chalkboard that leaned against the wall next to him. He was careful not to smudge the drawing—a set of ragged lines running down from a childlike drawing of the lighthouse—or any of the notes scrawled next to it. He drew a heavy, old-fashioned logbook across the tabletop to him, opened it—the pen was right where he always left it. He should have put his reading glasses on but often forgot and ended up squinting as he wrote. He jotted down the tides, visibility, temperature, barometric pressure, wind direction ... then the tip of the pen hovered briefly over the box for wind speed.

Owen cocked his head to one side, listening to the loose hinge rattle a little on the door above the regular hum of his lighthouse motor. He filled in the wind speed, noting that the wind must have picked up to just over twenty knots to rattle the hinge, so he jotted down twenty-two in the box, then a quick scribble of his initials and he closed the logbook. Then he took a deep breath as he stood and moved the pickaxe from where it leaned against a drawer. Inside the drawer he found a screwdriver and got to work on the loose hinge.

That small task finished, Owen took up the pickaxe and, cautious of the low ceiling, set it on his shoulder and went through the back door that led to the courtyard and the more important task beyond.

There was digging to do before he slept.

Having sailed along the track of the storm, wind and rain battered at the wheelhouse of the passenger ferry *Granuaile*. Ryan O'Reilly loved this part—bringing his boat to the dock in bad weather. Maybe the weather wasn't really that bad, the storm starting to let up— he'd seen heavier seas, too—despite only being twenty-five, he was an experienced seaman and felt like the only man in the world who could pilot that boat with its heavy, difficult-to-coax-into-motion arse right into the slip as sweet as you please.

The *Granuaile* ran back and forth between Clare Island and Roonagh Quay on a regular schedule, which meant sometimes a boat built to carry ninety-six passengers went across with only one or two. The wheelhouse rose above the bow, with the passenger compartment and sun deck directly behind.

The other half of the ship's crew was Ryan's younger-by-three-years brother, Derry. He actually managed to get himself to the rail, even had the rope in his hands to secure the *Granuaile* to the Clare Island quayside—and all without having to be told for what would have been the thousandth time. Light from the small harbor and from his own wheelhouse reflected in the rain-spattered glass, but Derry was easy enough for Ryan to make out in his luminous yellow rain gear.

Ryan watched Derry move and, when it seemed

he'd tied them up, slid down a window in the wheelhouse, calling out, "If things don't improve, I might have to sell your body to science."

"Ah ..." his brother shot back, "they wouldn't have a test tube big enough for my organ." Then Derry gave the hand signal that they were secure to the dock.

"It was those girl's hands on a man's body that I was thinking of," Ryan said with a wink that Derry couldn't see anyway. His brother's hands were no more delicate than his own, but Ryan knew it worked Derry's last nerve, this talk of him having girly hands.

"What are you talking about?" Derry said as he finished securing the ropes to the quayside then moved a few feet forward to let down the passenger gangway.

"That's not a knot ..." Ryan said, more loudly, shouting through the open window, "Look at it."

Derry looked back at the rope. "You're having the *craic*," Derry said, and gave the rope a kick, "that would hold a battleship."

"It would have to be a very small one," Ryan quipped, but his attention was already back to his vessel, setting her in neutral, readying to secure her for the night as the handful of passengers stepped off onto the quayside.

. . .

Having washed the dust from his hair, Owen set a half-empty bottle of whiskey on his nightstand, on top of the plastic pouch that contained the still unopened letter from Boston, and climbed into bed, wincing a little, stretching a little, feeling a little stiff and a little old. He put on his reading glasses, leaned back against the headboard and something clanked against the wood—something heavy, made of ...

He turned the chain around his neck and moved the ornate gold key from behind his back. It felt warm—or not cold, anyway—against his chest. He lifted it and touched the bow to his lips and didn't really kiss it, but something about that gesture calmed him.

He held the key for a few minutes, feeling the familiar weight of it, his calloused thumb tracing the outline of the crown-and-anchor carved into the bow. The wind refused to die down as the rain lashed at the side of the lighthouse, but cutting through it was the dull throb of his light's motor. He almost thought he could hear his own heartbeat—in time with his light.

With a quick exhale of breath to clear all this nonsense from his head, Owen let the key fall back to his chest and reached out for the bottle of whiskey. Dispensing with the niceties, being alone in his bedroom, he popped the cork and took a swig from the bottle. He coughed a little at the familiar burn of the drink, but it warmed him inside.

On the bed next to him, lying open, was a copy of *Grace O'Malley: The Pirate Queen*.

"The Pirate Queen," he whispered to himself as he picked up the book, put down the bottle, and started flipping through the pages. He found a dog-eared page, then another, then three more until he stopped and started to read again. Every word was familiar, as were his own hand-scribbled notes along the margins and in the text itself—a word or sentence circled here, underlined there—but he read them again, each one as carefully as if he were still learning his alphabet—but they steadfastly refused to give up any further information, divulge any unexpected secrets.

Something made him look at the letter again.

He lifted the bottle off it and took another sip of whiskey. But he hesitated a little before he put the bottle back down. When he did, the sound of it hitting the table was louder—too loud. It was as if he'd slammed the bottle down, but—and the sound came again.

It sounded too close to be thunder. Then the thud came again—someone was knocking on his door.

Owen rolled his eyes and set his book back down on the bed next to him.

"Ah, fer the love of …" he grumbled, then louder: "I'm comin', damn it."

Dragging himself out of bed, he didn't even bother putting on a shirt, but he turned a few lights on as he pounded down a staircase and through the lighthouse residence to the front door.

He opened the door to be greeted by a face he hadn't seen in … how long had it been?

"Hello Owen."

"Paddy?" Owen asked. He could barely believe his eyes. But there he was standing on his doorstep in the pouring rain—his brother Patrick.

"Will you let me in?" Patrick asked. "I'm soaked to the skin."

Owen's hand clenched into a fist on the doorjamb. His cheeks burned, his lips went thin, and a little muscle in his neck began to twitch. Then he slammed the door shut in his brother's face, and with shaking hands and dry mouth, he turned off all the lights in the place but the lighthouse lantern, which continued to sweep across sea and stone.

• • •

Ellen O'Malley closed her eyes and took a deep breath in through her nose, savoring the aroma of bacon and cabbage. Even the sea-and-plastic smell of her cousin's boys' blazing-yellow raincoats drifted into the background against that all-but-forgotten scent. People in LA didn't eat like this.

Mary put a plate down in front of her, and Ellen opened her eyes, letting a smile and wink suffice as a thank you. The plate in front of her seemed lost on a tabletop filled with salt and pepper shakers of seemingly infinite variety. The sideboard against the wall behind her was similarly crowded with little statuettes and picture frames—and Ellen spotted the little plastic Hollywood-sign snow globe she'd sent Mary as a joke a few years before. Who'd have thought of a snow globe commemorating a trip to Los Angeles? It had been years, and Ellen hadn't seen a single flake.

But there it was, mixed in with all the rest—some things she recognized as having belonged to her aunt and uncle, and to the grandparents she and Mary shared.

Mary headed back for the kitchen, but before she could go, her oldest boy, Ryan, took her lightly by the wrist, stood, and sat her down for all the world as if they'd been transported to Buckingham Palace. Mary played along with a smile and a sort of seated curtsy. This young man, exhausted from a day at sea, dripped a mixture of rain and seawater on the table, chair, and floor, but he served his mother a helping of bacon and cabbage like a regular gentleman.

Ellen had to look away then, and something in her chest tightened a bit.

"How was business today, lads?" Mary asked both her sons as she waved off a few more strips of bacon.

"Quiet," Ryan replied, "as always."

Ellen frowned a little at the sound of easy resignation in her cousin's son's voice, a young man Ellen always thought of as a nephew—a simpler relationship reinforced over the years by both women and nurtured over transatlantic phone calls.

"Things will pick up," Mary said. "You'll see."

Ryan and Derry shared a quick look, and it was obvious that neither thought there was the least possibility of that happening.

As though to cover the brief lapse in conversation, Derry said, "We had a fella on yesterday saying there's work in Galway."

"I can't run the boat on my own," Ryan replied quickly, and with an air of finality.

Derry's eyes narrowed, his forehead creased. "I didn't say I was going. I was just saying."

"Well why say it if you didn't mean any—"

"So Ellen," Mary said loudly, interrupting both her boys. "Tell us about your book."

Ryan and Derry stared at each other in silence, eating their bacon and occasionally widening their eyes at each other and shrugging in an exaggerated fashion.

"Well," Ellen said, content to help Mary bring whatever sort of peace to the table the two boys would allow, "I've always had something of a fascination for our heaven-knows-how-many-times-great grandmother Grace O'Malley. I'd like to find out a little more about her."

"I think that's a lovely idea," Mary replied, though Ellen wasn't sure she meant it or had even really heard her.

Ellen watched as Mary looked first at Ryan, then at Derry, then back to Ryan while the two boys—two young men—continued to eye each other. Ellen tried to think of something to say—thought maybe a comment on the Hollywood snow globe, but then Ryan scraped his chair back across the floor and stood up, moving to the door in a single long stride.

"I'll get the pots on the boat," he said to no one in particular.

"Finish your dinner, Ryan," his mother demanded.

"I'm not hungry, Ma—"

And if Ryan intended to say anything more, he swallowed it when his mother bolted to her feet and, in a long stride of her own, blocked the door with her body. Ellen cleared her throat, then started nibbling on a slice of bacon in order not to stare.

"You're a long time dead, Ryan O'Reilly," Mary said through gritted teeth. "Remember that." It could be she thought no one but Ryan would be able to hear her if she spoke like that, but the room was small and cramped, and even over her own crunching, Ellen heard every word. "Now go do your pots, and when you come back, you'll be brothers again. You hear me?"

Ellen couldn't help it. A slice of bacon still in her hand, her teeth working through a salty bite, she let her eyes twitch back and forth between Mary and Ryan while the young man thought about it for a moment. Then Ellen looked back down at her plate when Ryan nodded and took his mother up in a damp embrace.

The boys had lost their father, and Mary her husband—Cormac O'Reilly—five years before when his fishing boat ran aground and capsized off of Inishark Island. The tear at the corner of Mary's eye was clear enough to see. Ellen was sure Ryan had seen it, at least.

"Sorry, Ma," he said, and though Mary didn't seem to mind his wet clothes, he released her and she moved aside to let him go.

Derry didn't bother waiting for him to leave the house before grabbing his brother's half-finished plate and going to work on the bacon.

Still chewing, Derry, clearly having fully shrugged off that odd confrontation with his brother, asked, "So Auntie Ellen, where's your fella at?"

Ellen hoped her own face didn't look like Mary's. If a mother could stare daggers at her own child, then Derry was well and thoroughly slashed. She sat back down and said, "Derry, I told you. Remember?"

Ellen cleared her throat, thought about maybe trying for a forkful of cabbage.

"Nobody tells me anything," Derry protested.

His mother's answer came fast and final: "You just don't listen."

"It's okay," Ellen spoke up finally, for her own sake as much as young Derry's. She turned to him and said, "We broke up a couple of years ago."

Ellen thought how hollow that sounded, how trite. She'd said it as though her husband were just another schoolgirl crush, some transitory fling easily enough shrugged off. But there had been nothing at all easy about the utter disintegration of their marriage.

Not for Ellen, anyway.

Derry had taken another bite of his brother's abandoned bacon, and he stopped chewing when it appeared that both his mother and his aunt expected him to say something.

"Sorry ..." he muttered around a mouthful of bacon.

"Don't worry," she said, and he wasn't looking at her anymore, instead aiming for the cabbage with a fork. Ellen, not sure what came over her, put her hand on his, startling him. "I'm so happy to be here."

Derry was at a loss.

So was she.

• • •

All trace of the lightning gone, the only light outside Owen's bedroom window was the steady pulse of his light. Inside, only the little lamp next to his bed burned, the shade tipped so it would spill the majority of its light on the pages of his copy of *Grace O'Malley: The Pirate Queen*.

He looked down at a page and individual words registered, but he knew he'd had the book open at the same page for the better part of an hour and hadn't yet read a full sentence.

He tossed the book on the bed near his feet, not caring particularly that it landed open a bit, creasing a few of the pages.

Owen banged his head back against the headboard, which in turn bounced off the wall. Then he dragged himself out of bed.

Ignoring the cold wood floor against the bottoms of his feet, he went to the window and looked out as the lighthouse cast its beam of light over the cresting sea.

After a few seconds, he decided that was it for any sleep tonight.

Might as well get a head start on tomorrow's digging.

CHAPTER 3

The tunnel was just big enough for Owen to fold his heavy frame into. He didn't need it to be any bigger, and it was hard enough digging it out to be as wide as it was. The air was equal parts oxygen and dust, and Owen coughed by reflex. The dim orange bulb behind him flickered, if anything only making the darkness thicker somehow.

The low, murmuring rumble of the generator was enough to send some of the particulates into the air around him, but the tunnel itself was safe.

At least as safe as he could make it.

With the generator rumbling above, Owen hefted the drill and found a steady enough hold in the cement wall in front of him—a wall of crude lime-cement mortar buried deep in the foundations of the Clare Island Lighthouse—and then the noise was deafening, and the dust even thicker. He breathed through his nose and squinted.

He used a drill bit designed for making one and a half inch holes in wood. It didn't make holes in the cement so much as grind it into chunks that fell out around it. Strangely enough, the blunter it became, the better it worked. There was the smell of smoke—that was normal—but something about the vibration of the drill seemed off. Owen pushed harder, forcing all his weight against the old drill. The machine was almost as old as Owen, but he was still digging, so the drill could, too.

Then a screaming sound stung his ears, and he grunted and swore at the pain in his head, the vibrations in his hands and arms, and smoke that filled the tight little space in an instant.

He choked, and so did the drill.

There was a grinding sound like sheet metal being dragged across gravel, and then the vibration was gone at least.

Owen blinked in the dense smoke and squeezed the trigger on the drill over and over again. It made a couple more dying noises, and that was it.

The generator still rumbled away. The drill had power, but something inside it had come undone … he could feel it.

He grumbled, then swore his way through a fit of coughing and tossed the drill aside. His pickaxe was behind him, and Owen, not for the first time, went at it the old-fashioned way. He smashed the implement into the cement wall, and a few chips came out. Then he smashed it again for a few more chips, then again and again and again and forgot that it was hard to breathe and forgot that it was hard to see, and forgot the pain in his hands, the pain in his arms, the pain is his neck, and just smashed and smashed and smashed at that cement wall until his body gave up on him, and he hit it one more time—barely a tap—and fell back coughing, hacking, wheezing, and blinking.

He lay there for all of three difficult breaths, and the lights went out.

Plunged into utter darkness and a dense quiet, Owen sighed. The generator wasn't rumbling anymore. Owen slid around and crawled out, leaving the pickaxe but dragging the old drill with him. Despite having to feel his way out in almost complete darkness except for the dull yellow floodlight, it didn't take him long to emerge from the hole and into the little shed above. The morning sun struggled through the dirty little window, the first indication Owen had that he'd worked through the night. After stomping out of the narrow door of the shed and around to the generator, he went though the little ritual to start it again, pressing this, pulling that …

A splutter.

Then nothing.

Cursing himself in a hissing whisper, he unscrewed the fuel cap and … mystery solved.

Owen stomped across the courtyard, straight

through the kitchen and the living room, and out the front door. After gathering up the electrical cord, he tossed the drill into the bed of his old truck.

Then he stopped just long enough to cough up some of the dust and smoke and spit it on the sparse grass next to his truck. He wiped his mouth with the back of his hand and climbed up into the truck bed. In the bed of the truck was a jerry can—empty.

Owen crawled out and went to the truck's fuel cap—and found a siphon tube hanging out of it—right where he'd left it.

Fists on his hips, he said, "Shite."

He grabbed the empty jerry can with one hand, slung the old drill over his shoulder with the other, and headed off for the small village that clung to the ferryboat quayside in the southeast of the island as though he were some kind of giant striding the earth with single-minded purpose.

He trudged down the path he'd walked a thousand times, and as he crested the hill, his legs started to shake a little. He usually tried to stretch when he came out of the tunnel, get the blood moving right again, but having stomped off directly from the hole, lugging the jerry can and that heavy old drill, having barely paused to take a breath of clean air … in the end Owen had to give himself permission to take a minute. The village was still a good forty-five-minutes' walk away without the burden of the extra weight.

He let the empty jerry can fall from his fingers and dropped the drill on the ground next to him. He sat on a rock he'd sat on before. He liked this rock. Not because it was any more comfortable than any other rock, but because it had a view of the most beautiful cove on the island and the soothing sound of a stream that flowed by the side of it, then ran off the end of the cliff and turned into a waterfall. The sun shone on the blue water in the little inlet, the breeze barely rippling the surface. As he looked down into the cove, to his left past the waterfall was an almost-straight-line rock face jutting out into the sea with a headland rising from it that framed the north of the inlet. A trio of red-billed chough fluttered overhead, spinning around the cool updrafts over the cove, their black-feathered bodies self-silhouetted against the blue sky.

The same breeze the birds played in felt good on his face, cooling him off. He wiped away a little sweat and the dust of pulverized lime-cement from his brow. He coughed up a bit more dust and spat it on the short grass, then stretched his back, which argued with him a bit.

That made him think maybe he should make the tunnel a little taller.

His eyes followed the path that ran down to the right of his little rock, and as he sat facing the sea, part of him wanted to jump up from the rock and get on his way, but a slightly bigger part was content to take it easy for at least a few more minutes. The path was littered with old lobster pots, and a little fork led down to the cove around the other side of the hill where it transformed into a stone jetty that framed the south of the inlet. An old bicycle leaned against the cliff face next to a rusty ladder that dropped down into the water from the jetty. Owen had helped replace that ladder when the old one rusted through. How long ago was that? Twenty years already …

The only boat in the cove was the lobster boat *Quinn*. The little boat wasn't much more than a round-bottomed skiff, ten feet long and open to the air, a small rusty outboard engine clinging to its stern. It was tied up with long ropes at three points around the cove to prevent it from being dragged onto the rocks in a storm.

The shallows showed as a patch of blue the same color as the perfect sky, the water so clear Owen could make out the shape and color of rocks underneath. He blinked in the sunlight and took a good, deep breath and didn't have to cough.

Turning his attention back to the cove, he blinked at something in the water he hadn't noticed before, then leaned forward a little as if the couple of inches would actually help him see …

A head of long auburn hair breaking the surface, gleaming in the sun, followed by the body of—the naked body—of a woman swimming …

And even from a distance, Owen knew it was Ellen.

He felt color rise in his cheeks and thought he should look away but didn't. The sound of Ellen singing, her voice echoing against the rocks of the cove, drifted up to him—it sounded Gaelic, but it was too faint for him to make out the tune.

He watched her swim slowly, leisurely, to the rusty ladder. He thought again that he should turn away but decided again not to. As she climbed up, the sunlight played on the water as it slid off her skin. *Los Angeles has been good to her*, he thought.

Women her age didn't—shouldn't—have that sort of figure, that sort of skin, that sort of way of moving. He watched her dress as if she were a dancer, as if that simple act were a form of art.

The bicycle was hers, and it wasn't until she started walking it back along the path up from the cove that Owen stood. His little break was over. The old drill felt a little less heavy when he slung it over his shoulder, and the empty jerry can felt a little emptier. And his back and legs had shed the stiffness of the tunnel, and his step had found a spring to it. Owen let himself smile as he strolled rather than stomped on his way along the path, not down to the cove but along the headland.

Gulls circled above him, maybe wondering if the drill or jerry can contained anything like food. The east coast of the island stretched out in front of him.

In the distance the sturdy square of Grace O'Malley's castle keep squatted over the quayside. The ferry *Granuaile* chugged away from the harbor, a couple of passengers leaning on the rails, watching the island shrink behind them.

Owen made his way along the headland and followed an old shortcut of his down to a pebble beach to avoid an arduous section of coastline. He stopped at the remains of a scuttled tugboat rusting away in front of him. The spring was still in his step, the image of Ellen O'Malley still in his head, a sight even the old tug, being slowly digested by the sea, didn't push from his thoughts. But the old drill dug into his shoulder, and though he may have felt content and at peace, a jabbing pain had a tendency to make itself known regardless. He slid the drill from his shoulder, dropped the jerry can, and leaned up against the rusted old boat.

He looked out to sea while he rubbed the tense pain from his shoulder.

"Lovely morning."

Owen jumped at the sound of the man's voice—right next to him. Blood seemed to drain from his head, and he blinked and took a deep breath, then turned to his brother Patrick and said, "Jaysus! You frightened the life out of me."

Patrick glistened in the bright sunlight, and his eyes sparkled with humor behind a pair of expensive glasses. He looked old, Owen thought as he glimpsed his bushy eyebrows streaked with gray, but then so did Owen.

We are old, he thought.

Patrick gestured to the rusty tugboat and said, "Can I?"

Owen looked his elder brother up and down: a dark green cashmere sweater, khaki pants, a color-coordinated beige checked shirt, hair slicked back over a high forehead, a gold watch, and shiny shoes that were probably made by the same company as his glasses. He could have been an American dentist or lawyer on holiday. The rusty hulk was going to ruin his outfit.

"Sit where you like," Owen said with a shrug, "I don't own it."

Patrick nudged his pant cuffs up and sat, apparently paying the rust and dirt and kittiwake droppings no mind. Owen turned to look back out to sea and sighed to himself.

After a long few minutes, Owen said, "Why are you here?"

"I figured over thirty years of silence was probably enough," Patrick replied without a pause to think.

"Did you now?" Owen jabbed. He didn't bother trying to hide anything—let all the baggage between them stay in the tone of his voice.

"Did you read any of the letters I sent?" Patrick asked, not so deftly changing the subject.

45

Owen shrugged and replied, "They kept the fire going through the winter." He'd imagined saying that dozens of times, should Patrick ever find his way to Clare Island and ask him that question. It was more satisfying in his imagination. Something told him not to turn to look at his brother's face.

But he couldn't resist it. Patrick was smiling.

"Well," he said, and Owen looked back out to sea, "I'm glad you found a use for them."

Not standing up, Owen said, "I can't be sitting here chatting. I've got things to do."

He sat there for a heartbeat or two before realizing he should actually stand up, so he did. He leaned over, ignoring his still-stiff shoulder to pick up the old drill.

Without looking back at his brother, Owen said, "There's a regular ferry service back to the mainland."

"Will you not just give me a few minutes to talk?" Patrick asked. "I've come a long way."

Owen, the drill resting painfully on his shoulder, grabbed the jerry can and could have started walking, but he didn't.

"What is done is done," he said, still not turning to look at his brother. "You go back to your life, and I'll get back to mine. Goodbye, Paddy."

Then Owen did start walking, fully conscious of having lost that spring in his step, not even sure he could remember why it had been there. He could feel his brother behind him, standing still and staring out to sea.

As he kept walking away from the beach and back inland, a little faster, the drill too heavy, the empty jerry can bouncing off his knee with every step, Owen refused to think about his brother, standing back there by the old tug. He didn't think about where Patrick was staying, why he was here, what he hoped to get out of Owen. He was trying not to think about anything when the Gaelic song Ellen sang as she swam floated into his consciousness.

He had heard that tune before—couldn't recognize it back at the cove—but now it was just as clear as …

Owen stopped and for the first time in several minutes, looked up from the path in front of him. An art easel stood outside the open door of a cottage. The old bike from the cove leaned against the wall next to the door. Ellen must have ridden along the main road. He hadn't seen her pass.

The song drifted out from inside the cottage. Her voice was beautiful, a thin, wavering soprano, and Owen paused to look through the open door.

The little cottage was filled with paintings—leaning here and there—and books sat stacked in orderly, if temporary, piles. The voice moved through the interior of the cottage, and Owen couldn't help but follow it to an open window. He peered inside, and there she stood, drying her now wild auburn hair, wearing an old t-shirt that only just covered her—Owen was pretty sure there was nothing underneath.

He struggled to remember the name of the old Gaelic song she sang but like the tired old drill, his memory failed him.

Not startled, just surprised, Ellen turned to see him looking through her window, and Owen's blood seemed to harden in his veins, gluing his feet to that spot. Ellen smiled as though there was nothing the slightest bit odd about the old lighthouse keeper staring at her through her window when she was barely half dressed. She wrapped the towel around her, holding it with both hands.

"Good morning?" she prompted. The look on his face must have made him appear … Owen didn't even want to think about it.

"Hello …" he said, then knew in the single breath that passed that he'd paused too long. "I …" and his face grew hot, like the sun had shifted in the sky just to pour all its heat onto his cheeks. A noise kind of like a gurgle came out of his throat.

Ellen's eyes darted to the drill on his shoulder, and she said, still smiling, "You've come to hang some pictures for me, have you?"

"No," Owen said too fast. He cleared his throat and shifted the weight of the old drill on his shoulder. "No … it's broken. I'm just off to Dougal's to get it repaired …"

Owen tried to smile but might have managed a grimace. He could feel that he'd sort of let that sentence hang there, but had no way out of it.

"Would you like a cup of coffee?" Ellen asked.

"No …" he said, because that's what he thought she wanted him to say, "busy day."

"Building?" she asked.

Owen shook his head and blinked at her. Her eyebrows went up on her forehead, and she pointed at the drill.

"That's right," he said, letting out a breath he didn't realize he'd been holding. "I'll be on my way now."

And without waiting for a response, Owen turned to get the hell out of there.

"Oh, Owen?" Ellen called after him.

He stopped and turned back to see her, drying her hair with a hand towel and still smiling at him.

"I would really appreciate it if I could visit the lighthouse," she said, looking a bit sheepish. "It's for my book."

Owen had to clear his throat before he was able to say, "The place is a real mess now …"

"I won't stay long," she said, her eyebrows up on her forehead again, her wet hair framing her face and catching the sunlight. "Promise."

She really smiled at him now, and Owen almost took a step back. A single sentence came to his mind as though someone else was thinking it for him: *She's beautiful.*

"Friday," his mouth said before his brain could screw things up. "Sixish?"

Ellen's smile turned into a self-satisfied smirk, and she said, "Will I get to see your uniform?"

His mouth was dry and he really wanted to go, so as he turned he said, "Hanging in the wardrobe."

She graced him with a laugh and then started singing the enchanting Gaelic song again, the words distinct for the first time, *"Leag mé síos ..."* her beautiful voice following him as he made his way as fast as he could to Dougal's.

By the time he got there, his "fast as he could" had gotten pretty slow, and Owen staggered into the yard.

Everywhere were rusty bits and pieces of old machines. That thing over there might once have been a car radiator, and next to it the valve cover from a boat diesel, and sitting like the leaning tower of Pisa was an old soda pop machine that advertised brands Owen hadn't seen in decades.

And lording over this mechanical graveyard stood a gap-toothed, wiry old man with a few tufts of gray hair left and skin that was one-half pale and blotchy and the other half grease. That was Dougal, wiping his dirty hands with an even dirtier rag.

Owen marched right up to him and unslung the drill into Dougal's waiting hands. He coughed into his handkerchief as Dougal looked over the drill, then he stretched his aching shoulder as Dougal held the tool up to his ear to shake it.

Owen could hear the rattle as plain as day.

"She's knackered," Dougal drawled at him with all the finality of an undertaker and tried to hand the drill back to Owen.

But Owen didn't budge. "I know it's knackered," Owen said. "I want you to *un*knacker it."

Dougal shifted the weight of the thing, realizing Owen wasn't going to take it back, and shook his head. "I must have patched her up twenty times for you, Owen, but finally she's given up the ghost. What are you doing to the poor old girl?"

"Never you mind," Owen said, his tone leaving no room for argument. "How much?"

Dougal raised the drill to his ear again and rattled it a bit more gently this time.

"Knackered ..." he said, still listening to the rattle, "... *kaput!*"

"Twenty euros," Owen offered.

Dougal didn't even seem to hear him. "I can't fix it," he said. "I don't have a drive shaft for the drill, and it'll take at least a week to get one."

"Thirty," Owen said without pause.

"Owen," Dougal said, holding the drill out to him again, his skinny arms shaking under the weight of it, "buy a new drill."

"And where shall I do that? I don't have the time to go to Westport," Owen replied.

Dougal looked down at the old drill, turned it over a few times, and when he looked back up at Owen, there was a mischievous twinkle in his eye. "All right …" he said, and his smile revealed some missing teeth, "forty euros and you tell me what you're building up there."

Owen didn't flinch. "You're a tight arse," he said. "Thirty-five and mind your own business."

Dougal was already nodding before Owen stopped talking. "You're an enema, Owen, that's for sure."

"What?" Owen asked.

Dougal's forehead crinkled, and he set the drill on the ground at his feet and took something out of his pocket—an old paperback book, barely held together at the spine—and started flipping through it. Owen peeked over the top of it, and Dougal, noticing him, hid the pages against his chest. Owen smiled when he revealed the cover: a dictionary.

"No," Dougal muttered to himself, "… no … that's an *enigma*."

"What are you doing, man?" Owen asked, hiding his smile.

"Never too old to learn, Owen, you know," Dougal said, looking a bit sheepish. "Thought I might find myself an educated woman …"

Owen shook his head and drew in a deep breath. Wanting to move the conversation back in the right direction, he thrust the empty jerry can at Dougal and said, "Fill her up."

Dougal appeared more than happy to get back to commerce and replied, "Right you are."

Owen followed him to the door of a shed and waited while he unlocked a big rusty padlock. An old hand pump was inside. The odor of diesel fuel wafted out as Dougal started filling the jerry can.

"I'd like your advice on something," Dougal said, taking Owen a bit by surprise.

He motioned Owen closer, clearly wanting him to take over the hand pump. Owen didn't bother complaining about Dougal's peculiar brand of customer service, just took over pumping diesel while the old man scurried off into his workshop.

The can was almost full when Dougal ran back, clutching a different shirt in each hand. He held them up for Owen to see—one blue, the other red.

"What do you think?" Dougal asked. "The blue or the red ... for the Seafarer's Festival? I want to look my best, you know. I've got my eye on someone." Dougal winked at him, and Owen shook his head.

"The one with the fewest grease stains on it," Owen advised, not looking up from the pump. He didn't have to look at Dougal to know he was looking at the shirts, then his hands, then Owen ...

"You're probably right," Dougal said after an uncomfortable pause.

One last pump and the jerry can was full. Owen screwed the cap back on, then fished in his pocket for Dougal's money. He came out with a ten-euro note.

"You should come to the Seafarer's Festival for

once," Dougal suggested, taking the money from Owen.

"No," Owen said, "I'll not be there."

He lifted the full jerry can, his arm, shoulder, and back already protesting, and started off while Dougal examined the ten-euro note as though it was the first one like it he'd ever seen.

"Twelve euros a can …" Dougal called after him, but Owen didn't break a stride.

"Self service," he shouted back, "is two euros."

Dougal's voice was a dozen steps more distant when he called out, "What about the drill?"

Not worried whether or not Dougal could hear him as he marched away, Owen replied, "Payment on collection."

CHAPTER 4

Derry had worked up a sweat scurrying around the boat, preparing the ropes for docking. He'd held out all morning, but he would have to take his coat off, even risking someone complaining about his t-shirt. It was the only thing he had clean that morning, but the boss wouldn't like it. The shirt had one arrow pointing up that said "The Man" and another arrow pointing down that said "The Legend."

It was funny when he bought it, anyway.

Ryan steered the ferry into its slip in a flat calm, and Derry tied off the bow rope. With the engine in neutral, Ryan climbed down out of the wheelhouse to help his brother. He squinted in the sunshine and pulled down the passenger gangway. A friend of his mother's came off the boat first after a morning spent with her sister on the mainland. Derry helped her off with a smile and a friendly if abbreviated greeting. She smiled at him and went on her way. Then, before Derry knew what had happened, there was another hand in his, a little rougher, must have been an old lady, but when Derry turned he was surprised to see a man.

Derry swallowed his surprise and blinked as the thin, pale gentleman allowed himself to be helped across the short steel gangway and stepped cautiously onto the quayside. He was dressed more for the city streets of Dublin than Clare Island, with a trilby and a tightly cinched tan mac. Derry noticed his cheap gold-plated watch on a leather band that might not even have been real leather. It was as if he were going to a fancy dress party as "a successful businessman."

"You staying long?" Derry asked the man. There was something about him …

"No," the man said, in a faux cultured accent Derry saw right through, "I hope to be back in civilization as soon as possible."

"Is that right?" Derry asked, trying not to sound too confrontational.

The thin man looked him up and down and obviously didn't like the t-shirt one bit.

"Now," the man said in a tone so condescending Derry thought he must have practiced it, "what would be the quickest way to the lighthouse?"

"Turn right at the end of the quayside and keep walking," Derry said with a smile, knowing that the only thing his brother Ryan hated more than that t-shirt was when he'd occasionally have a go at one of the passengers. "If your feet get wet, then you've gone too far."

To his credit, the man knew Derry was winding him up and with pursed lips replied, "I'll be sure to remember that."

The man turned, his mac swishing around him despite being tied so tight, and started making his way up the quayside. Ryan stepped up next to Derry, nudged him gently with his elbow, and called out to the man, "Are you that fella from the council?"

The man stopped and turned to look at the two brothers, chin up. "That's right," he called back.

"You come to help us out, have you?" Ryan asked. Derry smiled a bit wider.

The man cleared his throat, turned to face the two young men, and replied, "I'm here on council business, if that's what you mean. Why?"

Derry shrugged, and Ryan said, "Well, I know that some of the islanders have applied for grants and suchlike and haven't heard anything back."

The man blinked and shifted his feet, starting to turn away, but said, "That's not my department."

"Is that right?" Ryan said quickly, not letting him go. "But could you—"

"Do you know anywhere that'll have a room available?" the councilman cut him off.

Derry looked at his brother, curious to hear an answer to that himself. "No," Ryan said without seeming to pause to consider it. Derry shrugged and looked at the councilman. Ryan continued, nodding at the O'Malley guesthouse on the quayside, "Me mam's guesthouse is full."

Derry folded his arms across his chest and shrugged again, smiling at the councilman standing there, shifting back and forth on his feet. "I should try over the other side of the island," Derry said.

He looked at his brother and returned Ryan's smirk.

"I see," the councilman said and turned fast, staggering the first step, then quickly recovering to walk up the quayside. Derry shrugged him off again and went to tie the aft rope.

"Smarmy suit!" Ryan muttered under his breath after the receding stranger. Then he turned to Derry and said, "Tie 'em like a man, would ya?"

"Get away before I box ya ears," Derry replied.

Ryan came up next to him and grabbed at the rope, Derry pulling it just out of reach. "It'll be more of a slap with those girl's hands."

Derry let go of the rope and grabbed his brother instead, and Ryan was already laughing before Derry had him on the ground.

. . .

With a generator full of diesel, Owen turned the lights on in the tunnel and went back to work. The low-wattage light bulbs bathed the tunnel in a dim, orange-tinted glow. He wasn't exactly doing precision work, not yet anyway—so it was plenty enough light to bang away at cement, and the brighter bulbs made it too hot.

Owen only got in one good swing with the pickaxe before an alarm chimed shrilly, pinging back and forth in the cramped tunnel and stinging his ears.

He leaned the pick against the wall and half walked, half crawled out of the tunnel and back up to his lighthouse. Already covered in dust, he left a thin trail of it across the courtyard, then the kitchen and living room, but brushed the rest off before he got to the bottom step of the spiral staircase. Up into the lantern tower he went, peering at the weathervane, when there was a knock at the door.

He cursed under his breath, as irritated at having been startled by the noise as at the interruption itself.

Owen turned and went back down the curved stairs and barely set one foot in the living room when the knock sounded again, a little impatient, a little insistent, and a whole lot more aggravating.

Owen's jaw tensed, his teeth started to grind. He grabbed the door handle tightly, his hand a sort of stiff claw, and even before he had the door open a crack, he started to tell Patrick, "I thought I told you to—"

But it wasn't Patrick.

The man in the doorway was the tall, thin, stiff, all trussed up in a mac councilman who stepped off the *Granuaile*. Owen had never seen this character before in his life.

"You only have to knock once!" Owen said a little too loudly, too angrily maybe, but he'd been ready to let his brother have it, and that needed to go somewhere.

The man seemed a bit dazed by that. His eyes went wide, and his thin brows shot up on his forehead, disappearing under his silly hat.

"Do I know you?" Owen asked, taking control of his own voice but still not bothering to hide the fact that this stranger had interrupted his work.

The man pushed his hand through the open door as though he expected Owen to shake it and said, "My name is Mr. O'Connell."

For a second it seemed as though the man thought that name might mean something to Owen. He kept his hand there, maybe hoping Owen wouldn't close the door on his arm. Owen thought about doing just that but shook his hand instead. It was clammy and weak, and Owen pulled away as fast as he could. Mr. O'Connell looked down at his own palm then and grimaced. Owen's hands were dirty, O'Connell's weren't—until just then.

O'Connell brushed some dirt and cement dust off

his hand onto his uncomfortably tight coat, and that brought about another grimace while he said, "From the Mayo County Council."

"I see," Owen replied.

O'Connell looked Owen up and down in a way that made Owen sincerely want to punch the skinny councilman in his skinny, smug face.

"Can I come in?" O'Connell asked, his ratty little eyes glancing over Owen's shoulder.

"What do you want?" Owen asked.

"This won't take long," O'Connell replied.

Owen searched the man's face for a few seconds, long enough to get the idea that he wasn't just going to go away, then finally said, "Well I suppose you'd better come in then."

Owen let go of the handle and headed into the kitchen. O'Connell pushed the door to make the gap wide enough for him to enter, then took off his hat and followed Owen inside. By the time O'Connell got to the kitchen, Owen was turning the chalkboard around so it faced the wall.

For a minute or so, neither man said a word. O'Connell might have been soaking up the sight of Owen's lighthouse kitchen, cluttered with broken bits of cement and a layer of fine dust. He might have noted the titles of the books Owen closed and stacked to clear a bit of the tabletop.

Owen didn't rightly care what the man was looking

at or noticing and instead flipped the logbook open and jotted down his weathervane readings.

"Into your history, I see," O'Connell said, nodding at the top book on the small stack on the table, a copy of *The History of the Spanish Armada*.

"What is your business, Mr. O'Connell?" Owen asked, not looking up from the logbook. "I'm a busy man."

There was a pause that Owen ignored, and then O'Connell answered, "Very well, Mr. Kerrigan. We sent you a letter some weeks ago informing you that your job as the keeper will cease on the day that the new automatic lighthouse starts operating …"

As O'Connell chattered, Owen tipped his head, listening for the thin, faraway shriek of the wind from the lantern tower. He jotted the wind speed down in the logbook, then said, "That isn't for months yet."

"Saturday, Mr. Kerrigan," O'Connell said, and Owen held his breath. "It was clearly explained in the letter. The new lighthouse starts operating this Saturday. Your last watch will be on Friday night."

Owen had finished noting the wind direction and speed, but the tip of the pencil was still on the logbook page. He pressed down—hard—and the pencil lead snapped.

Owen looked up at O'Connell sitting there, and piercing him with his rodent eyes.

"Letter …" Owen said. "What letter? I … I … this is my light!"

Owen flushed at that and felt the fool, but that passed quickly back to anger when O'Connell appeared briefly sympathetic.

"I wasn't expecting to be delivering the news like this," the councilman said. "It's all explained in the letter."

Owen looked across the living room to the little pile of unopened mail.

O'Connell continued speaking. "We already have potential buyers, and your residency of the property does expire when you cease employment."

"I can't move out," Owen said, still looking at the unopened letters, "not just like that …"

A full minute might have passed before O'Connell said, "This isn't negotiable."

Owen closed his eyes and held his breath again for a few seconds. He could feel the blood drain from his face, sweat begin to mix with the dirt and cement dust on his palms. He let out the breath and swallowed, but his throat was dry. He coughed a little and opened his eyes but only stared at the logbook, still open in front of him. He just then realized he was still holding the pencil.

"How long do I have?" Owen asked. His voice didn't shake. He didn't scream the question or shout it. He just needed to know the answer.

The man from the council made it harder by saying, "The council simply can't afford to maintain the property—we have to sell it as quickly as possible. It will be a big burden off our budget. Now, we have some potential buyers coming on Saturday at ten o'clock. I'll need to show them around."

Owen felt his head moving back and forth. Was he shaking his head?

"Saturday, ten a.m., Mr. Kerrigan."

Owen's eyes didn't move up from the logbook, but still he could see O'Connell smooth down the front of his fancy coat.

"And you'll have to vacate the property by the end of the weekend. I'll let myself out," the man from the council said.

Owen kept his eyes down on the logbook, and just as O'Connell stepped out and shut the front door behind him with a distinctive *click*, Owen snapped the pencil in half in his right hand.

He reached over and turned the chalkboard back around, then examined the diagrams that charted his progress with the tunnel. The drawing wasn't perfect—Owen wasn't an architect—but he'd drawn the foundations of his lighthouse from precise measurements he'd made himself and any records he could find both on the island and on the mainland.

He was close.

Each day's progress was marked on the board. He looked at the current page in his logbook—Wednesday. A few days wasn't enough time. He had weeks of digging left to do.

He tossed the broken halves of the pencil across the room, then thumped his right fist hard on the tabletop just once. It stung, and the heel of his hand went numb, tingly.

He stood fast then and went into the living room just a few steps, but then why was he in the living room? Then he turned and took two steps, then turned and took one more. Where was he going?

So he sat in the armchair—dropped into it, really. Across the room from him was the black-and-white photo of the two boys, and he whispered a word that started with *f* and stood and took a few steps again, then a few more in the other direction.

Then he cursed again and grabbed his fleece jacket and went straight for the door.

CHAPTER 5

Owen's pickup truck rumbled and coughed to a stop at the quayside and was still knocking and shuddering when Owen climbed out. He left the door open and trudged along with just enough urgency to catch up to Patrick. The O'Reilly boys were preparing the ferry for its next passage, the passenger gangway not yet up in the hope that they might get at least one passenger for their voyage to the mainland.

Owen had a few minutes then. He squinted into the setting sun and called, but not too loudly, "Paddy."

The O'Reilly boys looked up. Owen avoided looking at them. He kept his eyes on his brother, who didn't turn to face him but stopped walking at least.

A gray-winged fulmar squawked in the sky over his head, and Owen was relieved for the interruption, however momentary. He looked up and watched the bird—a sort of pudgy little gull—swoop out to sea, and when he looked back down, Patrick had turned to face him.

Patrick's face was blank, and Owen couldn't tell

what he was thinking. He just seemed to be waiting. Owen took a step closer to him and looked over Patrick's shoulder at the two young ferrymen. They'd gone back to their work, coiling ropes and stowing empty produce boxes.

"No need for another goodbye," Patrick said, his face now reading disappointment. Owen wondered what it was that Patrick had really come to Clare Island for. "I get the message," Patrick went on, "I won't be coming back."

Owen didn't want to look his brother in the eye just then, even though he knew he should. He took a deep breath and felt a sort of pressure pushing in around him, as though he'd sunk to the bottom of the ocean.

Patrick was about to turn back to the ferry, so Owen said, "Paddy, look, I ..." He had to stop and clear his throat, trying to push the words out through whatever was making his chest feel so tight. "I've changed my mind."

Patrick raised an eyebrow, even flinched a little, as though Owen had lunged at him, even slapped him, but neither of them had moved a muscle. The fulmar squawked again, having turned over the end of the quay to slide back inland on a draft of air.

"You sent me packing a few hours ago," Patrick said. "Why the sudden change of heart?"

Owen sighed, and his eyes darted about the quayside. A young couple, obviously on holiday, passed by them, and Owen looked down at the ground, waiting for them to pass. They paid him no mind. The fulmar, perhaps a different one, squawked again.

"Stay …" Owen said. Then he paused to clear his throat once more. "Stay … for a while, anyway."

Owen cleared his throat a third time and pretended to be distracted by something up the hill from the quay.

Even without looking at him, Owen knew his brother was smiling.

"It may have been thirty-something years," Patrick said, "but I still know when you're lying to me."

"All right, I need your help," Owen said quickly, like ripping off a plaster.

Patrick shook his head, looking down at the ground the same way Owen had, then turned and started off again for the ferry. He didn't turn around, even turn his head when he said, "Goodbye, Owen."

Owen raised his hands to his waist, palms up, then dropped them back to his sides. Patrick kept walking.

Owen thought of a few rude comments he might leave his brother with, on his way to the ferry and the mainland and a flight back to wherever he was …

"I didn't burn them," Owen shouted to his brother.

Ryan looked up at him, and Owen turned his head to look at the same spot on the hill. That fulmar—Owen was sure it was the same one—stood at the top of a telephone pole, looking down at him. Owen and the bird made eye contact, and the gray-winged fulmar tipped its head to one side. Owen looked back at his brother, and Patrick had stopped walking and turned to face him again. Behind him, the O'Reilly boys had started up a game of football with one of their orange floats.

"I just haven't read them," Owen said to his brother. "I couldn't."

Patrick nodded, then shook his head. Owen knew he was thinking, confused ... he'd had that same look ever since they were kids.

The O'Reilly boys raced past them then, and the younger one nudged Owen as they passed. Patrick ignored them, but Owen grumbled, "Watch where you're going lads!"

The two young men chased their orange float, kicking it back and forth between them. The older one turned and said, "Sorry ... sorry, Mr. Kerrigan." Then he gave the float a solid kick. With an echoing thump, the float bounced off Ryan's toe and arced up past the two older men. Owen watched it soar across the quayside and bounce off the ferryboat's mast with a clank.

"Goal!" the older of the O'Reilly boys squealed. His younger brother gave him a playful shrug, and together they chased off after their makeshift football.

Patrick didn't notice any of it. He just stood there.

"Well?" Owen asked.

Patrick didn't move or look at him for a little bit.

Then just all at once, he started walking toward him, and Owen walked with him, side by side, to the truck.

• • •

The sun was setting, and Owen went straight up the spiral staircase to the lantern room. Despite everything else, there was still the regular work of a lighthouse keeper to be done.

With the lens mechanism hatch open, Owen kneeled on the floor, unpacked his tools and carefully inspected the works. He'd been keeping an eye on the lens drive gear teeth for several weeks and grunted when he saw another couple of them showing outward signs of wear. It was the kind of thing that could keep working for a year or suddenly just shred itself. He disengaged the clutch and with a bit of elbow grease pulled the thing around a quarter rotation while keeping a fingertip just at the edge of the underside of the gear, trying to feel how well it was engaging with the lens wheel as he turned it. Actually engaging the drive shaft would have helped with the lens turning on its own, but the chance he'd get his finger chewed up in the wheel was too great. He sat back and sighed, looking at the rotation-gear assembly while nibbling at the inside of his bottom lip. He polished the underside of the lens drive gear with a rag where he'd touched it before he reengaged the clutch.

Owen had to admit to himself that if the council was ready to throw him out on his arse and sell the building to God knows who to do God knows what with … It would take him a whole lot longer than that to get a new lens drive gear in from Michigan—the last place he knew of to buy one.

"I like what you've done with the place," Patrick called up from the bottom of the staircase.

Owen could hear the sarcasm in his voice—Patrick wasn't trying to hide it.

He may not have been the best housekeeper when it came to the living room and the kitchen—especially since he'd started in on the tunnel—but his brother hadn't bothered to climb the stairs of the lantern tower.

Owen wiped a bit of stray grease from the regulator housing.

"Whose are all these books?" Patrick called up.

"Mine!" Owen shouted in response.

He put a few drops of oil into the mechanism, making sure with the rag that it didn't drip.

Patrick's voice came up from below again: "I've never seen you read a book."

Owen would never dream of taking out his mounting frustration with his brother on the lantern works, so he closed the housing gently, checking to make sure it was properly latched.

"Never had any reason to," Owen answered his

71

brother finally, though he wasn't sure his voice was loud enough to be heard in the living room.

Not that it mattered.

Owen stood and took a deep breath, riding through the odd aches and pains. He felt his years only when he had to stand up from the floor, and a bit more even since the old drill had given out and he'd had to dig with the pickaxe.

He squeezed the steel lever closed, pushed it down to start the lens rotating, and listened to the motor for a few minutes. It sounded right. Perfect.

He replaced his tools, took a deep breath, then flicked on the big cast iron switch to turn on the lantern lamp and went down the stairs, wiping his hands on the rag.

"I thought all of the lighthouses were automatic now," Patrick enquired.

Owen said, "Will be soon enough."

He came into the living room where Patrick sat in his armchair, staring at the black-and-white photograph of the two of them as boys.

Owen's jaw tensed, and he said, "The new lighthouse starts on Saturday. I have to be out of here at the end of the weekend."

Owen came closer to Patrick and couldn't help but stare daggers at him, sitting in his chair. Patrick looked up, and though they hadn't seen each other in years, they were still brothers. Standing, Patrick smirked at him in that way he had of giving in but making sure it was clear that he didn't really care either way.

"The weekend?" Patrick asked, beginning to pace the room, hands behind his back as though he was looking to buy the place himself. "It's Wednesday today … there isn't much of the week left? What will you do?"

"I have a retirement plan," Owen replied with a smile. Now it was his turn to look as though it didn't matter either way.

Patrick didn't bite. Instead he asked, "So you want me to help you move out?"

Owen shook his head and walked into the kitchen, knowing Patrick would follow him.

"No," Owen answered. "Dig."

"Dig? For what?"

Owen turned to face him, and looked him dead in the eye. "Gold."

Patrick's eyes went wide, and the right corner of his mouth curled up ever so slightly. Owen knew that look, too—the same look he'd had since they were kids. It was how he looked when Owen, age ten, had bragged that he was going to go to America to be an astronaut, or five years later when he said he'd kissed Maeva Murphy behind the church. It was precisely the look Owen expected, except this time he wasn't lying.

"What?" Patrick prompted, obviously realizing Owen wasn't going to crack.

"You heard me," Owen replied.

"No," Patrick said, as though he were talking to a not-terribly-bright four-year-old. "I heard 'gold.'"

"That's right," Owen said, entirely serious. "Gold."

Patrick didn't pause to think before he roared, "Owen! You're not the full shilling."

"The tunnel," Owen growled back, "it's almost finished."

Owen pointed at the chalkboard. Patrick stood by Owen's side, his eyes flicking from notation to notation, an engineer taking in the specifications of a project. The drawing of his lighthouse was crude, even childlike, but the layout was right and the measurements, though not to scale on the drawing, were as accurate as Owen could make them.

There were two drawings, one a bird's-eye view of the main building, showing the kitchen/living room, his lantern tower and the back door that opened out from the kitchen into the small cobblestone courtyard. The tower house, drawn as a wobbly circle, stood on the other side of the yard. This was the original lighthouse, until it was destroyed by fire in 1813 when a wick from the old lantern was left to smolder after it fell out of the tub in which spent wicks were normally discarded, and set fire to the lantern.

Next to the tower house and at the far end of the courtyard was the shed drawn as a little square building, and inside the square was a circle colored in with hash marks, with lines trailing from it like the tail of a comet.

The second drawing showed the cluster of buildings from the side with a chest-high wall running around their perimeter, the comet's tail now recognizable as a tunnel coming down at about a fifty-five degree angle from the floor of the shed, then taking a sudden turn back on itself. There the lines went from straight, or as straight as Owen could draw them, to dotted lines until it reached the end of another set of dotted lines marked "catacombs." At the end of his tunnel, at the far northwest end of the "catacombs" was a little square identified by an arrow and the words "treasure chest."

With a wave to tell Patrick to follow him, Owen grabbed the chalkboard and a couple of books from the kitchen table and went out the back door into the courtyard. With his lighthouse light to guide him, he made his way across the cobblestone yard to the shed just off the tower house and unlocked the door. Struggling a bit with the books and the chalkboard, Owen started up the generator that sat near the shed wall across from his lighthouse tower. While it rumbled to life, Owen stopped in the doorway of the shed and let his brother step into the room. Patrick flashed Owen a look of suspicion as he passed, which Owen returned with an impatient smirk.

Patrick stepped up to the mouth of the tunnel, now awash in the dim orange glow of the work lights shining up from below and looked at it as though it were an open grave. He leaned in a little closer to try to see deeper into the interior.

"Remember the story of the Spanish Armada?" Owen asked.

Patrick shook his head first, then blinked and nodded instead. Of course he remembered.

"Well," Owen said, propping the chalkboard up on a workbench and leaning it against the shed wall near where the heavy-duty outdoor extension cord from the generator snaked into the room and down into the hole, "what was left of the Armada had to contend with the Irish coast to get back to Spain. One of them, *El Gran Grin*, was shipwrecked on Clare Island."

"You have been in the books," Patrick said.

Owen ignored him and said, "Do you remember the story of Grace O'Malley?"

"Granuaile?" Patrick replied.

Owen nodded and continued, "She ruled these islands at that time from her castle on Clare. Now, she didn't like the English, but she wasn't stupid. She knew that if she was seen to be helping the Spanish that England would send everything they had after her."

"The Spaniards knew it as well, but they also knew that money talks. They carried ransom money in case they were captured so they could buy their way home."

Owen paused and licked his lips. He couldn't help but grin at his puzzled brother and said, "I'm talking about treasure chests … gold coins … wealth beyond your wildest dreams …"

Patrick stared down the tunnel, and Owen wasn't sure if he was even listening. But he didn't care. He was talking about something he'd kept inside for so long, had never spoken about even once, and now he couldn't stop.

"Nobody ever spoke of it because Gracie also knew that if another clan got wind of their haul, they'd have every bounty hunter in the land trying to get their hands on it. So she buried it, and buried it deep."

Patrick squatted at the lip of the shaft Owen had dug into the foundation of his lighthouse complex and squinted at the rough lime-cement walls. Owen moved the string of lights, trying to help him get a better look.

"How long have you been digging this?" Patrick asked, and Owen couldn't tell if he was impressed or worried.

"Too long not to finish it," Owen answered.

Owen had dug the tunnel to be just big enough to climb down into and work in—not more than five feet in rough diameter—a little less in some spots, but not much more. From the roof of the tunnel at the end, where he'd turned back to the west and started leveling off, there were just a few inches over twelve feet of earth above him. While Patrick appeared to be visually inspecting the tunnel's structural integrity, Owen flipped through one of the books and found a drawing of a watchtower—a very old structure that originally stood where the lighthouse now resides—and the catacombs beneath it.

He held it up for Patrick to see. "I started to read," Owen said, "and piece it all together, and I soon realized that I was quite literally sitting on a gold mine."

"If nobody ever spoke of it," Patrick replied, not looking up at the book, "then what makes you think it even exists, let alone is buried here?"

"Look at this poem that Gracie left on her tomb," Owen said, setting down the book in his hand and flipping through the other book. After a minute or so of trying to find the note he was looking for, Owen, frustrated, opened the book and shook it, the pages hanging down. A folded-up piece of paper wafted to the floor, and he snatched it up, unfolded it, and shoved it in front of his brother.

Patrick looked at the note with clear reluctance, as though the paper was coated in some kind of poison.

Owen nodded at the paper and said, "Look …"

Eventually, Patrick obliged and looked down at it. Owen turned it right-side up and began to read aloud:

> "Lions of the black-browed sea
> Wrecked the ships by wind and mighty crest
> A king's ransom for the return of the lions
> A tower to watch over the beautiful bounty."

"The 'lions' are the Spaniards," Owen explained. "The 'king's ransom' is the gold they carried to pay for their safe passage. My light was built on the site of Gracie's watchtower. It had catacombs beneath it."

Owen picked up the book with the drawing of the watchtower again and held the handwritten poem next to it, then proudly announced, "This is the tower that watches over the beautiful bounty. The catacombs were filled in with lime-cement to make the foundation for my light when it was built in 1806, before they bothered with archaeology. But Gracie left clues in her poetry so that her descendants would know where the loot was buried."

Owen knew he was talking fast, faster than he'd ever talked before, but it was as if someone had opened a valve in him, letting it all out at once.

Patrick barely glanced at the book and said, "And you worked it all out, did you? You're crazier than I thought."

"Paddy," Owen started.

But Patrick talked right over him. "You've been digging for I don't know how long because of some poem. Get a hold of yourself, man. That is *your* handwriting."

"I copied it off Gracie's tomb," Owen said, frustrated that that was what Patrick thought to comment on, being purposely obtuse. "And it's not just a poem. There's a story that's been passed down that Gracie's clan were seen bringing a chest to the watchtower that used to sit where my lighthouse now stands."

Patrick went back to examining the tunnel while Owen went on, "I don't have far to go. By my reckoning there should only be a few feet of cement left, but I won't make it on my own in four days." He pointed at the book again, then at the chalkboard. "Look at the drawings ... it's there."

Patrick did look up at the book, squinting in the dim light, and gave the chalkboard a quick glance. He stood and read the poem again, silently. Owen watched his eyes track from line to line.

Finally, Patrick said, "I see catacombs all right, but I don't see an X marking the spot of any buried treasure." Owen stepped to the chalkboard, scrubbed out "treasure chest" from the board, then picked up a chunk of cement from the floor as Patrick continued, "And this poem doesn't even rhyme." Using the dry, crumbling cement as chalk, Owen drew a nice big X on the chalkboard right where he knew the treasure to be. Patrick ignored him and concluded, "The reason nobody spoke about it is because it doesn't exist."

"I'm asking you to help me," Owen said. He didn't know what he felt as he said those words again. Was it desperation?

Owen just needed to dig faster, much faster than he could dig on his own with a pickaxe.

"I was a designer," Patrick said, head tipped to one

side as though he felt sorry for poor, insane Owen, "of marine engines. I haven't gotten my hands dirty in years."

Patrick glanced at Owen's perpetually dirty hands.

"I can't finish it on my own," Owen reaffirmed.

Patrick shook his head and replied, "A few hours ago, you didn't want anything to do with me, and now you're asking me to get involved in some ridiculous treasure hunt." He looked out the shed's only window, just a black rectangle now, the sun having set in full. "I assume I've now missed the last ferry back to the mainland, so I'd appreciate a bed for the night. Then I'll be out of your hair in the morning."

Owen, still holding the poem to the open page with the drawing of the watchtower and the catacombs, slammed the book shut. "Come with me," Owen said, and he turned, picked up the chalkboard, and walked out.

Patrick followed him outside, and Owen went just a few steps from the shed and along the round wall of the tower house to another door. This one he didn't bother to lock, he just pushed it open and flipped on the light—just a single old lamp on a rickety table in an unwelcoming space.

"You can sleep in here," Owen said. "It's a bit dirty, but … well, no cause to clean it."

Patrick leaned to one side to peer into the dark little room in the base of the tower. There was a single bed surrounded by tools piled on the floor. A layer of dust seemed to glow in the moonlight. Owen expected Patrick to rail against the thought of spending a night in a tool shed but he just stepped past him into the dingy room. "Goodnight," he said, and Owen closed the door behind him.

CHAPTER 6

Only on a morning like this, with the seas calm, the wind but a whisper, and the sun only barely risen over the eastern horizon, could anyone hear the regular clank of a pickaxe against cement wafting up and out of the grounds of the Clare Island Lighthouse.

But there was no one close enough to hear it, and rarely was there.

There was a pause in the pounding, then another blow. Another pause. Another blow. Then quiet.

After a time, Owen's heavy-footed tramping echoed up the curving steps of his lighthouse to the lantern room. The rotating lens slowly ground to a halt, the bright light quickly fading. Then the footsteps again, through the living room and out the front door into the chilly dawn. Still covered practically head to toe in fine gray-white dust, he stood just outside the door and shook himself off. A few hard, ragged coughs cleared at least some of the dust from his throat, and after a couple of stuttering attempts, he managed to get in a deep breath of fresh air.

With a few more shakes of his arms and legs and a moment to stretch his aching back, Owen started off down the trail. He hadn't gone more than half a dozen steps when the hairs on the back of his neck stood on end. He looked behind him, stumbled, then stopped to turn around.

The dull gray silhouette of his brother stood in the small upper window of the tower house. Apparently Patrick hadn't found the dingy little room to his liking and had managed to find a more congenial place to spend the night in the top of the tower. Much as Owen hated the thought of anyone creeping around the grounds without him knowing, he could hardly fault his brother for assuming he must have been kidding, suggesting Patrick sleep in that grimy old room.

And maybe he had been kidding.

Owen shrugged and set off back on the path, absently brushing more dust and little flakes of cement out of his already gray hair.

There wasn't a cloud in the sky, and the chill was already coming out of the air as Owen made his way along the cliffs. He coughed a few times as he walked, breathing deeply to try to replace the dust in his lungs with the cool, pure sea air.

Heavy and slow with exhaustion, Owen made it to the rock at the crest of the hill overlooking the cove and sat down. He squinted, a little dust still in his eyes, and grimaced, trying to clear his face of powdered cement. Then he felt his face soften.

The sea glittered in the morning sunlight and, just as he'd hoped, there was Ellen O'Malley again, walking down into the cove with a spring in her step. She had a towel wrapped around her shoulders, her hair tied up. But then a sound interrupted Owen's reverie. His face hardened again when he saw a little lobster boat chugging around the headland and making for the cove.

• • •

Derry stood in the lobster boat, a fishing gaff in his hands. It was almost identical to Quinn's lobster boat, with a slightly bigger outboard engine that gurgled away and sounded fast but was all talk. Ryan steered the boat, leaving Derry the harder, wetter work of dragging up the lobster pots. Fishing for lobster was one way a few of the islanders could supplement their income, and with the Seafarer's Festival soon upon them, they should turn a tidy profit.

As they rounded the cliff toward the siding, they could see old Quinn's lobster boat bobbing about at the end of the cove, suspended between its three ropes …

Loathe as Derry may have been to admit it, Ryan had a deft hand with the little outboard and put the float—an old two-liter soda bottle—right along their port side. Derry slipped the hooked end of the fishing gaff around the rope, and the makeshift float caught against the rusty hook. He could tell just as soon as he started pulling up the line, the cold water of the soaked rope numbing his hands, that there weren't any lobsters in it. A few more seconds told the tale—no one home. The bait was still there, so Derry let the pot drop back into the water.

He looked over at Ryan, who'd seen the empty pot. The two brothers exchanged a shrug, and Ryan steered a little more to port, out a bit to sea. Derry checked his watch. They had just enough time to putter around the island back to the quayside to get the ferry ready for the first morning run.

He set the fishing gaff along the gunwale, and as he sat on the wet bench, he was looking off the starboard side and ahead a bit into the cove.

Still a ways out and getting a bit farther out, Derry couldn't tell who it was who had quickly disrobed and slipped into the water. But he was just close enough to know it was a she and not a he.

Derry sat on the wet little bench facing his brother and said, "Let's check the pot in the cove."

Derry's face flushed, and he couldn't help but smile. Ryan gave a quick nod and turned into the cove. Derry squinted as the rising sun glinted off the water, and it was hard to see … and there she was, just the top of a head, and a smudge of flesh just under the rippling surface of the water. Derry waggled his eyebrows a bit and turned to Ryan to point out the naked woman they'd been lucky enough to come upon when a familiar voice called out, "Good morning, boys."

It was their Aunt Ellen's voice, but where was she? Derry started scanning the rim of the cliffs, then realized the voice had come from the water, and his eyes bulged and his breath caught in his throat.

"Ah …" Derry said, blushing again, his heart racing. "Err …" He was having a bit of trouble breathing. "Morning Auntie …"

"Oh," Ryan said, apparently just having noticed her. Then he called back, "You haven't seen our pot, have you?"

Ellen pulled her bare arm out of the water and pointed, and Derry coughed. "That must be it there," she said.

Derry looked at his brother, and their eyes met. Derry shook his head, fast, his eyes still bulging, holding his breath.

Ryan looked back at their aunt, then back to Derry, and Derry was still shaking his head.

"No bother," Ryan called back to their mother's cousin. "We'll come back for it later."

And with that he turned the outboard and gave it the last little bit more it had. The boat chugged out of the cove.

"You eejit!" Ryan hissed at Derry, though they were already too far away to be heard.

Derry tried to swallow, but it was as if his throat had closed up. Though it was still cool out, he started sweating. "I think I might have seen her naked," he choked out. "Oh, sweet Jaysus, I'm going to ifreann for sure."

• • •

Patrick was sitting at the kitchen table when Owen stomped in.

"Morning Owen," he said. "Enjoy your walk?"

Owen walked past him, ignoring him. He switched on the kettle, went back into the living room and straight up the spiral staircase to the lantern room. He could feel Patrick's eyes on him the whole time, but paid him no mind.

He checked the instruments and went briskly back down the stairs, keeping the pertinent facts and figures in mind. Patrick watched him walk back into the kitchen. Owen pulled up a chair next to his brother, and ignored him entirely in favor of the logbook. He flipped through the book and scribbled down the readings. Patrick leaned forward to look over his shoulder.

"That poem," Patrick said. "It doesn't rhyme, you know."

Owen wasn't sure if it was Patrick's breath or a draft from the lantern tower that caught the back of his neck, but he shifted uncomfortably in his seat as he briskly rubbed the spot on his neck where his hairs had stood up. Patrick was forever standing over his shoulder and breathing down his neck as they were growing up, and even if it wasn't him on this occasion, the very thought of it still wound him up after all this time.

"It's half a poem," Patrick said, and Owen turned to look at him.

"I don't need an English lesson," Owen shot back. "I need a pair of hands."

Patrick smirked and held up his hands, looking at them in a mocking way, as though he'd just noticed he had hands.

"I'll give you twenty percent for a few days' work," Owen offered, the share only just then coming to him. He cringed, trying not to show that he thought he'd offered too much.

"I don't want your money," Patrick replied, putting his hands back down in his lap. The table was empty in front of him. He hadn't bothered to fix himself a cup of tea or anything for breakfast. "I want you to stop this before you kill yourself."

Owen scoffed and closed the logbook with an unsatisfying dull thud. "Then why did you come back here with me?"

"To talk things over before it's too late," Patrick replied without pause.

Owen opened the logbook back up and though his eyes wandered the page, chosen at random, he didn't read any of the old notes.

"I don't have time for talking," Owen said.

Patrick shook his head and with a sigh replied, "I can't watch you destroy yourself down there—"

Owen whipped his head up and around to stare his brother in the eyes.

They sat and glared at each other for a few seconds, then Owen checked his watch. "Fine," he said, "you'll make the first ferry … come on."

Owen pushed himself up to his feet, palms down on the table, and he headed through the living room and out the front door. Patrick reluctantly followed. Without another word, Owen went to his truck and climbed in, opening the passenger side door for his brother. As he started it up, Patrick climbed into the passenger-side and settled into his seat with another sigh. He seemed resolved not to even close the door of the truck himself, so Owen leaned across and slammed it for him. Owen put the truck in gear and rattled out of the gravel driveway in front of his lighthouse.

As they bounced along down the dirt road, the two brothers sat in silence for a long few minutes. Owen refused even to look at his brother. His lips were drawn into a tight line, his teeth clenched tightly together.

Eventually, Patrick broke the silence. "Did you not ever wonder what was in those letters?"

It took Owen a few seconds to remember what letters he was talking about, and then he replied, "There's nothing you could say in a letter that would change my mind."

"How about in person?" Patrick replied.

Owen steered around some deeper ruts in the dirt road and let his brother sit there for another long pause. "Save your breath," Owen said finally. "I'll not forgive you for what happened."

Then it was Patrick's turn to sit in intractable silence.

Though to Owen all this seemed to grind on through interminable hours, maybe half a dozen minutes passed before he gave in enough to say, "Look. We have the next few days to do something together. That's what you want, isn't it? Before it's too late?"

"Owen, please," Patrick replied, "will you leave it? As our father used to tell you, I think you may have lost the run of yourself."

Owen's lips twisted into a grimace and as though guided to that moment by the hand of providence, he drove up on the signpost. One sign pointed straight on and was marked "QUAYSIDE 2KM," and the other to the right: "CHURCH 1KM."

Owen swerved hard right, the truck fishtailing on the dry dirt and gravel road.

"Where are we going?" Patrick demanded.

"There's something you need to see," Owen grumbled back.

He glanced at his passenger but Patrick was looking out of the window. Owen wasn't driving too fast, but the kilometer to the church was eaten up by the truck soon enough.

The caretaker's cottage was a relatively new building for the island, barely more than two centuries under the sun. It sat amongst a stack of lobster pots and a low stone wall.

The lead roof of the church behind the cottage was new, as were the telephone poles running along the edge of the churchyard and some of the stones in the little graveyard. But the nave had stood since the 1400s. In spite of being worn smooth by hundreds of years of rain and some of the stones giving purchase to patches of moss, the gray walls rose straight up, unbowed.

Owen brought his truck to a rumbling stop in front of the little gate to the cottage. He turned off the engine, reached across Patrick's lap to grab a flashlight out of the glove box, and pulled out the key from the ignition, a clear sign to Patrick that he could sit in the truck and wait for him or follow. Owen wanted him to follow, of course, but he'd be damned if he was going to ask.

Patrick sat steadfast in his seat.

Quinn sat on a lobster pot, his eyes sparkling in the morning sun, and watched Owen approach. Though older than Owen by a decade or so, Quinn had a younger air about him and in some ways seemed like a strange sort of wrinkled little boy playing pirate. A patch covered his left eye, and a cigarette hung from his mouth, suspended by a single tooth. He reached into his pocket and pulled out a pair of thick-rimmed glasses that he rested on his crooked nose at a decided angle.

As Owen approached the cottage, a dog's sharp, loud bark startled him. Quinn's shabby old sheepdog Patch ran toward him, but stopped short. Owen had known the dog since it was a puppy, and Patch had never barked at him—then Owen realized the dog was looking past him at Patrick.

He remembered that Patrick was never comfortable around dogs. Maybe Patch picked up on it, but he didn't have time to give it any more thought. Patrick would be safe in the truck, and he didn't look like he had any intention of getting out anyway.

Quinn hadn't just been sitting on the lobster pot; he was carefully repairing his fish netting. He stopped his work as Owen approached and hopped down like a man half his age. He brushed his greasy gray hair back with his left hand, then caught Owen up in a short, comradely embrace. Owen looked back at Patrick, who was still sitting in the truck, staring at the barking dog.

"It's been a while," Quinn said, attracting Owen's attention away from the dog.

"Been busy," Owen said.

Then Quinn looked past him and scowled at his dog. "Quiet, boy."

But the dog only seemed to bark louder. Owen turned back to the truck and said to Quinn, "My brother, Paddy."

Quinn shouted at the dog again and said to Owen, "I can't hear a word you're saying." Then once more to the still-barking dog, "Quiet, boy!"

But the dog stood his ground, barking without pause. Quinn patted Owen on the arm and said, with a nod to his cottage, "Come inside."

Owen followed Quinn into his cottage, and not for the first time, it struck Owen that passing through that door was akin to stepping through a time machine into the 1950s. The dull blue, vinyl furniture sat on the dull pink linoleum floor. An old recording of an old song, played on an old record player.

Quinn slipped a bottle of malt whiskey out of a cupboard and showed it to Owen with a wink. Owen smiled and nodded once in reply. So what if it was half past eight in the morning?

While he poured a couple of glasses, Quinn said, "If you've come for the key, you can't have it."

Owen half-expected that but still asked, "Why?"

"Father O'Brien has decided that no one goes into the church without his permission," Quinn proclaimed as he handed Owen one of the glasses.

Owen retorted, maybe a bit too emphatically, "It's a community church for cryin' out loud!"

Quinn shrugged and downed the whiskey in a single gulp, then said, "You know what he's like. Been reading the newspapers again. All these stories of church robberies … He's convinced that we're next."

Owen looked down at his own drink but didn't put the glass to his lips. "A thief will hardly get very far … we're on an island."

"I know," Quinn replied with a shrug. "He's had me up there taking down the spire this morning. He'll have me stripping the lead off the roof next."

"The spire?" Owen exclaimed. Then he downed his own whiskey, coughing a bit at the burn so early in the morning.

"It's worth something. Father O'Brien reckons it's off one of the Spanish Armada ships … you know," Quinn said. "Bloody heavy, I'll tell you that much."

"I just need the key for two minutes," Owen said, the word "minutes" coming off as too loud. The music stopped. He glanced over at the old record player as it automatically lifted the needle off the record and shut itself off. "He won't even know I've been," Owen finished.

The dog had stopped barking, too.

"Well," Quinn said, "you can ask him yourself."

"He doesn't like me," Owen retorted.

"Maybe you shouldn't have told him to feck off,"

Quinn replied with a wink, then waggled his glass to ask Owen if he wanted another. Owen shook his head.

"I didn't mean it," he said.

Quinn poured himself another. "Your obsession with old Gracie is not healthy, my boy. Can't you find yourself a woman with warm blood in her veins?"

Owen stood his ground against Quinn's sly grin and wink.

"The *key*," he demanded.

Quinn just shook his head, staring at him over the lip of his whiskey glass.

With a sigh, Owen turned to leave. Then he stopped and asked, "How's my old generator holding up?"

With an eyebrow raised, he turned to look at Quinn, whose face had dropped. Owen imagined he could smell smoke, the little old man was thinking so hard.

After a while Quinn put his glass down on a counter, picked up the bottle of whiskey, and opened the cupboard. He put the whiskey away, and when his hand came back out, he held a huge, rusty iron key.

"Two minutes," Quinn sighed. "And don't get caught."

He handed the key to Owen, who smiled, nodded, and showed himself out. Patch had wandered off, but Patrick still sat in the truck. Owen looked at him, caught his eye, and held up the key.

He could see Patrick sort of sag, so he opened the truck door and stood there impatiently until Patrick climbed out, then slammed the door behind him and stomped off. By the time he got to the door of the old church, Patrick had caught up with him.

"Why are we here?" Patrick asked.

"To see Gracie," Owen replied.

Owen opened the old lock with a practiced touch and swung the heavy doors inward. The hinges let out a ghastly creaking that, despite his being well acquainted with their every squeal, gave Owen a bit of gooseflesh.

Patrick at his side, Owen shook that off and stepped into the church, saying, "Grace O'Malley was one of the greatest Irish women that ever lived. She was a lady, a scholar …" Owen paused to swing the creaking door shut with a dense thud. "… and a *pirate!*"

CHAPTER 7

A grand Gothic cathedral it was not.

If anything the church seemed even smaller on the inside than it appeared from without. And inside it appeared even older.

In the dimmed light that passed through the thin, arched, dirty, thick-glassed windows, the walls at first appeared to be made of marble. But as Owen's eyes grew accustomed to the dim lighting, the walls once again revealed themselves to be as dirty and old and faded and patchwork as the windows themselves. Still, Owen could spend a whole day just gazing at the ceiling, painted with images of men and animals, more reminiscent of cave paintings than the work of modern men. This was folk art, not Michelangelo, and Owen found it infinitely more beautiful.

Inside the door was a small nave, probably always too small even for the island's population back when it was built. Past the brick-arched crossing, there wasn't much if any of a transept on the left wall, really more an arched niche, and to the right, just a bit more space. The apse, with a lone small window in the far wall, felt like the end of a dank and narrow cave.

Owen clicked on his flashlight, and the beam played across the elaborate spire that Quinn had laid on its side just inside the door. It occurred to Owen that picking the padlock to get onto the church would be an easier job for a thief than climbing onto the roof of the church to pull it down. About four feet long and topped with a crescent-shaped disk, it was a peculiar artifact from the Spanish Armada, but it wasn't what Owen had come to show his brother.

"Over here," he said, stepping through the vaulted crossing into the apse.

He shined his flashlight on the arched niche in the left-hand wall. The once-ornate decorative carvings were rounded with age and grayed by dust. Mold grew in verdant patches, eating away at the centuries-old plaster surrounding it.

"This is the tomb of Grace O'Malley," Owen whispered to his brother, nodding at the little alcove.

"This is it," Owen whispered, leaving his light on the tomb. "Look. That's the poem. Just as I told you." Then Owen couldn't help but raise his voice well beyond what anyone would call a whisper: *"All of it!"*

Patrick shushed him and grudgingly stepped to his side and began to read aloud:

"Lions of the black-browed sea
Wrecked the ships by wind and mighty crest
A king's ransom for the return of the lions
A tower to watch over the beautiful bounty."

With a sigh, Patrick looked at his brother, shook his head, and whispered, "It's half a poem, I'm telling you."

Then Owen's flashlight beam found the plaque on the wall just to the left of the alcove. Set a couple of inches deep into the wall, and framed as though it were a window, the upright rectangle was carved in bas-relief.

The black slate carving was bordered on both sides by stylized knotted ropes. At the top was a prancing horse, its too-long tail up high and curved back down. Most of the center of the carving was a shield topped with what always looked to Owen like a bird but may have been an armored knight in profile wearing a pointy-visored helm. A stack of arrows crossed through that figure.

Below that, in the middle of the shield, was a wildly stylized boar with quite a fierce grimace, its open mouth lined with exaggerated fangs and a protruding tongue. A rough crop of hair ran along its back to a curved tail making almost a complete figure eight. Three bows with arrows drawn—two on the top and one on the bottom—pointed at the boar. Then, almost as an afterthought, a box on the bottom left corner of the shield contained

100

a crude sailing ship riding the waves with a pennant fluttering from the top of its mast.

Under the shield, packed in so the last two letters had to be turned up toward the shield, were the words "TERRA MARIQUE POTENS"—*mighty by land and sea*. And under that, in letters much larger and prouder, the name "O'MAILLE."

"That's Grace O'Malley's coat of arms," Owen said as he stepped back, watching his brother's eyes play over the carving, when the door creaked open.

The blood dropped right out of Owen's face, and the flashlight beam went this way and that. Before the big old door had swung entirely open, Owen had clicked off the flashlight and whispered, "Quick," to his surprised brother, "hide."

The brothers then pressed into a gap behind the little archway.

Owen peeked around the corner and wasn't surprised to see Father Finbar O'Brien framed in the morning sunlight. The man was no older than forty but acted sixty. His hair had started thinning in a fuzzy patch high on his forehead, over thick, black, arched eyebrows that gave him just the right perpetual condemning scowl for a parish priest. He always looked like he needed a shave, and when he smiled, his lips looked tight and insincere.

"Well," the priest said, "it's lovely to finally meet you, Ellen."

Owen almost let out a gasp but just managed to contain it.

"Mary has told me all about you and your book," the priest finished.

Owen pressed harder into the wall, trying to disappear behind the arch. He heard Ellen and Mary step into the church as the priest held the door open for them. The sound of the padlock bouncing and scraping against the door made Owen cringe. Father O'Brien must have been examining it; surely he had seen the church was unlocked.

Footsteps approached the archway. Owen pressed himself harder still against the wall as Patrick stared back at him with a disdainful glare for getting them into their predicament. Neither of them could speak for fear of being discovered only a few steps away.

"So," Father O'Brien said, "here we are."

Owen fought back a twinge of fear that the priest was talking to him.

"The last time I was in here, I was just a child," Ellen said, her voice echoing a little.

"Nothing much will have changed," Father O'Brien replied, a touch of pride in his voice.

"Wasn't there a rumor that Gracie isn't actually buried here?" Ellen asked the priest.

Owen bit his lip to stop himself from answering.

The priest chuckled in a condescending fashion that made Owen cringe again and said, "People do love a mystery, don't they? Would someone really go to all the trouble of building a tomb and then have themselves buried somewhere else?"

Owen heard the scratching of a pen on paper. Ellen must have been taking notes or drawing a quick sketch.

He could feel himself start to sweat.

"Is there anything behind the tomb?" Ellen asked.

A moment of blind panic shot through Owen, and he tensed all the more.

"Plenty of dust, but that's about all," Father O'Brien replied dismissively.

Owen closed his eyes and considered praying.

"I'd like to take some photographs if that's okay," Ellen said.

Father O'Brien answered, "No problem," and a couple of flashes pierced Owen's eyelids.

"Thank you, Father," Ellen said.

"Yes," Mary added, "thank you."

"You're welcome," the priest responded, and Owen wasn't sure if he'd truly detected a sense of impatience in the priest's tone or if that was just wishful thinking.

Their footsteps receded, and the door creaked a little, then a little more.

Owen risked a peek around the archway and saw that they had indeed left the church, the door beginning to creak slowly closed.

"Come on," Owen whispered to Patrick, "before he locks us in."

Then a thin-fingered hand wrapped around the closing door and Ellen looked in—had she heard him?

That hardly mattered; their eyes met, and Owen, feeling a tightness in his face and jaw, mouthed the words, "Don't tell him," and patted the air in front of him.

Ellen, clearly confused, nodded and slipped back out the door.

"Ellen," Mary's voice filtered in from outside, "was that—?"

• • •

"Nothing," Ellen cut in, shaking her head, eyes wide.

Mary looked at her, confused, but got the message not to say anything about Owen being in the church, though it was obvious she didn't understand why that was a problem at all.

And as Ellen brushed past Father O'Brien and stood next to her cousin, she shared in that confusion. She couldn't fathom why Owen didn't want the priest to know he was in the church just then, but as she pondered that, she remembered the puzzled look on Father O'Brien's face when they first got to the church door and he found the padlock hanging there unlocked. Ellen hadn't thought anything of it at the time. After all, who would lock up a public church?

Ellen barely registered the small talk passing

between the priest and her cousin. Her hands shook a little, and her face must have been noticeably red. This lighthouse keeper was quite a mystery. And one, at least in that moment, she wanted to play along with.

"Ellen." She jumped a little at the sound of her name, and from the look on her cousin's face she must have been standing there, oblivious to the world, for at least long enough to miss some question or other.

"So, you're not married?" the priest added, more of a statement than a question, and Ellen bristled at the look on his face and the tone of his voice, as though he were speaking to an errant toddler.

She carefully stepped to the side and around him so that the priest stood with his back to the door, which was still grinding its way closed with that awful screeching noise.

"Ellen?" Mary prompted, jabbing a thumb in the direction of the priest.

"No," Ellen said, afraid her voice was too loud. She softened it and her demeanor, letting her weight shift onto her right foot and unconsciously reaching out to touch Father O'Brien on the arm. "No, I've come back to Clare for a fresh start."

Father O'Brien smiled, and the look made Ellen draw back slightly. He didn't notice and instead turned to reach for the padlock. Ellen drew in a sharp breath and touched his arm again to turn him around.

"And you?" she asked without thinking.

"The Lord only allows me to window shop, I'm afraid," he said with a glint in his eye and an uncomfortable toothy smirk that made Ellen have to work not to cringe.

"Of course," Ellen said after clearing her throat.

Owen slipped out the door, right behind the priest. Ellen almost gasped; then she quickly grabbed the priest by the arm and turned him toward her. She took three steps back, dragging the befuddled clergyman along. Owen looked back at the door, and Ellen thought he was waving to someone in the church to follow him. But she had to turn away to keep the priest from looking, too. The door creaked and creaked again, and to keep him from turning at the sound, Ellen said, "I beg your pardon, Father."

Owen having slipped around the corner of the church and out of sight, Ellen released Father O'Brien, and the priest turned and padlocked the church door. "Well," he said, turning back to look at Ellen, "I hope to be seeing you ladies at the Seafarer's Festival on Saturday."

Ellen hardly heard him. Instead she started thinking of Owen Kerrigan, the enigmatic Lighthouse Keeper ...

"We'll be there," Mary answered for them both.

"That's grand," Father O'Brien said, grinning with a smile full of crooked teeth turning slightly gray.

•••

Owen wound his way through the tombstones in the churchyard as quietly as he could, Patrick reluctantly in tow. Knowing they'd made good their escape—the priest would have said something had they been spotted and would no doubt have reinforced the defenses in his precious church to prevent Owen from making any more uninvited incursions. Owen slowed a bit and even backtracked through the cemetery.

The tombstones ranged in age from all too recent to centuries gone. The newer ones stood straight at attention, only making it clear that in time, like those whose graves they marked, they would begin to sink into the loamy mud.

Owen stopped at a particular stone. Not too ornate, seemingly put up only out of a sense of religious obligation, the old stone had seen more than its share of wind and rainstorms. The name on it was barely legible, but with a little effort, it could still be read.

Pointing to the headstone, Owen said to his brother, "Unusual name for an Irishman, don't you think?"

Patrick glanced at the stone and clearly wasn't able to make out the name. Owen crouched in front of it, and Patrick followed suit, leaning in and squinting, then reaching out a finger to touch it—though he never quite made contact.

"Quickly," Quinn said from behind them, and

Owen almost toppled over. Before he could scold Quinn for almost giving him a heart attack, the old caretaker said, "I need the key. And you'd better get off before he sees you now."

Owen put a hand on the tombstone to push himself up, leaving his brother to squint at the name "Sebastian Aguado" and the inscription "Died 1588." Owen gave Quinn back his key and watched the old man shuffle down the path back to his cottage.

CHAPTER 8

Owen's truck ground to a stop on the quayside, sliding a bit on the loose gravel. He stopped a bit faster than he'd intended—and he'd intended to stop fast—and had to try to cover up for the fact that his gut bounced him off the steering wheel.

Patrick grunted at the hard stop, looking sideways at his brother.

Owen didn't look back. He put the hand brake on and just sat there, resting his head in his right hand, elbow up in the open window. That same chubby fulmar circled lazily overhead. Three little girls Owen didn't recognize alternated between hopping, skipping, and dancing along the quayside, tossing stones into the water. The sunlight played across the water, flashing in what seemed like Morse code, but Owen couldn't translate the message. The sun struggled slowly up to its zenith.

It was a beautiful day.

The two brothers sat in silence for a full minute, which even to Owen felt like a damn long time.

Patrick spoke first. "So what if *El Gran Grin* did wreck on the island?" he said. "There's no evidence it was carrying a treasure chest."

Owen bristled at the way he said "treasure chest," as though it was the most absurd pair of words anyone had ever uttered. The two brothers sat there for another long pause, both refusing to speak to each other.

The quayside was starting to get a bit busy—busy by Clare Island standards anyway. There might have been a dozen people out and about. More fulmars and a few nesting gannets swooped overhead. A nice-looking young couple in nylon jumpers and dark blue jeans had joined the little girls, watching them cavort around with cautious smiles as the wind began to pick up and occasionally splashed a bit of spray at them. Two of the three girls hugged each other, then exchanged courtly bows. The other stopped throwing stones in the water to look on, her arms folded across her chest.

"You've not changed have you?" Owen grumbled. "Will you just believe me for *once*?"

One of the O'Reilly boys dropped the gangplank of the ferry with a great clattering that startled the young family and a few other passersby. Another young couple holding hands smiled at the ferryman, and he stepped out of the way to let them board.

"So …" Patrick said, "sending me packing, then?"

Owen didn't move, even though he had a pain in

his upper back and would have liked to have at least sat forward a bit.

With no change in his voice at all, Patrick added, "So this is goodbye?"

Owen stared out of the truck's windshield, and his eyes played along the quayside and the people strolling about, the businesses opening—not a lot of businesses—but his gaze lingered on what the locals called simply "the Castle." This was Grace O'Malley's stronghold—Castle Granuaile.

Legend had it that when Grace was a child, she had begged her father to allow her to sail with him. To put her off, he said that her hair would catch in the sails, so she cut it off and he gave her the nickname Grainne Mhaol (Grainne the Bald), which was Anglicized to Granuaile. Even when her flowing locks grew back, the nickname endured.

The castle itself was a great box of gray, weathered stone, now open to the public. It had once been home to a woman who was both a fearsome warrior and an educated scholar. The same woman who had refused to bow to Queen Elizabeth I and lived to tell the tale.

Grace O'Malley, immortalized in Irish legend as the renowned Pirate Queen.

To Owen, Castle Granuaile was more hallowed ground than the old church. He glanced reverently at the castle as he popped open the door of the truck, ignoring Patrick's sigh. He went three steps when he realized Patrick was just going to sit there. Then Owen went around the truck and opened his brother's door for him and stood aside, sweeping a hand, play-acting as a butler or doorman but with eyes that clearly communicated the next gesture would be less polite.

Patrick rolled his eyes and stepped out of the truck.

He may have made some grumbling protestations, but Owen ignored him and stormed along the quayside to the cluster of little houses, following the signs to the visitor center which resided in a small house at the end.

It didn't really know what it was. Part museum, part visitor center, and part shop. He hated that there were all these trinkets for sale to tourists, but at least it paid for essential works on the castle. Owen felt like crossing himself, entering into this shrine to Grace O'Malley. The walls were covered in posters and paintings of Grace, documenting some of her infamous adventures. It was quiet, and Owen was pleasantly surprised that he and his brother seemed to have the place to themselves. There was a sign on the desk that read: "GONE TO LUNCH. PLEASE LEAVE 1 EURO IN TIN."

And next to it, the tin.

Owen dug in his pockets and counted out two euros in coins, then dropped them dutifully into the tin.

Without turning to look at his brother, Owen

waved Patrick over to one side of the cramped little visitor center, saying, "Over there."

They stepped in front of a statue of Grace O'Malley, and Owen took a deep breath. There she was, as though frozen in time. She was a captivating woman. Her auburn hair swept back behind her and over her left shoulder, a thin headband rimming her forehead. Her eyes seemed strangely alive, her features—prominent nose, gently arched brows, big, red lips and defined cheekbones—reminding Owen, and not for the first time, of Ellen.

Grace wore a flowing dress, two sheathed double-edged swords hung from her rope belt, and her right hand was clutching a ship's tiller for all the world as if she meant to hit the brothers with it. *And she would have, too,* Owen thought.

"You see the key?" Owen asked his brother, indicating the ornate gold key that hung around the statue's neck.

Patrick leaned in to get a better look, then shrugged.

Owen pulled his gold key out from under his shirt and presented it to Patrick, still hanging from the chain around his neck. Owen's key was identical in almost every detail to the one on the statue, except Owen's was made of gold and the one on the statue of cheap painted plastic.

"This is the original," he told an already skeptical Patrick.

Owen took a step closer to his brother, who grudgingly gave the key a second look, then glanced back at the key hanging from the neck of the statue, then back at Owen's key once more. His face softening, he started to blink.

"Where did you get it?" Patrick asked.

"It's where it all started," Owen replied. "I found it washed up in the cove. It's from *El Gran Grin*. It's the key to the treasure chest."

Patrick looked at the key again but shook his head. "It can't be."

"It is," Owen fired back.

Owen dropped the key back into his shirt and stepped back to look at his brother. Patrick stood there for a bit, thinking.

"Even if it exists," Patrick said, his voice quieter now, "how do you know that it's under the lighthouse? It was probably taken off the island years ago."

Owen shook his head and said, in no uncertain terms, "The treasure is *here*, and it's under my light."

Patrick took a deep breath and looked around at the various museum displays and memorabilia. "I can't do this on my own," Owen said. "I don't have enough time, and I've just lost another morning with all this shite."

"Why me?" Patrick asked without pause.

Owen thought he had an answer ready but had trouble forming the words. His tongue stuck to the roof of his mouth. He tried to clear his throat, but that didn't help. His face flushed, his skin growing hot all at once.

"For feck's sake …" he finally managed. "Because you're my brother."

Patrick blinked, and his eyes went from hard to soft; then he looked away. Owen thought he might be blushing, too. Patrick turned his head this way and that as though he was looking around at the displays again, but Owen could tell his eyes were focused no more than a few inches in front of his face. He was thinking.

"I must be mad," Patrick said, so quietly Owen almost couldn't hear him.

Owen flushed again and couldn't resist a short smile, which he quickly suppressed by wiping his knuckles across his lips.

Owen went for the exit with Patrick in tow.

Once out of the visitor center, they walked back to the truck parked at the quayside under a wheeling flock of black-feathered, red-billed choughs.

• • •

Dougal must have heard Owen's truck rumble up his gravel drive. Before Owen even ground to a stop, the old man was walking toward him, the old drill in hand. Owen smiled at the spring in Dougal's step, which boded well for the condition of the tool.

"Now take it easy on her," Dougal warned, resting the old drill safely in the truck's bed.

Owen had counted out the thirty-five euros ahead of time, and without reply, he passed the wad of bills to Dougal through the open window. The old man accepted the money with a wink, not bothering to count it—at least not in front of Owen.

Voices—female voices—caught Owen's attention before he could thank Dougal. The short list of questions he had about the state of the drill fled his mind when Owen glanced up at the rear-view mirror and caught sight of Ellen and Mary. The cousins were chatting happily and strolling down toward the quayside. Mary's foot slipped on something—Owen couldn't see what—and Ellen's hand shot out to steady her, though it didn't appear that Mary was in much danger of falling. That brought a little round of giggles from both women. Owen was vaguely aware of Dougal moving around, and just as he realized he probably shouldn't be staring in the rear-view mirror in silence, a man approached the cousins.

It was that stuffed shirt from the council—Owen couldn't remember his name—all trussed up in his mac. The man was coming up the opposite way, and they stopped, apparently introducing themselves. Owen's eyes narrowed when the councilman shook Ellen's hand. Then movement to his right caught Owen's attention—Dougal waving at Mary and Ellen.

"Are we going to be seeing you ladies at the Seafarer's?" Dougal called. He smiled, and Owen sighed, grimacing. "I'll be dee-jaying …" Owen closed his eyes, rolling them at the same time. "I do requests …" Dougal added.

The women waved back. The councilman grimaced at Dougal for distracting the ladies from his attention.

Owen put the truck into gear and pulled away—not so fast anyone would notice, just enough to get the hell out of there.

· · ·

The drill, as loud as ever, drove into the cement at the end of the tunnel, sending out a dense cloud of dust, grit, and smoke. Owen kept his lips clamped tightly shut against it, and his eyes were almost closed, too. The drill bit screamed through the hard material, but it went all the way in. The drill still on, the shriek still deafening, Owen slid it in and out a few times, then pulled the bit out of the wall and set the drill down.

The pickaxe lay on the floor of the tunnel next to him, and he grabbed it up. In a single motion, he moved it from his left hand into position to strike the wall and—no time like the present—gave the lighthouse's foundation a good solid whack. Larger pieces of concrete flew out. One bounced off Owen's forehead, and another scraped against his hand, though neither hard enough to scratch him.

The hole was small—he hadn't gotten enough of a swing with the pickaxe. Patrick sat scrunched into the tunnel behind him, limiting how far back Owen could set the pickaxe. Owen wasn't sure what his brother was doing back there, but as sure as the day is long, he wasn't working. Of course, Patrick had been doing that ever since they were teenagers—getting out of work with complaints of a "bad back." Owen didn't believe him any more now than he did back then.

"Would you have ever tried to contact me if I hadn't come?" Patrick asked.

Owen cringed. It felt as though Patrick had been sitting there waiting for enough of a quiet, relatively dust-free moment to ask that question. And it was a question Owen had no intention of answering, and Patrick should have known better than to ask it.

But as though answering for him, the tunnel shed a few flakes of cement from the rough-carved ceiling, raining down on them for a few admittedly disconcerting seconds.

Owen looked up at the ceiling, holding his breath, and when he turned a little to see if there were any significant cracks behind him, he saw his brother doing the same.

"Is this tunnel safe?" Patrick asked.

Owen swallowed.

When Patrick looked back down from the ceiling to Owen, Owen replied, "Safe enough to finish the dig …"

Patrick's eyes widened as he shook his head, "Are you sure?"

Owen retorted, "According to my chart, I'm no further along than I would be on my own. Now get some dirt on those hands and dig!"

Patrick looked around the cramped tunnel as though casting about for any sort of tool, then looked back up at the ceiling as another little chip of cement fell onto Owen's head and slowly slipped off to clatter on the floor. Patrick struggled to his feet and retreated to one of the few parts of the tunnel a grown man could stand in.

Owen turned his attention back to the end of the tunnel and took advantage of the extra room to give it a really good whack with the pickaxe.

• • •

One thing on Clare Island that came cheap—relatively speaking, at least, and for locals only—was lobster. Enough were dragged up creeping and snapping out of the surrounding waters that Owen was able to put on quite a little spread on the outside table.

He went at the boiled beast with bare hands, Patrick watching him as though he were some kind of laboratory animal. The lobster itself looked like some giant spider, a mutant conjured up in the laboratory of a wizard with expensive tastes and the courage to eat something that might have been a louse seen through a microscope.

Owen sat near the lighthouse wall, the table set right up against it. He didn't always eat outside, but after a particularly long day's digging, it was good to get some fresh air. The night was cool, but not cold. The stars were out, and the breeze came in off the sea to help wash the air clean.

Owen's lantern beat out a rhythmic pulse of light above him.

He didn't want to look but had sat down facing that way. The new automatic lighthouse gleamed from a rocky outcrop just north of the island.

Owen watched it blink on, then pulse a few times and fade out. He ate the perfect, tender meat from a lobster claw, and by the time he swallowed, the new lighthouse blinked on again. Its light beam crossed over with his this time, and the beams looked like two jousting knights, the new light a usurper to his throne. When the automatic light faded out again and went off, Owen couldn't help but feel he'd won the little skirmish.

But then the new lighthouse blinked on again, pulsed, and faded out. Each test cycle the same as the last. The bloody thing worked just fine.

Owen looked down at his plate but didn't take

any more food. He cracked open a bottle of stout and poured it into an almost-clean glass, but didn't take a drink; he knew he had to wait for the black nectar to settle if it was to be fully appreciated.

Patrick sat in the pool of dim yellow light shining from a fixture on the lighthouse wall. Owen thought the light made Patrick look pale, even sick. He drew in a breath and was surprised at how hard that was. Owen's hands were shaking, his throat tight. Patrick didn't seem to notice any of that. He just sat there.

Shaking his head, Owen turned back away from his brother to join him watching the new lighthouse run through one more test cycle, and then at last took a good gulp of his drink.

"I guess machines will replace us all someday?" Patrick said, his inflection making it sound, oddly, like a question.

Owen resisted the urge to ask how a machine might replace Patrick's former profession as a marine engine designer as he knew that Patrick probably would have an answer for that. So instead he took another swig of stout and set the glass back down on the table, then patted the cool plaster wall of the lighthouse next to him, leaving a couple of melted-butter fingerprints on the whitewashed surface.

"What a waste …" Owen said with a sigh. "Two hundred years old and she's still running like a dream."

Patrick turned away from the new automatic lighthouse to look at his brother. As Owen cracked open another lobster claw, he asked, "What will you do – if by some miracle you actually find your treasure?"

Owen shrugged and chewed a bite of lobster meat. When he'd swallowed he replied, "I have no idea." Then, looking all around as though throwing a net around his light, maybe all of Clare Island with it, he added, "This is my life."

Owen had another bite of lobster, but he could hardly taste the meat.

"Ciara …" Patrick started. Owen could hear the strain in his voice. Patrick looked down at the table in front of him, at the untouched lobster on his plate, his mind obviously not on eating. Apparently finding some reserve of courage, all at once he said, "Ciara wanted me to pass on her regards."

Owen felt his body jerk forward a little. Could Patrick have seen it? His brother wasn't looking at him. Owen's stomach tightened, and all at once he was aware that he was holding the empty shell of a lobster claw and he just wanted it out of his hand. He didn't want anything in his hands. He threw the shell down on the table, and it clattered to an unsatisfying quiet stop somewhere between the two of them.

Owen stood up fast, ignoring all the little aches and pains, all the stiffness of the years spent in the tunnel—and the years just in general.

He downed his glass in one huge gulp, then said, "I need a drink."

"Owen," Patrick said, looking up … toward him, but not looking him in the eye, "we have to talk about this."

There was some pleading in his voice, but Owen had already turned to go back into the house for a bottle of whiskey or just to go back inside the house. His legs made the decision for him to stop and turn around. He even took a step back closer to the table, standing next to his overturned chair. Through a tightly constricted throat, Owen said, "What is there to talk about? How many times do I have to tell you?"

Owen grabbed the table with both hands and squeezed until his knuckles protested. He leaned in closer to Patrick … closer, and closer still …

Owen sprayed a few shreds of lobster and a few drops of stout from his mouth when he shouted, *"I won't forgive you!"* Each word seemed to explode out of him.

Owen tried to take a deep breath and ended up coughing, almost stumbling as he stood up straight and stepped back, letting go of the table.

"If that's the only reason that you're staying, then you can leave now," Owen said, his voice back to something approaching normal. But it still had to pass through a throat so tight it felt as though someone was strangling him.

Patrick looked his brother in the eye and said, "There isn't a day that's gone by that I haven't thought about what happened. If I had my time again, I would have done things differently."

Owen shook his head and turned his back on his brother. He forced out a breath that ended up as a cross between a sigh and a grumble as he reached back to steady himself on the table. He took a deep breath, rattling with cement dust and something else—something Owen didn't want to feel there.

"Get yourself to bed," Owen said without turning around. "We have a big day tomorrow …" He thought for a few seconds about what to say, then took another deep breath, steadier this time. He turned around, bent over—glowered at Patrick as he blew out the kerosene lamp on the table. Then he picked up his own plate, then Patrick's, still full of unfinished lobster, and said, "Save your energy for the digging."

It sounded like good advice for the both of them.

Owen didn't wait to see if Patrick went straight to bed, or if he even left the table. Maybe he cleaned up the empty bottles, maybe he just left them there. Owen tossed his brother's untouched lobster in the trash, did a few minutes of washing up, and then his shaking knees forced him to sit.

His shoulders tensed, and Owen started to be concerned, he was shaking so much. "God help me," he whispered to himself, then thought, *Is this a stroke now? Is that what this is?*

But he wasn't having a stroke.

He was remembering something he'd steadfastly avoided remembering. And he'd been steadfast in that determination for years—decades even.

An image of Ciara began to form in his mind, blurry and diffuse as though she were coming up out of the water. Her features didn't quite coalesce. She was beautiful—Owen knew that. He remembered that much, at least. He closed his eyes and swallowed a sob.

He sat there and counted to ten, then started over and counted to ten again. His heart stopped racing so much, and he could finally breathe. But still he couldn't form her face in his mind's eye. She rose to just below the surface of the water, her eyes ... blue? Brown? He remembered a blue dress, but it might have been purple.

Then a laugh shot out unbidden between his lips.

He swallowed the next laugh the same way he'd swallowed the sob.

He couldn't remember her face—the woman for whom he'd refused to speak to his only brother over for year after lonely year.

Pressing his eyes tightly closed, Owen tried once more to force her face to come up out of the water, but when it did, it was Ellen O'Malley's face.

Owen laughed again, wiped away the beginnings

of a tear, and let himself smile in the silent darkness of the unlit room.

Through the windows the harsh glow of his light made shadows run along the walls, expanding and contracting like people coming closer, then farther away, then closer, then even farther still.

Owen sat there in the dark for a little while, having given up trying to remember anything else he never wanted to remember. Then he went back down into the tunnel to dig as the close to full moon rose over Clare Island.

• • •

The next morning Owen awoke stiff, exhausted, and covered in dust. After struggling up out of bed, staggering into the shower, and grimacing through the chore of dressing, he skipped breakfast and made his way back down to the cove and the rock that had become the only thing he looked forward to.

He didn't even check the weather instruments that morning. He didn't polish the railing running up the spiral staircase of the lantern tower. He didn't make an inventory of his parts and make sure he had more than a week's worth of engine oil and other consumables.

Instead, he sat on his rock and watched Ellen O'Malley walk down the path to the water.

In the same way she had each time before, Ellen

disrobed and eased down the ladder into the clear water. She glided through the water and swam around Quinn's lobster boat that was still tied up in the cove. Owen knew he was staring at her. He knew that if she saw him, she would probably think he was some dirty old man sitting up there on a rock watching her swim naked. As he toiled with his thoughts, a voice cut through the gentle breeze—

"She's a beauty," Patrick said, and Owen all but jumped out of his own skin.

"You scared the bejaysus out of me," Owen said. His face went hot, and he coughed out a little cement dust. Owen glanced at his brother, who wore the same green cashmere sweater and identical khaki pants, the beige checked shirt, the ever-present gold watch, expensive glasses, and those shiny shoes that never seemed to have a scuff on them. Had Patrick not brought a change of clothes with him? Maybe he wasn't expecting to stay for long enough to need them.

Shrugging off that thought, Owen pressed his lips together to see Patrick watching Ellen swim slowly away from the ladder. "Keep down, man," Owen stage-whispered.

Patrick sat down next to him on the rock, and Owen, eyebrows furrowed, inched away from him a little. Patrick's eyes remained glued on the cove.

"Who is she?" he asked, and at first Owen wanted

to punch him square in the jaw, or maybe the nose—no, he thought finally, the eye. But he didn't hit his brother. Instead he found himself shaking his head and chewing the inside of his bottom lip. He felt like a schoolboy caught with a *Playboy* under his mattress.

Owen cleared his throat and said, "Ellen." He almost smiled, so pleased at how light and normal and conversational he thought he sounded. "She was in the church yesterday."

"She's writing the book?" Patrick asked, then started nodding as if answering his own question.

"Apparently so," Owen answered.

"What's it about?" asked Patrick.

"No idea," Owen replied. "She wants to come to my light this evening. Something about research …"

Patrick smiled and turned from the cove to look at his brother. "I'll make myself scarce."

"There's no need," Owen said, maybe a bit too fast and a touch too loudly. "We'll be digging. We don't have time for visitors."

With a sigh Patrick said, "Owen, wake up."

Owen felt his blood starting to boil again. *One nice, puffy, red-rimmed black eye*—slipped back into his mind.

"That tunnel is a pipe dream." Patrick pointed down at Ellen O'Malley. "This is life, right there in that cove."

Owen pushed himself up to his feet even as Ellen climbed back up the ladder out of the water. He turned his back on the cove and followed his brother's gaze up into the sky, where half a rainbow showed itself in the approaching rain.

"Well," Patrick said, "someone's smiling on us."

"That's a wind dog," Owen corrected him. He waited for Patrick to look at him, then said, "Bad weather's on the way."

CHAPTER 9

"Crap," Ellen O'Malley said under her breath.

That had been one of her favorite coffee mugs. A friend from work had given it to her after a vacation to Florida. Ellen couldn't remember why that particular woman had thought to get her a souvenir … had Ellen ever returned the gesture?

Anyway, the mug was a collage of all things "Florida": a flamingo, the space shuttle, a bowl of oranges, the skyline of Miami, a couple dancing the cha-cha … and in her continuing efforts to get unpacked she'd dropped it in the sink, and there it sat, in a dozen jagged pieces.

Ellen picked up one of the bigger shards, careful of the sharp edges, and stepped back, her weight all on her right foot. She turned the broken bit of cheap souvenir porcelain over and then back, and then this way and that, studying the shape of it, the way the front half of an alligator seemed to charge from it, fang-lined jaws agape …

She set that piece on the counter and gingerly picked

up another. This was part of an orange hibiscus flower, and then another—the top of the giant rocket that the space shuttle sat atop: a slightly different orange.

"Pretty," she whispered to herself, then went about placing each piece of the broken mug carefully on a dish towel next to the sink. She thought maybe a mosaic, or maybe she could do something with a flower pot, arranging them around just as splashes of color so that someone would have to look very carefully, very closely to maybe catch a glimpse of an alligator or a dancer or a water-skier.

Then something caught her eye through the window over the sink. A man was rooting around in the weeds across the road. She carefully placed the last piece of the broken coffee mug next to her, then squinted out through the window.

"Is that …" she whispered to herself. "Oh, what is his name?" *The cheerful man who looked like he was born in a toolbox*, she thought, "Dougal?"

Sure enough, Dougal tramped out of the weeds and onto the road. He seemed somehow … dressed up. Anyway, he wasn't wearing oil-stained coveralls but a proper shirt and navy blue pants. He might even have combed his hair.

Ellen smiled at that, then smiled even wider when she saw that he held a makeshift bouquet of various flowering weeds, clutched tightly in his right hand as though he was afraid they might try to escape.

And then another man strolled up the road, coming over the crest of the hill and slowing down to speak with Dougal. This was the man from the council that she and Mary had met yesterday. Try as she might, Ellen couldn't remember his name.

The rain had stopped, and the sun was struggling out through the dispersing clouds. Ellen pushed open the window, but slowly, as quietly as she could. She almost laughed aloud when she realized she didn't want to scare the two men off who now stood facing each other.

"It's a fine morning, Mister …" Dougal started. "Mister …?"

"O'Connell," the councilman provided with a polite smile. "Now the rain has stopped. I'm sure you get twice as much rain on this island than we do on the mainland."

"You're up early," Dougal said to Ellen through the open window, and Ellen thought, *Is it early?*

"I like a morning walk," O'Connell replied, or at least that's what Ellen thought he said. They were just far enough away that it was difficult for her to hear every word.

"Me too," Dougal said with a grin. He looked down, then glanced at Ellen's cottage, which was odd. "Goodbye now."

Mr. O'Connell looked as surprised by that sudden turn as Ellen felt. She smiled and shrugged to herself, and O'Connell nodded. Dougal started off down the road, and Mr. O'Connell walked right along with him for a few steps before both men stopped and looked at each other.

"Well …" Dougal said, not relaxing his death-grip on the little bouquet, "enjoy your day."

"I will," a clearly confused O'Connell replied. "Goodbye."

Then both men proceeded to just stand there.

Ellen wondered if maybe she should say something when a third man bobbed up over the brow of the hill—Father O'Brien, cradling a Bible and whistling some unknowable tune.

"Morning gentlemen," the priest said, his voice projecting clearly even as far as Ellen's kitchen window. "What a lovely morning it is."

Dougal nodded, and O'Connell stuttered through some kind of agreement—Ellen couldn't hear him.

Then all three men just stood there looking at each other, then trying not to look at each other, each apparently waiting for the other two to be on their way.

"Well I am popular this morning," Ellen whispered to herself. Then she called out, "Is everything okay?"

As though they'd spent hours rehearsing, they said in perfect three-part harmony, "Just passing …"

Ellen laughed and said, "Should I make us all a coffee?"

And then again the chorus: "Tea?"

The three men looked at each other, all horrified.

"Tea it is," Ellen said with a wide, gleaming smile at the Clare Island Welcoming Committee.

. . .

Owen hammered away at the cement wall like a man possessed. Sweat rolled down his forehead and into his eyes, where it mixed with the cement dust to all but plaster over them.

Owen couldn't see but didn't really have to see. It wasn't precision work—not yet. He'd been digging all day, and there were still hours and hours and hours of banging and banging and banging away to be done …

Patrick sat farther back in the tunnel, his gentrified arse on a pile of pulverized cement.

Not a drop of sweat on him.

"We've been in here digging all day," Patrick said, and Owen thought, *We?* "Take a break, man. You'll give yourself a heart attack."

Not that Owen hadn't considered that, a man of his years singlehandedly tunneling through age-old cement …

But he was fine, aside from the occasional ache and pain. Still, Owen slumped to the floor next to his brother and wiped the cement-and-sweat slurry from his eyes and face with a damp rag.

Owen looked at his brother while he ran the

already grainy rag against the back of his neck. "Not much chance of *you* getting a heart attack, sat on your arse there."

"This is a waste of your time and mine," Patrick insisted. "I should be at home with my family, not sat in a stinking hole with you."

Owen tossed the pickaxe against the tunnel wall— hard—harder even than he'd intended. Patrick lurched back, and Owen took a deep breath to tell his long-lost brother that he was free to get lost for another long time but was interrupted by a low, guttural rumbling like some kind of dragon was snoring itself awake somewhere in Owen's tunnel.

Owen looked at Patrick, and Patrick looked at Owen. Then both brothers looked up at the rough-hewn ceiling of the tunnel. A small lump of congealed dirt and cement landed on Owen's cheek, not a centimeter from his left eye. A slightly larger flake just missed Patrick's head. Then there was more— little flakes of cement and little clumps of dirt, and Owen whispered, "Shite." Then, after a couple of fast heartbeats, he shouted, "RUN!"

The two of them scrambled faster than any two men their age had any right to scramble, up over the bend in the tunnel, then slipping a little and struggling for footing on the upward slope. Second by second they clicked back and forth between feck-you panic and fraternal protectiveness.

All the time dirt and dust and cement and rocks rained all around them in a cacophony of crashing and thudding, and then they were out and sprawled on the floor of the shed. Owen was covered head to toe in a fine white dust streaked with dirty brown, but Patrick had somehow managed to keep his immaculate clothes relatively unscathed. They lay shoulder to shoulder, Owen coughing and spluttering and bringing up great wads of dusty spit.

Then the roaring noise stopped all at once, and they lay there for a bit longer, Owen's heavy, rasping breaths punctuated by the occasional tap, tap-tap-tap of a few last loose bits falling from the tunnel ceiling that echoed up and out into the shed.

Patrick sat up slowly, resting on his elbows, and he looked down on Owen and said, "I told you it wasn't safe."

Owen's eyes narrowed as he clenched his fist and gritted his teeth … but instead of giving in to the urge to thump his brother, he struggled up to his feet and half stepped, half fell back against the wall of the shed. He coughed once more and looked down into the tunnel from which dust still gently billowed out into the shed, looking for all the world like smoke.

Then Owen turned the word "Shite!" into the longest, loudest, angriest word anyone's ever bellowed. They might have heard him in Dublin, if not Mumbai.

Owen put his hands on his knees and bent forward, forcing air into his lungs. He closed his eyes, hoping against all hope that Patrick wouldn't say anything else. Owen thought at that moment he'd give every last coin of Grace O'Malley's treasure if his brother would just sit there and not say another word.

And Patrick must have sensed it. He just sat there tight-lipped, staring at his brother, slowly shaking his head in silent disapproval.

Finally, the need for water sent Owen limping across the courtyard and back into the lighthouse kitchen. As he rinsed the dust from his mouth, he wondered just how bad the cave-in had been—how many hours, or even days, he'd lost.

Then his thoughts were interrupted by a tap, then a proper knock on the front door.

Owen's face flushed, and he stood up straight, now keenly aware that he was covered in dust and looked like he'd just been dug up.

Staggering to the front door, he peered through the dirty little window beside it to see Ellen O'Malley beaming back at him.

Owen couldn't breathe.

"Oh," he managed to barely exhale, "shite …"

Owen recoiled from the window to see Patrick now sat in the leather armchair. "It's Ellen," Owen whispered to his brother.

"Well let her in then," Patrick demanded.

"Look at the state of me!" Owen half whispered, half shouted.

"If it's not convenient, I can come back later on," Ellen called through the door.

Owen leaned against it. His heart quickened. *Yes I'll tell her to come back later.* He was just about to utter the words when—

Patrick's face was stern, almost paternal, when he said, "Don't you dare send her away, you hear me?"

After a long, conflicted pause, Owen banged the back of his head against the door in frustration and growled out in a whispered tone, "God help me, okay … okay …"

Then he turned to Patrick, who sat there, arms folded across his chest, smirking at him.

"Well, on yer bike then!" Owen fired at Patrick, wiping the smirk from his face.

"I could do with some fresh air," Patrick replied as if he was intending to leave anyway.

"Back door," Owen said definitively as he blocked the front door.

He watched Patrick get up from the chair and walk into the kitchen, ensuring that he'd gone, and then unlocked and opened the front door to let Ellen in.

Before Ellen could catch sight of him, Owen ambled as quickly as his tired legs would carry him out of the room and into the kitchen. Calling out as he left, "Give me a minute."

"No problem?" Ellen said as she walked in holding a cake tin and closing the door behind her.

The lighthouse complex had been added on to and rebuilt over the years, adding a shed here, a room addition there, and more than one back staircase. Owen trundled up a staircase so narrow his arms rubbed against the rough plaster walls as he went. He left trails of dust and grit along the walls but got to his bedroom. Even as he entered, he started stripping off his dust-covered clothes, waving away the cloud that puffed up around him and quickly settled into piles on the floor. When he threw open his wardrobe, he was confronted by weeks of having set aside his regular household duties in favor of the tunnel.

He hadn't done any laundry in a while.

Most of his clothes lay in a heap hardly less dusted with powdered cement and dry dirt as those he'd just stripped out of.

But hanging from the rail in the wardrobe was the only clean garment in his lighthouse. It had been years since he'd last worn it—would it even fit him anymore?

Owen grimaced, but when he heard Ellen singing downstairs, he sighed and whispered, "Come on Kerrigan, you can do this."

• • •

Ellen stood in the lighthouse living room—at least, that's what it seemed to be.

The furnishings were rather spartan, but that just added to the allure of the lonely lighthouse keeper in his unassuming garret.

After a few minutes, she started to feel a fool, standing there with her cake tin.

On further examination, the place was a mess. There was a thin layer of dust over everything, and a strangely thicker layer of dust in other parts. Ellen walked over to the curved housing of the lighthouse drive shaft, some kind of steel shaft covered in chipped black paint that ran down the middle of the lantern tower, and there was the end of a brass rail hinting at a stairway. Nudging up against the tower, she peeked up the spiral staircase into the lantern room—she loved the idea of breezing up that tightly winding staircase, up to the top of lighthouse to look out over the island like a queen looking down from the highest minaret of her castle.

The thought made Ellen smile, but then she was startled by a thumping sound, and footsteps on wooden stairs—heavy footsteps that echoed through the lighthouse. Ellen swallowed and her mouth felt dry, and she cleared her throat and went quickly to the leather armchair. Should she sit down? Was it better if she was sitting there, more casual, as though she belonged, and not standing there as if at attention in a stranger's living room? She ended up taking two steps toward the chair, then stopping and taking a single step back and a little to one side and fetching up again next to the spiral staircase.

She stifled a laugh, then felt obliged to clear her throat again—more loudly this time—so no one thought she was hiding or sneaking around.

Owen emerged from the kitchen and stood there, seemingly at attention. Ellen thought he looked like a policeman. He wore a jet-black uniform: a double-breasted jacket with shiny brass buttons and sharply creased black pants. A simple white shirt underneath and a black tie finished it off. It all looked either brand-new or freshly pressed, at least—impeccably clean. On his head was a peaked cap with a brilliant white top and a patent-leather black band and visor. A silver badge shone from the center of his forehead. A wreath of shamrocks with a crown on top surrounded the words "Irish Lights" embossed on a stylized belt that encircled a maritime scene of an iconic lighthouse tower with a three-masted ship sailing past in the distance. The principal lighthouse keeper's badge had been replaced with a cloth one years ago, but Owen refused to change his.

And it was a tight fit, as Owen had feared, but he managed to pull it off. Anyway, Ellen admired the effort. He seemed to be putting on the whole show for her; then she thought maybe he was wearing his uniform in honor of the old lighthouse's last day of service—not for her.

He had this charmingly perplexed look on his face that didn't go with the suit at all. The lighthouse keeper was clearly at a loss for words.

"I brought you a cake," she said with a smile, and lifted the cover off the cake tin.

Owen looked down at the cake, which was in the shape of a lighthouse, and his eyes moved across it, reading, "GOOD LUCK OWEN" and "LIGHTHOUSE KEEPER OF CLARE" in script Ellen was rather proud of.

Then something fell out of his hair: a speck of … Ellen wasn't sure. A little rock or bit of plaster? He didn't seem to notice it.

He swallowed and was still at a loss, so Ellen said, "It's a fruitcake."

"Cake," Owen said, "doesn't agree with me."

Ellen's smile faded and Owen's eyes went a bit wide, so she smiled again. She liked the sound of his voice. It sort of rumbled up from out of him.

Their eyes started darting from here to there, neither of them apparently quite knowing what to look at. Ellen thought of a few things to say but didn't say any of them, and Owen's lips opened and closed a few times, too.

"Do you have anything to drink?" Ellen asked.

He appeared surprised by the question but answered, "In the kitchen."

He pointed to the kitchen as though it wasn't obvious. "Grab me one as well, would you? I have to get my light ready."

Quite the dashing host, Ellen thought but didn't say. She wandered into the kitchen and thought she'd put the cake down on the table but found the tabletop littered with books, most sitting open or partially open, with pencils and other items—a spoon, a screwdriver, what looked like just a stick—marking pages. The titles all seemed to share a theme: Grace O'Malley ... the Spanish Armada ... and the history of Clare Island.

After finding a bit of space to leave the cake, Ellen took a wild guess and opened a cupboard at random. It was empty.

Then Owen's voice rumbled in from the other room, "There's a bottle in the sink."

Sure enough, there was a bottle of whiskey sitting in the sink. Not precisely the place she would have put it, but something about that odd decision made her smile.

She took the bottle out of the sink and found it half full.

After a couple more tries, she managed to locate a cupboard that at least held a few mugs. Taking two that looked reasonably clean and watertight and the bottle of whiskey, she went into the living room and stood at the bottom of the spiral staircase leading up to the lantern room. She could hear Owen scuffling about up there. Tentatively placing a foot on the first step, she glanced at the gleaming brass handrail and thought best not to touch it.

"Can I come up?" Ellen asked, raising her voice a little, though the lantern tower itself wasn't that tall. "Owen?"

Feeling a bit like she was crossing into sacred lands, she crept up the steps into the tower, her eyes following the graceful curve of the brass railing that wound around and up.

She looked up to see Owen at the top, bearing down on her. He waved her up, and Ellen felt like a schoolgirl. She couldn't quite tell if she'd been invited to the school dance or into the headmaster's office, but holding the bottle and two mugs in her right hand, she instinctively reached out for the railing with her left, forgetting that only a moment ago she had thought best not to touch it.

"Mind the rail," Owen grumbled from above, and Ellen snatched her hand away from the gleaming brass.

Holding her hand a few inches above the rail, she started up the steps again, only vaguely aware that she was singing that old Gaelic song she'd been unable to get out of her head for days now. "*Leag mé síos…*"

When she got up to the top, she stopped singing and watched as Owen carefully closed a metal door under the lantern lamp in the center of the round, glass-walled room. He was so delicate with the thing, cleaning off where his fingers touched it.

Her cheeks grew hot, and her lips pressed into a tight smile. It wasn't just that he was cleaning, but that he was so … and she searched for the word while she watched him work … *attentive*. Careful. Considerate. Precise.

Ellen had never thought of herself as being the sort of woman who looked for a man to take care of her, never thought of herself as the sort of woman who needed to be taken care of. But something about the way he was around that brass and steel mechanism made him seem like the kind of man she wouldn't mind having take care of her.

That, added to the books, his gruff manner, and the dust in his hair. He had secrets, too, this mysterious old lighthouse keeper.

She poured some whiskey into one of the mugs, and when Owen stood up from the floor, she handed it to him and came to the sudden decision to ask, "What was the thing with Father O'Brien in the church yesterday?"

Owen was slightly taken aback by the question, but by the time he'd taken the mug from her he'd shrugged it off. "Ah," he said, "he's taken a bit of a disliking to me ever since I told him to feck off."

Ellen laughed—really laughed—and it felt good.

"You did what?" she prodded.

"Well …" Owen tried to explain, his face getting a bit red in the cheeks, "he knocked my drink over me …"

Ellen's eyes went wide—she'd done the very same.

With a mischievous glint in his eye, Owen continued, "I didn't know it was him."

Ellen sighed and smiled and poured herself a splash of whiskey. She raised the mug up for a toast. "Hopefully we'll keep this one in your mouth or your mug."

Owen smiled, and Ellen wondered if she'd ever seen him smile yet.

"*Sláinte*," she said with a wink.

"*Sláinte*."

They clinked mugs gently. Ellen took a sip, Owen a gulp.

"What was that you were singing?" Owen asked.

Ellen shrugged. "It's old … something that I learned when I was a child. It's strange, you know. I haven't sung it for years, but since I've been back on Clare, it's been in my mind all of the time. It's a bit of a family heirloom I suppose."

"I've heard it before, but I can't remember its name—what's it called?" Owen asked.

Ellen shook her head. "My Gaelic is a little rusty, but I think it translates as 'Lay Me Down.'"

Owen took another swig from his mug, pleased that he'd fathomed the name of the song at long last, then looked at his watch and said, "We still have a couple of minutes before I light her up."

Ellen had been eyeing the balcony with its iron railing running around the outside of the lantern tower, and she nodded at the glass door leading out to it. "Can we?"

Owen nodded and stepped aside. Ellen went to the door and fumbled with the old-fashioned handle. Owen took the bottle of whiskey from her hand to help her—or did he just want a bit more? As she stepped outside, Owen did pour himself a bit more.

Though the deck didn't look terribly comfortable, Ellen slid down to sit with her back to the glass. She beckoned Owen over to join her.

Ellen looked out toward the harbor, then up at the sky. The sun was setting, and the gray clouds were streaked with a dull orange. Patches of blue sky seemed almost green, as though reflecting the brilliant green of the moss-covered headlands towering over the silvery water. She couldn't see them but could hear waves—not too big—break against the rocks beneath them.

A breeze took some of her long auburn hair and toyed with it.

She found herself smiling.

"I used to let the lighthouse hypnotize me when I was a child," she said as Owen sat next to her. "I would watch it from my bedroom at night for hours. It would take me places." She looked over at him, pleased that he was just sitting there, listening. "Truth is, I had a bit of a crush on the lighthouse keeper." He smiled, and she added, "Mr. Flannigan."

Owen looked out to sea and shifted his weight. His uniform seemed even tighter when he sat.

"So …" he said, struggling to find something to say. "Why did you leave the island?"

Ellen looked back out to the gray, flat water and said, "My father died when I was fifteen. My mother didn't see a future for us here. Work was offered in America, so off we went."

"Why would you want to come back?" Owen asked. It was a question a few islanders had asked her in the past few days.

Ellen had never told anyone else but Mary and her boys the truth. Until now. "I split with my husband," she said in a matter-of-fact way.

"I'm sorry," Owen said, shifting again, moving just half an inch away from her, "that's none of my business."

"It's okay," she said, then paused to take a little sip of whiskey. It burned her lips. "There's not much to say. We married very young and grew apart. He's remarried now."

She looked over at Owen and saw him chewing on the inside of his lip, eyelids drooping a bit over his eyes and color in his cheeks again.

Ellen wondered why he seemed so embarrassed. She didn't tell him that her ex-husband had met his new wife while they were still married, that adultery came as easy to him as lying did. She didn't say that he'd left her in a city that was one sun-baked car park after another, as though the plan had been to pave the whole damned thing in concrete. She didn't inform him that though it seemed like a good idea in theory, the incessant sunshine and dry heat made it feel as though she was always inside a particularly uncomfortable, brightly lit building. She didn't admit that eventually she just wanted to see the color green again, like she'd grown up with. She didn't want to tell him she thought maybe if she got away from Los Angeles, changed her name back to her maiden name, O'Malley, and got all the way home—she might even meet an honest man.

But by the look on his face, she'd told him all of that and more.

"It's okay," she said, and even nudged him gently with her elbow. "I've come to terms with it."

"Really?" Owen asked, looking at her.

She smiled back at him. "Change what you can and have the courage to accept what you can't, and be thankful for the time that we had. At least that's what my two-hundred-dollar-an-hour therapist told me."

Owen laughed, and she liked the sound of it. Like his voice, it seemed to rumble out of him. It came up from very, very deep. And it was honest, not forced.

"So," she said, "the impenetrable fortress has a sense of humor."

Owen shrugged, and drank a little more whiskey.

"How about you?" she asked. "Why did you come to Clare?"

"I needed a change." He paused in a moment of reflection. "That was over thirty years ago," he murmured.

Then he realized that if Ellen left the island before he arrived, when she was fifteen, then fifteen plus over thirty years made her probably closer to fifty …

"Ever married?" she inquired.

Owen shook his head and seemed to want to say something, but instead he grabbed hold of the railing with his free hand and pulled himself to his feet. Ellen's smile faded from her lips.

"I have to turn on my light," Owen said. He stopped and looked out to sea. Ellen swallowed and took a shuddering little breath. Then Owen added, almost in a whisper, "One last time."

He turned to go back inside, then stopped. Ellen held her breath, watching him. She felt a hot tear in the corner of her eye and a dull ache slowly building in her throat.

He turned, not all the way, and looked down at her and asked, "Would you like to?"

Ellen stood, careful not to spill the whiskey in her mug. "That would make me very happy."

Owen turned and went back inside, and Ellen wiped away the tear and replaced it with a smile.

Excited now, she followed him through the narrow glass door and back into the lantern room.

He stepped up to the big steel lever.

"Show me," she said.

He set down his mug on a little worktable, took hers and put it down, too, then the bottle. Then he put his hand on the lever. Ellen reached out—not too far, they stood only a foot apart—and placed her hand on top of his.

He squeezed the lever closed, and Ellen felt his knuckles tighten his rough skin. His hand was warm and dry. Together they pushed the lever down, and Ellen jumped a little when the mechanism ground into life. She giggled and thought she sounded like a little girl, but she didn't care. Gears started turning, and then Owen flicked the cast iron switch on with his other hand and the lamp came on—but not all of a sudden. It slowly grew in intensity even as it started to rotate, as if the lighthouse knew this was its last night and wanted to draw it out for as long as it could.

Ellen took her hand away from Owen's to shield her eyes from the light as the lens rotated around. Looking down, not into the light, she saw Owen's hand shaking as he took it off the lever and put it behind his back. Then the old mug was in his other hand, and he took a generous swig.

They both turned away from the lantern to look out to sea again through the windows.

"So," Owen said, "you're writing a book are you?"

"It's been a dream of mine for a while," she replied, having to raise her voice a bit over the grinding of the lighthouse mechanism.

Owen asked, "What's it about?" and took another swig of whiskey.

"Grace O'Malley," she replied.

He turned away, appearing to be distracted by something, so she couldn't see his face. "Anything in particular?"

"She was a fascinating woman," Ellen answered. "I'll see what I can uncover."

Owen turned back to her and took another sip of whiskey, then almost coughed it up when she said, "I read somewhere that the lighthouse was built on the site of Gracie's watchtower."

"Is that right?" he coughed and then swallowed, forcing the whiskey down his throat.

"I see you have some books on her," Ellen said, smiling.

Owen regained his composure and said, "Just some light reading."

Ellen smiled a bit more at that. She'd seen the books—light reading? He had enough research material on his kitchen table to get a Master's in Irish History.

She was about to say so, too, when something in his reflection in the window caught her eye—something under his uniform shirt, hanging around his neck. It looked like a gold key.

"That's pretty," she said, reaching for it. "Where's it from?"

Owen backed away, tucking the key into his shirt. "Oh … it's just a key."

Ellen stood there with her hand out, not sure what to do. Owen stepped farther away, almost as if he were running away from her, or getting ready to. "I …" he stammered, "I … must be getting back to my duties … and I need to pack."

He said the last line with such finality, Ellen pulled her hand back and stepped away from him.

"Of course," she said.

Though she hoped he would say more, Owen took her mug from her—gently—and nodded at the spiral staircase. She turned, blinking in confusion, and headed down the stairs. Ellen could hear the stairs creaking as Owen ambled down behind her. She'd never felt so hurried out of somewhere before.

They went down the stairs and through the living room, and Ellen couldn't stand the idea that she was being herded like a sheep.

They came to the front door, and Owen opened it for her.

She stopped, looking at him, but he didn't say anything. She thought maybe he wanted to say something to her just then.

"Is everything okay?" she asked him.

Without looking her in the eye, he replied, "Fine."

She stood there for another second, but it seemed like an hour so finally she just said, "Well, goodnight."

She stepped out, and Owen said, "Goodbye," and closed the door behind her.

Ellen stood there for a moment, absolutely sure that she'd just been summarily put out of the Clare Island Lighthouse, and with a definite finality.

• • •

Owen leaned against the door, certain he could feel her standing out there, just on the other side.

He held his breath until he heard her walk away, then he turned and headed into the kitchen where Patrick was sitting at the table. Owen gasped and jumped a little and swore.

"You blew it," Patrick said, disappointment clear in his quiet voice.

"Just leave me be," Owen said. "I'm doing just fine on my own. I don't need some … woman messing up my life. Anyway, she was snooping."

"Snooping?" Patrick repeated, his voice dripping with contempt. Owen bristled, but let his brother have his say. "Snooping. For what? You're scared she's going to uncover your treasure? Piece together the *clues*?" The mimicking emphasis on that last word was crystal clear.

"Are you blind? She didn't come here for buried treasure, she came here to flirt with you. You damn fool!"

Owen just then realized he was still holding a mug of whiskey, so he drank some.

"What did you mean in the tunnel earlier when you said 'family'?" Owen asked.

Patrick slumped a little in his chair. "We have a boy … a man now. Liam. It was all in the letters."

Owen went to the window. It was getting darker fast, but he could still see the faint silhouette of Ellen tramping back down the road.

"Liam," Owen said, his voice barely above a whisper. "How old is he?"

"Just turned thirty," Patrick replied. "He has his own family now."

Owen looked down at his mug but didn't even try to drink any more.

Ellen had disappeared behind a hill, but Owen stared after her just the same.

It took him a moment to be able to speak, "What's it like … having a child?"

Patrick took a deep breath, and took his time before answering, "It's like falling in love again."

CHAPTER 10

The sun had barely crested the horizon, and shafts of brilliant yellow light stabbed through the grubby window of the shed. Fine cement dust sparkled in the air, fanning out in waves for all the world like miniature faeries dancing to the slow but regular rhythm of the dull thump each time Owen dropped another bag of dirt and cement chips on the floor next to the tunnel entrance. He'd been using tough old burlap sacks—made to be sandbags—to haul the loose material out of the hole, and over the years he had lost a few to the occasional errant pickaxe or drill bit. Some had just gotten too old.

He dropped the seventh bag and it almost fell over, but he caught it before it did. Standing in the tunnel, he had to twist his back and reach up to get the bags out of it, and the muscles in his lower back sent out a sharp protest.

Owen grunted, sighed, and swore, rubbing his back to loosen it up, but it didn't loosen up.

He'd been working all night to clear the debris

of the tunnel collapse. He leaned back against the entrance to the tunnel shaft and put his hands on his knees. His head sagged forward on his neck, and he had to stand there for a little while, breathing the dusty air in and out, waiting for the cramp to pass.

Patrick stood next to the bags, looking down at him. Owen could feel his disapproving gaze, but at least Patrick didn't say anything. The two of them stood there for a few minutes, just waiting.

"It's over," Owen said decisively. He looked up at his brother, standing in silhouette against the dawn flooding through the window. Dust faeries danced around him. "It'll take weeks still to dig through to the chamber."

"It's a blessing in disguise," Patrick said. Owen couldn't hear any emotion in his brother's voice at all. It was the voice of a machine. "There's nothing under there."

Owen shook his head. What was he going to say? What else did Patrick expect him to say?

"Get some fresh air. You'll see things more clearly," Patrick said, a gentleness creeping into his tone.

Patrick squatted next to the hole and held out his hand. Owen looked up and could see his face now, hair carefully slicked back over his high forehead. His crease-free cashmere sweater and his clean, sharply pressed khaki pants. He must have polished his shoes that morning or the night before. There wasn't a scuff on them, despite their having to flee the tunnel. His light blue eyes squinted behind his glasses in the harsh light.

"Come on," Patrick urged.

Owen glared straight back into Patrick's eyes, waved his brother's hand away, and dragged himself out of the hole, dispirited and thoroughly exhausted.

• • •

Wearing the cleanest clothes he could find under his fleece jacket, Owen tramped over to the cove.

He didn't sit on the rock. Something made him keep going.

Owen patted his saggy pocket, and the paper and plastic pouch crinkled inside.

He coughed up a bit of dust and spat it in the grass.

The sun was rising slowly into a blue sky. It was meant to be a nice day, but for all Owen cared, it might have been raining. It might have been snowing for all that.

And after some time of refusing to think about anything, he found himself at the rusted old tugboat. He stumbled on a rock and steadied himself against its cool, rough hull. He left his hand on the side of the hulk and just leaned, listening to a kittiwake squeal in the sky above him but not looking up at it.

Owen's other hand went unbidden into his pocket and drew out the letter in its plastic pouch. Still unopened, it looked a bit the worse for wear, having been in his pocket for how many days now? Owen wasn't even sure he remembered—not that long, but it may as well have been years.

"Are you going to open that letter?" Ellen asked. Owen pulled his hand away from the old boat as he slipped the letter back into his pocket, all in one jerking motion.

She smiled, and Owen felt the corners of his own mouth turn up, despite some effort to scowl instead. He didn't like people sneaking up on him … but she hadn't really snuck up on him, had she? Like he knew the kittiwake was still wheeling above him by its tell-tale squawk alone, he'd just chosen not to look up, opting instead to keep his eyes focused on nothing—a point a few inches from his face so he could neither read the address on the letter nor count the stones under his feet.

"I didn't see you at the cove this morning," she said.

Owen shook his head, just then noticing that she was standing next to her bike and had her towel wrapped around her shoulders, her long auburn hair wet and alluringly disheveled. In the bright morning sun, he could see the odd strand of gray in it, but that didn't make her any less beautiful. She wore no makeup, but she didn't need any. Her soothing blue eyes washed over him, and he realized he was just standing there, staring at her.

"I …" he said, then said it again. Then he sighed and wouldn't look at her.

"It's okay," she said, and it was as if her voice both smiled and laughed, telling him it was okay even without having said it. "I'm flattered that someone would want to see me naked."

Owen coughed, and wanted to cough some more, but made himself stop. He leaned back against the boat but almost tipped over. He looked to his left, then to his right, unable to make up his mind which way he should start running.

Ellen said, "This is the bit where you say," and she effected a sort of rumbling brogue that was obviously meant to be him, " 'Are you havin' the *craic*? You have a beautiful body.' "

Much as he silently railed against the idea that anyone might think his voice sounded like that, Owen blushed not because he was angry at the imitation but because she'd said precisely what he'd wanted to say but couldn't. And it hit him then, too, that she'd seen him watching her swim naked, and had seen him more than once. Owen cringed and blood started to rush to his cheeks, but then she hadn't slapped him or called the police on him or sent her cousin's boys to set him straight with a roundhouse to the jaw … Was this what they meant by "flirting"? *God help me*, he thought, and said, "I'm a little out of practice."

"I can see that," she said, the smile still in her voice. "Would you like a cup of coffee?"

Owen nodded, then stopped himself and blinked, thinking, *Damn it, this woman switches gears fast.*

"Tea?" he said, looking at her finally.

Ellen nodded, smiling, and replied, "I guess I'll have to become a tea drinker again sooner or later."

She tipped her head in the direction of her cottage and started off, not too fast, pushing her bicycle along with her as she went.

Owen, still leaning against the boat, pushed himself away from it and followed her. He didn't try to catch up with her at first but stayed a few paces behind while he surreptitiously patted the rust away from his trousers. Then he adjusted his shirt a little, and made sure that the letter was in his fleece pocket and not visible, though she seemed to have forgotten about it anyway.

Then he quickened his pace just a bit and caught up with her.

"You threw me out pretty soon after I asked you if you were married," she said. "Did I touch a nerve?"

To himself he said, *Yes, you touched a nerve, and a mighty sensitive one at that.* Then aloud: "My brother ran off to America with my fiancée so, no, I've never been married."

Owen swallowed—had he just said that?

Black spots floated across his vision, and he blinked,

trying hard not to stumble or otherwise appear as though he were about to faint—or drop dead. He'd had no intention of saying that, of uttering those words.

"You've never met anyone else?" Ellen asked, as though what he'd told her wasn't the slightest bit out of the ordinary.

He took a deep breath, his thoughts only coming together as he spoke them. "I didn't think that I ever would," he said.

They walked a little, gradually picking up their pace. That same squawk called overhead, and Owen squinted up into the blazing blue sky to watch a single kittiwake turn barely ten feet over their heads, its wings rigid, floating like a kite on the salt breeze coming in off the sea.

"How are things with your brother now?" Ellen asked. Owen looked at her, surprised again by her candor, but when he stared at her face, he saw no judgment there. He didn't think she was waiting for him to say any one particular thing.

"I don't know," Owen replied. "He's staying with me for a few days. It's been a long time."

That clearly surprised her. "Oh," she said, "I didn't realize he was staying with you. I'd like to meet him."

Owen started shaking his head but forced himself to nod instead.

"Will you both be coming to the Seafarer's?" she asked, and this time Owen did shake his head.

But she wasn't looking at him, concentrating instead on guiding her bike around a hole in the gravel track.

"No," Owen said, but then he didn't like the way he'd said it—too final. "I don't think so."

Ellen shook her head and looked over at him. She seemed cross with him, or disappointed. "Let your hair down a little," she said. "You might just enjoy yourself."

Then there was that smile again—no judgment, no irritation—and Owen smiled back at her and shrugged. He really had no intention of going to any party on his last weekend at his light, the last hours in his tunnel. But maybe, he thought, a part of "flirting" was leaving some things unsaid.

They walked a little while longer without saying anything. Owen felt a pull coming from her, though, as though she had a sort of gravity. Every half-dozen steps or so, he would have to consciously move a little farther away from her, having been pulled in closer.

At last they came to her cottage, and as they passed an easel set up in her little front garden, Owen slowed to take a closer look at the painting leaning on it.

"Is that the cove?" he asked.

The painting had the colors of the water just right. The sea was rough, pounding at a lobster boat; Owen could almost see it being tossed about. A heavyset man stood in the bow with an oar, or it could have been a pole set in the water as though he was trying to fish something out of the churning sea.

"That's right," Ellen said.

"Rough night," Owen said, nodding at the painting.

"That's what the muse wanted when I picked up the brush," she replied with a warm smile, then leaned her bicycle up against the side of the house and held the front door open for him.

He passed very close to her as he went inside. She smelled of seawater and fresh air, and Owen wanted to take her in his arms and …

He stepped quickly into the little room and got to the far end of it as fast as possible.

Inside were boxes, most half full of books, plates, and towels. The paintings stacked up against the walls were mostly cityscapes—Owen didn't recognize which city. Anyway, he liked her painting of the cove better.

Ellen closed the door behind her and went to the kitchen, saying, "I'll make some tea."

Owen nodded and squinted at one of the paintings. Blurry, stylized buildings stood alongside a hill rendered in dark green and a desert brown. White letters written across it spelled out "HOLLYWOOD."

From the kitchen, Ellen said, "I hope you work things out with your brother. I was an only child …" She paused, maybe a bit reluctant, but then said, "I always wished for a brother or sister. Though I guess Mary has been like a sister to me."

"You can have mine if you like," Owen said, moving from the paintings to a small sofa cluttered with books.

There was a copy of *The Life of Grace O'Malley*, and next to it *Contemporary Irish Heritage*.

When Ellen came into the room, Owen straightened and stepped away from the sofa as though he'd been caught … doing what? He wasn't sure.

"Well," she said, "if he's come all the way from America to see you, he must really want to sort things out."

As she spoke, a drawing resting on the end table next to the sofa caught Owen's eye. He picked it up and saw the familiar shield. A boar, three bows and arrows pointing at it—two on the top and one on the bottom. In the bottom left corner of the shield, a ship riding on the waves. Under the shield—the words "TERRA. MARIQUE. POTENS." And "O'MAILLE."

"Grace O'Malley's coat of arms," Owen said. Thinking he might impress her with his knowledge.

"Nearly right," Ellen replied quickly with a smirk. Owen watched her leaf through a stack of papers—mostly handwritten notes—until she produced another drawing. She stood very close to him, shoulder to shoulder. Owen held the drawing he had mistaken for Grace O'Malley's coat of arms and Ellen the other so they could both see. "If you look closely, you'll see it's different. "This one"—she waved the drawing in her hand "—is Grace O'Malley's coat of arms." And then pointing to the drawing Owen held, she said, "*That* is the O'Malley family coat of arms." With a thin, long, delicate finger, Ellen traced the line of the keel of the ship. Then she did the same with the drawing she held, and Owen saw the clear, if subtle difference. "On Gracie's coat of arms, the ship is resting on the sand; on the O'Malley coat of arms, the ship is riding on the waves," she said.

Owen looked a little closer, squinting. He didn't have his reading glasses with him.

"You're right," he said—almost whispered, "so the coat of arms on her tomb is the O'Malley family crest."

"Correct," Ellen said, her voice betraying some part of the excitement Owen felt just then. "Someone of her stature would have had her personal coat of arms on her tombstone."

Owen took a step away from Ellen and asked, "So the rumors might be right?"

Ellen held her hands up, showing him her palms as though calming him, but she was the one who looked as if she were about to burst. "Might just be ..." she said, "that Gracie isn't buried there."

Owen rubbed the beard on his chin. "Why would somebody have a tomb built and bury themselves somewhere else?"

Ellen shrugged and said, "Maybe she was hiding something."

Owen shook his head and took a step closer to Ellen, handing her the drawing. She put a hand out but didn't take it. She leaned closer, and Owen didn't pull back.

Her eyes were so blue, and she had those cheekbones and those lips, and then the bloody phone rang and it was as if ice water had been injected into his veins and he stepped back, and Ellen looked this way and that and then picked up the phone and Owen could see her hand was shaking.

"Hello," she said loudly, then less so, "oh, yes, hello Mr. O'Connell. Yes, I'm fine … you're welcome." She listened a bit; then her eyes narrowed, and she asked, "Owen?" She looked up at Owen. "Sure, he's here. I'll put him on."

With a curious frown, Ellen held the phone out to Owen, who was entirely at a loss as to … but she'd said, "Mr. O'Connell."

Owen took the receiver and grunted out a quick, "Hello?"

"Mr. Kerrigan," the councilman squeaked out over the line. "I've rung half the island trying to find you. We had an arrangement. Ten o'clock on Saturday morning, yes? Remember?"

Owen didn't, actually, but asked, "What's the time?"

"Ten fifteen," O'Connell replied.

Owen looked at Ellen, who stood there watching, impatient for some explanation. Then he looked down to make sure she knew he wasn't talking to her and quietly said into the phone, "Shite. Give me ten minutes."

"Hurry up," O'Connell insisted. "The buyers have to be back on the next ferry. Don't make me lose this sale. You hear me?"

Owen hung up the phone—slammed it really, startling Ellen a little, and that was enough to shock Owen back from imagining the receiver in his fist was a heavier blunt object and the phone cradle the councilman's face.

"What's wrong?" Ellen asked.

Owen put up his hands in some effort to wipe away his little outburst and said, "He has some suits who want to buy my light and turn it into … I don't know what … it's not right."

He put his hands on his hips, and Ellen said, "I'm sorry."

"I have to go," he said, and stepped to go around her to the door, but there were boxes on the floor and he had to try to get around them. He was forced to get a little close to her, then a little closer, and she didn't move away.

She put out a hand—why? To steady him?

He tried to do the same thing; then his hand was on her arm and then on her side, and she was warm and soft and there and perfect, and he drew her into his body and kissed her full on the lips.

Her body went rigid, and Owen pulled away and almost tripped over a box full of old sketchbooks. He thought she was about to say something, but she didn't.

Her jaw seemed tight. He couldn't tell what she was thinking, and he took a couple of steps closer to the door, stepping over boxes. "I …" he began, but it took him a couple more steps to say, "I don't know what came over me. Sorry …"

He got to the door and stopped there and looked at her, and she looked back at him.

Owen had the feeling that his face looked just as confused and shocked and ill at ease as hers, and that made him feel in no way better.

He opened his mouth to say something, and she raised her eyebrows in reply. Then he opened the door and got the hell out of there.

CHAPTER 11

Owen came up the hill and bristled at the sight of three men milling about at his front door. He didn't bother trying to hide the scowl on his face, but did quicken his steps a bit when the councilman from the mainland looked up and noticed him approaching. Owen fancied he was charging at the men rather than walking toward them, but O'Connell didn't appear at all frightened.

The other two men were dressed smartly—not as old-fashioned as O'Connell but conspicuous on Clare Island, where a suit was a bit of a rarity among the local farmers and fishermen.

One of the two strangers spoke into his mobile phone. Owen wouldn't have listened even if he could hear what he was saying, but he didn't see the man wait for anyone else to speak, just kept jabbering away. His eyes looked dull, almost lifeless—as vacant as a cow's lowering stare. But his jaw worked around his torrent of words as though he was chewing them.

The second stranger was similarly engrossed in his

mobile, but this one tapped away at the screen with his thumbs. His face twitched a bit here and there around the corners of his mouth and his eyebrows, as though he could hear something or the little device could see his expressions and reacted accordingly. For all Owen knew, that's precisely what was happening. His clothes seemed somehow too small on him, as though he still thought of himself as a boy—at least when he went shopping.

As Owen got up to the door, O'Connell gave him a stern look and tapped on his cheap watch.

While he unlocked the door and stomped into the living room, not caring whether or not the three mainlanders followed him, Owen imagined various uncomfortable places that he would like to shove O'Connell's tacky timepiece. He kept going straight into the room, making for the lantern tower—habit making him want to check his readings.

"Mr. Kerrigan," O'Connell said from behind him, with that voice of his that sounded at once polite and patronizing, "would you mind if these gentlemen had a look around?"

Of course Owen did mind, but still he said gruffly, "Fine."

Owen stood there in the middle of his living room, realizing that not only was it no longer his living room, but he'd been going to his light to take readings he didn't need to take anymore. No one wanted his readings anymore. No one would do anything with his readings anymore. The new lighthouse would take the readings now, a robot sending data by radio to a bunch of computers to process and turn into lights on a screen. Owen didn't know what to do with himself now that it was no longer his living room, no longer his light even, so he just stood there.

The two strangers barely seemed to see him. One put away his mobile phone and produced a tablet computer from a little messenger bag he carried. He started the thing up, and his perfectly clean-shaven face looked corpse-like in the glow from the screen, which reflected in his dull eyes for all the world as if it was drawing the intelligence out of him to use for its own massive-networked purposes. He held the thing up, and a light blinked, then flashed. Owen blinked spots from his eyes.

The other man did the same thing with his little mobile.

Owen grumbled something unintelligible under his breath as he rubbed his eyes. Were they taking photographs with the bloody things?

A weak hand on his elbow made Owen twitch away, but it was O'Connell and the councilman just held on. Owen let himself be led to the corner of the room, out of the way of the two strangers.

"You will be out of here by the end of the weekend?" O'Connell asked. It was clear in his tone and his face that he didn't think that was remotely possible as the weekend ended tomorrow.

In fact, it *wasn't* remotely possible.

Owen hadn't even thought about packing, much less started. And O'Connell had easily picked up on that.

After treating Owen to another sideways, skeptical glare, O'Connell stepped over to his two buyers. His fingers steepled in front of him, O'Connell said, "So, gentlemen, this lighthouse was established in 1806, when …"

Owen tuned the man out—he knew more of the history of the Clare Island lighthouse than Mr. O'Connell could possibly imagine, and he certainly didn't want to hear some strangers' heads being filled with half-truths and assumptions.

Instead, Owen tramped into the kitchen, looking for a place to hide and maybe a glass of water. *Was it too early for a whiskey?* he thought. He could certainly do with one. He came to a sudden stop when he saw Patrick sitting at the table in front of one of the open books. Owen took a deep breath—he'd be kicked out of the place before he got used to Patrick being there.

Patrick stared at the chalkboard, which Owen had leaned back up against the wall where it belonged. Owen began to stare at it as well. In spite of clearing out the rubble from the roof collapse, there was still so much farther to go.

"How did it go with Ellen?" Patrick asked, still staring at the chalkboard.

"It didn't," Owen replied. When Patrick looked back at him, eyebrows raised, Owen explained, "I'm a fool—she was just leading me on. You both were." And Patrick's eyebrows dropped.

Patrick opened his mouth to speak but stopped when O'Connell called in from the living room, "What was that, Mr. Kerrigan? Did you say something?"

"Ah …" Owen called back, "mind your own business."

O'Connell stepped into the kitchen, looking rather perturbed, and said, "I'd like to take them up into the lantern room."

Owen shook his head but replied, "Just don't touch anything."

Mr. O'Connell gave him another condescending look.

Putting more than a little threat into his voice, Owen said, "And keep your hands off my rail."

O'Connell swallowed and nodded quickly. He turned on his heels and went back into the living room, speaking loudly to the two buyers.

"He seems like a nice guy," Patrick said to lighten the mood. Owen just gave a mumbled growl in response. "What happened with Ellen?" Patrick asked, and though Owen wasn't delighted with the subject, he was happy to talk to anyone but the councilman about anything but selling his light out from under him.

"I don't know what came over me." Owen leaned

against the sink and folded his arms across his chest. "I kissed her, and she froze to the spot."

Saying it aloud like that brought the sensation of it flooding back. Owen grimaced and it looked as if he blushed a little, or maybe that was just the veins in his cheeks sensing that the whiskey bottle wasn't far away.

Patrick laughed a little and said, "Maybe she just needs some time."

Owen listened to the sound of footsteps going up into the lantern room.

Patrick pointed to the chalkboard and said, "You might want to hide that."

Owen glanced at the chalkboard … then the blood drained from his face, and he thought his heart skipped a beat. It had been sitting there right in front of that pen-pusher from the council, and …

Owen took three steps to cross the kitchen, turned it around and stood it back up against the wall, careful not to smudge or erase any of the chalk markings.

"If they go outside," Patrick continued, "they'll see the entrance to the tunnel."

And before his brother had even finished speaking, Owen was on his way to the back door, fishing the keys out of his pocket. O'Connell's voice echoed down from the lantern room. Owen couldn't even listen to his nonsense. But what did it matter? These two didn't ever have to light the thing—in fact, with the new automatic lighthouse in operation, they would be specifically prohibited from lighting this thing. They didn't have to take weather readings, either. They were probably planning to knock it down, for all he knew. *If she has to be sold, at least sell it to someone who'll care for her like he has. She deserves a worthy retirement.* Then an unbearable thought slipped into his mind. *What if they know about the treasure and reap the rewards of all my hard work when I'm gone?* He quickly forced the thought from his mind. It was too unpleasant to even contemplate, but he could feel his blood starting to boil, all the same.

Owen locked the back door, swore quietly under his breath, and stomped back to the kitchen table. The three strangers were coming down the stairs from the lantern room when Owen sat at the table across from his brother.

"As you can see, gentlemen," O'Connell said, "this would make a wonderful project."

One of the buyers asked, in an accent Owen couldn't quite identify, "It is complete, I assume? That is important."

"Complete, yes," O'Connell replied without a pause to consider if he were telling the truth. "Of course, it's fully functional."

And you two had better not turn the damned thing on, Owen thought. Then he thought, *if they want it intact, maybe they aren't after digging for my treasure,* which eased his blood pressure a little. But then he started to wonder if the men were intending to strip the lighthouse of its historical workings and sell them to the highest bidder, which raised his blood pressure again. It was only when O'Connell jiggled the back-door handle that Owen snapped out of his thoughts and smiled across at Patrick.

Still smiling, Owen leaned back in his chair to look over at the three men, stymied by the locked door. "Lost the key," he said.

"Is that right?" O'Connell said, turning quickly, then tamping down his anger for the benefit of his customers. He returned Owen's insincere smile. "How do you refill the lighthouse backup generator?"

"Jump over the wall," Owen replied with a shrug. "I'll give you a leg over if you'd like."

The two buyers looked at O'Connell, who turned to them and forced a smile.

"That's fine," one of the strangers said, waving a hand at O'Connell and clearly eager to just keep moving—or eager to get out of there.

Then the other buyer said, "We've seen enough."

The two strangers shared a look, rolling their eyes. Mr. O'Connell's jaw tightened.

"That's grand," O'Connell practically squeaked. He looked at his watch. "We'll just make the ferry."

Owen started to get up, but O'Connell held up a hand. "We'll let ourselves out ... let you get back to your *packing.*"

O'Connell's obvious emphasis on that last word, combined with the conspicuous lack of boxes, made the two buyers share another roll of their eyes.

Owen shrugged and sat back down. He sat there in calm silence for the few minutes it took for the three men to put away all their fancy electronic devices and leave through the front door. O'Connell probably gave him another scowl or two along the way, but Owen didn't bother looking.

When the door closed behind them, Patrick said, "There's something you need to see in this book." He nodded at the book sitting open on the tabletop in front of him.

Owen shook his head and replied, "Unless it's a design for a six-foot drill, I'm not interested."

"I'm trying to help," Patrick insisted.

Owen slammed his fist on the table—surprising himself more than Patrick at the outburst.

His hand stung a little.

"Paddy," Owen said, "I've read every book there is on the subject—that one you have there maybe half-a-dozen times. I've spent years of my life with this. Years. It's down there, and I will finish that damn hole if I have to use my bare hands."

Owen scraped his chair back, digging at the kitchen floor.

He looked down at his brother and tried to calm down. Finally Owen said, "I need a bath."

* * *

My bare hands, Owen thought, looking at the palms of his hands. His skin was as rough as sandpaper, and no matter how hard he tried, the grime wouldn't come out of all the cracks and folds of skin. He'd learned to ignore blisters but absentmindedly counted half a dozen of them.

With a sigh he turned off the water and climbed into the tub. Steam rose up around him, and though most people would have found the water too hot, Owen closed his eyes and reveled in the feeling of it as he sank in up to his chin.

His aching muscles started to relax—all but his jaw. He didn't even realize he'd been scowling, gritting his teeth, even grinding them all day.

He sank lower in the water, and some of it sloshed out onto the scratched, dull wood floor.

We'll let O'Connell worry about the mess, Owen thought.

He took a breath and put his whole head under the water. Rubbing his fingertips through his hair, he felt more grit there. He scratched a little harder, then did the same with his beard, which he realized could use a trim. His mind went to Ellen, as it had been doing more and more often. Of course she froze up, recoiled at his touch. It must have felt like a cactus was kissing her.

As he let the warm water sooth his aching muscles, his mind began to calm. Thoughts of Ellen and Paddy travelling halfway around the world to "talk" drifted from his mind. *The years of toil in that dark dingy hole, it can't have all been for nothing.* But he'd need an army to finish the dig now.

Owen brought his face out of the water to breathe and felt a presence in the room with him.

"God help me," Owen said, not opening his eyes. "Can I not get a moment's peace?"

"If you have to finish this thing," Patrick replied, "I think I've found your six-foot drill."

Owen opened one eye to see Patrick half-sitting, half-leaning on the sink, his ankles crossed and his arms folded over his chest. Patrick held his eyes open wide, waiting.

Owen opened his other eye, and Patrick said, "Come with me."

Patrick stepped out of the bathroom, looking like the cat that ate the canary, and Owen, jaw tight and scowling once more, got out of the tub—reluctantly, with the water still nice and hot. He toweled off as best he could, then wrapped himself in a threadbare old dressing gown.

He trudged down the stairs and walked through the kitchen to come out in the living room. Patrick stood at the base of the lantern tower, a self-satisfied grin on his face.

"What?" Owen demanded. He wanted to get back to his bath—maybe drain the now dirty water and start over fresh.

Patrick pointed at the lantern drive shaft, then down at the motor that drove it, which was housed in a shallow pit in the floor beneath it. At first all Owen could see was the chipped black paint—another repair he wouldn't have a chance to make.

"What?" Owen demanded.

"It's the perfect drill," Patrick answered.

Owen took a moment as the realization of what his clearly insane brother was suggesting hit him. He ground his words out between gritted teeth, "Are you fecking crazy?"

"Calm yourself down, and think about it," Patrick retorted.

Owen took a step back and said, "No …" He turned and muttered, "It's …" He walked a couple steps, saying, "I can't …" Then he stopped, turned to look at the drive shaft, and almost shouted, "I *won't* …" Then he turned away.

"Do you want to finish your tunnel or not?" Patrick asked. He wasn't smug, in his voice or his face. He wasn't condescending either, wasn't teasing him.

"I can't do it," Owen said. "I can't tear her heart out."

Owen rubbed a drop of bathwater off his cheek—or maybe it wasn't bathwater. He cleared his throat and breathed in short little pants through his nose.

Patrick sighed and said, "You've looked after her for most of your life. I reckon she owes you. The light will never be used again anyway— "

Owen took a couple of steps and dropped into his armchair. He was sitting on a book, but didn't care.

"You know the workings of that mechanism inside and out," Patrick went on. "It's your only chance."

Owen sat there, not really thinking, not carefully weighing the advantages and disadvantages, not considering in detail the significant challenges of just removing the mechanism, much less converting it to a faster-moving drill. He didn't really consider the fact that it might take days to modify it.

Instead of all that thinking, Owen asked his brother, "Will it work?"

"Yes," Patrick answered without a moment's pause. "Trust me."

Shaking his head, Owen said, "Things didn't work out too well for me the last time I trusted you, did they?"

Owen leaned forward and dug the book out from under him. He looked at the cover: *Treasures of the Spanish Armada*.

He stared at the cover, then looked back up at his brother and said, "Show me."

●●●

They spent the rest of the morning in the kitchen.

Owen drew the plans, with Patrick standing over him, pacing the kitchen in circles. Owen was reminded of a time when they were both kids. Patrick had hatched a plan to steal wine from the church—some complicated, hare-brained scheme that would never have worked. They'd have stood a better chance just walking in and asking the priest if they could have a nip. Owen remembered playing along, the plan itself much more fun than the theft ever would have been. Patrick had paced the bedroom they shared in precisely the same way. They'd both fallen asleep tossing around ideas for which of the neighborhood kids they could most easily frame for the job.

It had been forty years since Owen had thought of that night—maybe longer. And they never did steal the wine … or even try.

But now Patrick was less the mastermind than the instigator. Patrick knew how Owen's stubborn mind worked, and if he was lulled into believing the ideas were his, he would be far more likely to actually do it. It was as though he meant to draw out what Owen already knew. After an hour of that, Owen realized he did know how to do it; he just hadn't been able to consider ripping the guts out of his light … for any reason. And he knew what his brother was up to, but he appreciated him letting him be the mastermind for once. To finish what he'd started.

Then there was a little time spent considering the necessary tools and gathering them up. Between the lantern room, the various sheds, and Owen's truck, he managed to round up everything he thought he'd need.

Seated on the floor of the lantern tower with Patrick looking over his shoulder, Owen carefully released the drive shaft from the lantern. While he worked he wiped away at the grease and oil that dripped from the exposed gearwork. Having raided the kitchen for teacups, saucers, and bowls of every size and shape, he devised, with Patrick's advice, a system to keep various screws and bolts set out in an organized fashion, each documented on a sheet of graph paper so that when— and Owen refused to think, let alone say, the word *if*—he put her back together, he'd know precisely where every bit went back in place. He remembered watching Paddy use the regimented system as a child when his brother would disassemble and rebuild anything he could get his hands on, much to their mother's frustration.

The drive shaft hung in place, not attached to the lantern, and Owen went downstairs to the base of the tower and went to work just as carefully, just as cleanly, releasing the shaft from the motor as well.

Patrick had made himself scarce when it came time

to lift the heavy steel shaft up and out of the motor. Owen realized he was wasting his breath asking him. If he heard the phrase "bad back" one more time from Patrick, he surely would lose his mind. And he figured this time he'd give him the benefit of the doubt for coming up with the ingenious plan—at least until he attempted to lift it.

He got it to budge maybe a couple of millimeters but that was all, and he could only hold it up for a fraction of a second.

"It's too heavy," Patrick said from behind him, with a flat finality to his tone.

"You don't say," Owen grumbled, but he knew that even if he could persuade Patrick to risk his precious back and lend a hand, the shaft was still too heavy for even the two of them. Had they been younger—forty years younger—then maybe …

"We'll never lift it out," Owen said, an idea forming quickly. "We need more hands."

Owen wiped his hands on the rag he normally used to clean the motor, then without thinking wiped the sweat off his brow, leaving a grease mark across his forehead, which looked like war paint. "Wait here," he said.

CHAPTER 12

"Lads," Owen barked out as if "the lads" were late for an urgent appointment.

Ryan O'Reilly recognized the lighthouse keeper's voice even though he couldn't see the man past the dozen empty plastic crates. He and his brother had brought them over from Roonagh Quay full of mail and whatnot—a produce order for the scattering of guest houses—and much more often than not returned them to the mainland empty. They stacked easily enough into each other, and it had become a game between the two of them, as to who could carry the most. That game eventually topped out at twelve.

Ryan took a few steps to the edge of the quay and handed the crates over to his brother, who was on the deck of the ferry, and said, "Mr. Kerrigan …"

"How much do you make on a crossing?" Owen asked.

Ryan frowned and considered both the question and the man. It occurred to him that Owen Kerrigan always looked dirty, as though he'd been rooting around in the garden—all day, every day. Still, he had that rugged face and barrel-chested body that skinny, boyish Ryan always secretly envied.

"At the moment," Ryan answered, "it barely pays for the fuel."

He paused when Derry dropped the empty crates on the deck with a great clattering of plastic against wood, followed by an even louder, "Ah—me foot!"

Ryan laughed but cut it short when he saw the impatient and utterly unamused look on the lighthouse keeper's face.

"Maybe twenty euros," he added. "If we're lucky."

"I'll double it for half a day's work," Owen said without pause.

Derry, limping comically, hopped off the deck and was about to say something, when Ryan quickly and loudly interjected, "We have to provide a service to the community." Then in a normal voice he added, "We can't just not sail."

Derry again tried to interject, but Owen interrupted him with, "Treble it."

That shut both O'Reilly brothers up for a second. Ryan looked at his brother, who shrugged and then flashed a smile.

Ryan looked up into the brilliant, clear blue sky and watched a chubby fulmar wheel overhead and added, "We do two crossings in an afternoon."

"Sixty euros, that's your lot," Owen fired back.

After a moment's hesitation, Ryan said, "Derry, get the bad weather sign."

Derry clapped his hands together and hopped back onto the boat, quickly climbing up to the wheelhouse.

"One condition …" Owen said then, and Ryan thought, *All right, here we go … "No* questions."

Surprising himself, Ryan quickly countered, "Well that's got to be worth another ten."

The old man's bushy eyebrows twisted on his forehead, and he growled back with a finality in his voice, "Sixty. And no questions."

Derry set up the little sandwich board that read, "FERRY SERVICE POSTPONED DUE TO BAD WEATHER," seemingly oblivious to the ongoing negotiations. Ryan watched him, screwing up his lips, pretending to be deep in thought, but when he turned back to the old lighthouse keeper and his burning eyes, he lost his nerve.

"Where are we headed?" Ryan asked, sticking his hands into his pockets.

Derry stepped up next to him.

"My light," Owen replied.

The two O'Reilly brothers looked at each other and shrugged.

"We'll follow you up," Ryan said.

Without another word—not a wave, not even a shrug—Owen turned right around and climbed back into that rattling old truck of his.

· · ·

"So what's the *craic* boss?" the older of the O'Reilly boys said, hands on hips, staring down at the scattering of parts Owen had managed to pull out of the mechanism.

Owen's living room floor had come to resemble a junkyard, and though it pained Owen to see the guts half ripped out of his light, he knew that with the boys' help, he could at least get the heavy steel drive shaft down.

"No questions, remember?" Owen replied. He looked both brothers in the eye and said, "We're making a drill, and that's all you need to know."

The lads nodded, and Owen snuck a glance behind him to where Patrick stood, leaning against the wall, his arms folded across his chest. Patrick smiled back, and Owen got himself and the boys to work. Thankfully, he didn't need Patrick and his "bad back" now that he had the O'Reilly lads.

"First," Owen said, "we need to get the drive shaft out of the housing."

"We'll not lift that," the younger brother—Derry—complained.

"Will you quit your blether," Owen growled back, which amused the older brother, then got them to work. With the two boys lifting it up, Owen guiding it, and Patrick still leaning against the wall, they got the bottom end of the drive shaft up out of the motor to rest on the solid steel flange in the housing pit. This brought it down just the couple of inches necessary to drop it out of the lantern above, and with that they had the weight of the whole thing. Derry made some funny noises, and Ryan grunted a couple times. Then the center of gravity took hold, and it started falling to one side. Owen looked up, gritting his teeth.

"Mind the rail!" he yelled.

"The what?" Derry gasped, but his older brother grabbed the shaft a bit higher up and leaned with all his weight in the other direction.

With Owen pushing the same way, they kept it off the rail with maybe an inch to spare. Then it was a matter of easing the thing down, inch by inch and out into the living room.

Owen and Ryan propped it against the wall whilst Owen set Derry scurrying about to set a pair of sawhorses so they could keep the drive shaft off the floor.

It took all three of them to lift it, the full weight of the thing almost too much for them. But with a few jabs of pain in his back and shoulders and a few colorful complaints from the boys, they rested the steel shaft up on the sawhorses.

"I hope these things hold," Ryan said, and Owen hoped the same thing.

There was a bit of creaking, but hold they did, and

Owen assigned Derry to hold the thing to keep it from rolling off.

"Hold on, lads," Owen said, leaving the two boys in the living room as he went into the kitchen.

Patrick followed him, and Owen sat in front of his hastily sketched plans. While the O'Reilly boys teased each other about who'd already done more work, Owen and Patrick went over not only the best way to fix the drill bit to the drive shaft but how to get the whole contraption into the tunnel and around the dogleg to the end.

"I just hope," Owen said, so only Patrick could hear, "that we don't get the thing most of the way in there only to find it's half an inch too long."

"Only one way to find out," Patrick said, sitting down into a chair at the table.

Owen looked across the table at him, over the piles of papers and books and plans, and said, "Well then, you just take it easy here, why don't ya? Leave the heavy lifting to us."

Patrick answered with a smile that made Owen grab the plans, stand up, and march right over to the boys, in the living room. He almost shouted, "Time to earn your money, lads!"

Neither of the O'Reilly boys had any idea what Owen was talking about as he briefed them on the plan and pointed at the sketch with his leathered finger. So Owen took a deep breath and explained it to them again. Neither looked terribly confident in the plan, and Owen didn't feel any more confident than they looked.

Owen motioned for them to follow him out of the back door.

"If you don't mind my asking, Mr. Kerrigan," Ryan said as he walked across the courtyard to the shed, "That fella off the mainland … what's his name?"

"Mr. O'Connell," Derry answered, affecting a lousy upper-crust accent, "of the Almighty Council."

"Yeah," Ryan said with a twinkle in his eye, "Mr. Almighty O'Connell. Rumor has it …" He paused to draw breath. "He's here to kick you out of the lighthouse."

"You heard right," Owen grunted.

"The council owns it, and the council wants to sell it. They've just asked me to do some work on the foundations before I move out."

"Is that right?" Ryan replied, knowing full well that Owen was having him on.

Owen pushed open the door to the shed, shuffled in ahead of them, and said, "Mind your step."

Derry was the first brother to see the hole.

"Would you look at that?" he effused.

Ryan barged past his brother to catch a glimpse. "Looks like the foundations are in need of a lot of work, Mr. Kerrigan."

Owen just nodded back.

"You dug that?" Derry asked, peering in as though he expected a dragon to come flying out of it.

Owen nodded again.

"How deep does it go?" Derry asked, risking another step closer to the edge.

"The deal was no questions, lads—remember?" Owen replied.

The lads glanced at each other, and Owen knew they thought he was crazy, and knew just as well that they were probably right, just as he knew that either way he needed his new drilling contraption in the tunnel regardless and the lads their sixty euros.

"Come on, let's get on with it," Owen insisted.

And with that they were back in the living room and, on Owen's three-count, they lifted the heavy steel drive shaft. It may have been that they'd become accustomed to the work. It was more likely that the weight was more evenly distributed with the thing horizontal, but Owen thought it seemed lighter.

The three of them carefully walked the drive shaft through the kitchen and out the back door, Owen taking the lead, wanting to be the one to start feeding it into the tunnel. He put the slightly more responsible Ryan at the rear to make sure they didn't rip the back door out of its frame coming out.

"Damn, this thing is heavy," Derry complained.

"Shut it," Ryan huffed at his brother. "Look at Mr. Kerrigan, why don't you? Three times your age and not …" Ryan trailed off. Then he cleared his throat and said, "Sorry, Mr. Kerrigan."

As they made the halfway mark across the courtyard, Owen said, "If you can work your arms as much as your mouths, we might be in with a chance of getting this finished."

Ryan smirked. He liked Mr. Kerrigan's dry wit and cantankerous outbursts.

And by then they were coming through the shed door, and that's where it got tricky. But with a few twists and turns and a good fifteen minutes trying the wrong angle, the drive shaft eventually slipped down into the tunnel.

"Hold it there, lads," Owen said, ignoring the grunts of protest from the brothers. "I'll climb down and guide her in from here."

The lads looked on as the thickset lighthouse keeper eased himself down into the confines of the tunnel after making sure the string of lights were on. It wasn't an easy fit with the drive shaft sticking through the middle of it, but he eventually slid around and shouted back up, "I'm gonna walk her down then, lads. Just try to keep as much weight off this end as you can."

"Okay, Mr. Kerrigan," Ryan shouted back down at him.

Even as deep in the tunnel as he was, as Owen carefully moved the long drive shaft down the first sloping passage to the dogleg, he could hear the O'Reilly brothers' voices drifting down.

"How long do you think he's been digging this?" Derry asked.

"If he dug this by hand, it must have taken him years," Ryan replied.

"Years ..." Derry said, and the tone in his voice gave Owen goosebumps.

He stopped momentarily, catching his breath in the dusty confines of the tunnel. He sighed, then took stock of his situation. Finally he called back up the tunnel, "All right then, one of you is going to have to climb down first ... who's the smallest?"

"That'll be you, then," Ryan fired at Derry before Derry could even open his mouth.

Owen heard a couple of rough slaps and a few bad words, then the sound of someone climbing into the tunnel behind him.

It wasn't easy, and it took them a long time, but they eventually got the drive shaft down to the bottom of the tunnel and onto a flatbed wooden trolley that Owen had knocked together from a couple of ripped out floorboards and some small metal wheels he'd found in his workshop. As the tunnel had an incline, gravity would do its thing and keep the drill moving forward as it carved out the cement. At least that was the theory ...

The two boys didn't seem to like the tunnel very

much, and the younger choked on dust and held a hand over his nose and mouth.

"You're sure this is—" the older brother started.

"It's fine," Owen cut him off. "Hold on here."

Owen started to climb back out of the tunnel and Derry said—whimpered, almost, "Are you leavin' us in here?'

"Man yourself up," Ryan shot back.

"I'm getting the drill bit," Owen said then and walked out of the tunnel, leaving Ryan and Derry crouched in the dingy hole.

Owen was up, then back in a few minutes, and he ignored the looks of terror on the boys' faces. Once he got them back to work, they seemed to calm down. He pulled a rusted, heavy masonry drill bit from under his arm. Two feet long and two and a half inches in diameter. It had been lying on the floor of his shed for years. Too big for any of his drills but he couldn't bear to throw it away. He figured it might come in handy for something one day … and he was right. He handed it to Ryan, and then he and Derry lifted the drive shaft a few inches up off the wooden trolley. Ryan went to screw the drill bit on, and Owen felt the shaft jerk to one side. Ryan leaned too far in and fell, scraping his knuckles between the drill bit and the rough tunnel floor.

Derry laughed, and Owen realized the shaft hadn't moved on its own.

"Lads …" Owen warned, but they'd already started wrestling—as much as they could in the tight confines of the tunnel.

Owen's first impulse was to slap one or both of them, but he steadied himself.

"How much longer do you two want to be down here?" he yelled.

They stopped so suddenly that it was as though Owen had thrown a bucket of ice-cold water in their faces.

Then Owen and Derry lifted the shaft again, and Ryan got the drill bit on the end of it and screwed it on.

Owen smiled and said, "Careful climbing out."

A few scrapes and bruises aside, the three of them climbed out of the tunnel no worse for wear, and Owen clapped the boys on their backs.

The O'Reilly brothers shared smiles, and Ryan asked, "What's next?"

"Help me get the motor and the generator in here?" Owen said.

The two brothers looked at each other again, shrugged, and followed Owen out of the shed.

Patrick leaned against the wall of the tower house in the courtyard, keeping to himself and out of Owen's way. As Derry started dragging the generator and lights cable from the courtyard, Owen and Ryan went back into the lighthouse for the motor that would drive the drill.

• • •

The sun was setting by the time Ryan led his brother out the front door of the lighthouse.

Ryan still didn't quite know what to make of this crazy old lighthouse keeper and his hole in the ground, but at least now he knew why Mr. Kerrigan always looked so grimy. He and Derry looked just as bad themselves.

Owen followed them out onto the driveway, pulling a little wad of cash out of his pocket. He offered it to Ryan.

"No," Ryan said, making the decision right there on the spot, "you can keep your money."

"What?" Derry asked, just as fast.

"Take it," Owen insisted with knitted brows, holding the money out to Ryan, who only shook his head.

Derry stepped forward, and Ryan put out his hand to push him back.

"Come on," Ryan said to his brother, then moved him away by the elbow, leaving Owen standing, scratching his head, behind them.

Ryan wasn't sure they were completely out of earshot when Derry said in a hoarse stage whisper, "What are you doing? Sixty euros?"

Ryan picked up his pace, Derry followed along, and waited until they climbed into their van before continuing, "He's madder than a bag of spiders ... probably tunneling to the center of the earth."

Ryan smiled and wrapped his arm around his brother's shoulder.

"But it'll be worth it to see the look on O'Connell's face when he finds that hole, eh?"

Derry smiled back, and Ryan started the van as Derry's smile turned into a chuckle and then full-blown laughter at the thought of the look on O'Connell's face.

CHAPTER 13

Not that there was a lot of room before, but with the motor reattached to the shaft and the diesel generator just behind it attached by a short, thick makeshift electrical cable, all of which was squeezed onto the flatbed trolley, there was hardly enough room for Owen. Still, Patrick had wedged himself in behind him.

Owen sat on the rough, dusty floor and looked at his brother. Patrick's eyes went wide, waiting …

"Have you removed the speed limiter from the motor?" Patrick inquired.

Owen held up a small metal unit with a frayed electrical cord dangling from it.

"Ready?" Owen said with a grin.

Patrick nodded, and Owen went through his ritual to switch on the generator, which coughed and spluttered into life. Then he took hold of the big steel lever on the drill. He glanced at Patrick again, who gave him one short, anxious nod, and Owen squeezed the lever closed and pushed it forward.

The lighthouse motor, which was now the drill's motor, made a disconcerting metallic grinding sound, vibrated, then shook the wooden trolley so hard that cement dust and clumps of dry dirt rained from the ceiling to patter over Owen's head and shoulders.

Then, all at once, it was still and quiet.

A few little bits of loose cement continued to drop around them for another few seconds.

Owen didn't say anything, and neither did Patrick. Taking the lever in his hand again, Owen closed his eyes and retracted it, paused to count slowly to three, then pushed it forward again.

It whirred and screamed again—and the smell that rose off it was burning oil and dust and hot metal. It didn't shake as badly this time, and very little dust fell from the ceiling.

But it shut down again, just the same.

Owen kept his eyes closed, his hand still on the lever.

"Let me see," Patrick said, and Owen cringed at the hint of pity in his voice.

Owen put up a hand to stop him as he opened his eyes and looked around for the pickaxe.

"She just needs a little gentle persuasion," Owen said.

He grabbed the pickaxe up off the floor and swung it over his shoulder as he eyeballed the drill's motor. Patrick moved out of the way, back up the tunnel. He started to say something but stopped—and then just blurted out, "It's the generator!" Owen froze to the spot with the pickaxe on his shoulder and looked across to the generator. He hadn't even heard it coughing and spluttering against the din of the motor, but Patrick was right. Derry must have dislodged something when he dragged it down into the tunnel.

Owen took a step back, retracted the lever, then jammed it forward as hard as he could. The motor jarred with an awkward thrumming as Owen slammed the pickaxe down on top of the generator. His ears rang with the echoing clang.

The generator answered with a more rapid series of coughs and sputters. Owen slammed the pickaxe down on it again and didn't wait for more coughing, more sputtering, before smashing it one more time.

Then the generator let out a cough as though it had finally expelled whatever was choking it. Instead of that wet, sputtering noise, it murmured slowly, filling the tunnel with a painfully loud, echoing drone. Then the drill motor seemed to skip into life, beating out a reassuring tone, as cement dust pattered across Owen's shoulders and sprinkled in his hair.

Owen blinked the dust from his eyes, set the pickaxe on his shoulder again, and waited, counting silently to three. Then he sat the pickaxe down.

The motor rumbled along. The generator still gave an occasional cough as it settled into an uncomfortable rhythm. But it was good enough; the orange bulbs in the tunnel sprang back to life and the drill bit spun—and Owen stared at it, almost hypnotized by its constant, spiraling motion.

Owen threw his hands up in the air, oblivious to the fact that he hit his hands—hard—on the ceiling of the tunnel. He let out what he planned on being a delighted whoop, but his voice broke in the middle of it. That made him laugh. His eyes watered and his vision blurred, his eyelids sticking with accumulated dust.

Barely able to stand in the tunnel, Owen trundled out a rough approximation of a jig—and Patrick joined him, with such comical results Owen started laughing even harder.

He slumped against the wall of the tunnel and got a hold of himself.

"Come on now," Owen said to his brother with a wink. "Stand aside, and let me put this beauty to work."

Patrick backed up a couple of steps, and Owen moved over to stand behind the drill. He pressed both hands against it, dug in his toes, his knees bent, and pushed the heavy machine forward on its flatbed trolley.

The drill bit screamed a little when it touched the cement wall at the end of the tunnel, but Owen just pushed harder, then pushed some more, even after he thought he'd pushed it as far as it would go.

The drill bit chewed into the wall ... and kept chewing like a hot knife carving through butter. Owen slowly took his hands away from it, and as it chewed, gravity eased the contraption deeper into the tunnel, just as they'd hoped.

Owen thought his skull would split apart from the grin on his face.

He turned to his brother and saw the same expression.

"I think this calls for a celebration," Owen said, practically screaming over the deafening rumble of generator combined with the whirr of the motor and the scream of the drill bit in the cement. "We'll be through this in no time at all."

• • •

The full moon drew a wide, white swathe of light across the rippling sea. The rocks, so jagged and broken in the daylight, calmed to impotence in the heavy darkness. The stars were mostly washed out by the bright moonlight, and the world seemed cut in half: a dense, comforting black on top, and beneath, a shimmering silver blanket at once cold and inviting.

Owen took in a deep breath of the cool, salt-tinged air, and as though the act of drawing it into his lungs had conjured it up, the wind blew harder and slightly colder in his face. The white light on the water rippled and threatened to break apart when the wind pulled the calm sea into a light chop. A wave crashed against the rocks at the bottom of the lighthouse cliff with a basso rumble.

Owen let out his breath with a satisfied smile. He set his hands on the cold iron railing of the lantern tower balcony in front of him and put his right toes up on the bar at the bottom. His knee tapped the back of the row of foghorns mounted to the railing in front of him.

Patrick leaned forward next to him, resting his forearm on the rail and looking up and out to sea.

A flash of light reflected in Patrick's eye, and Owen turned to the new automatic lighthouse—really just a sort of antenna with a light on it, stuck in the rocks just to the north of the island. Its frigid, lifeless light pulsed away.

Owen's smile faded, and he tightened his grip on the railing. He felt the vibration, scant but definite. A low, steady rumble underlay the whisper of the sea on the rocks and the whistling of the wind, the drill digging away deep beneath them.

"Remember when we used to sit out with mah-mee in the fields and watch the stars?" Patrick said. "She knew all of their names."

Owen nodded and looked up, tracing imaginary lines between the few faint stars in the moonlit sky. "She made most of them up," he said.

"So there's not a constellation called the Dancing Pope?" Patrick replied, his voice cracking with horror.

Owen looked at him sharply in time to see his lopsided grin, and they both laughed.

Then Patrick turned his face back up to the sky and said, "I don't think I've ever seen a moon so bright."

"That's the perigee full moon," Owen said.

"The what moon?"

"Perigee," Owen repeated with a trace of irritation. "A supermoon. It only happens every thirteen months, when the moon is closest to the earth and lined up with the sun. It brings the highest and lowest tides. But this one is rare—the last time the moon was this close and the tides this extreme was 1948.

"Is that right?" Patrick replied. Then, after a quiet pause, he said, "I could never have imagined that they would ever have put a man up there when we were kids."

"Rubbish," Owen grunted back. "They never put a man on the moon. Those Americans have you brainwashed."

After a pause long enough for a sharply drawn breath, Patrick said, "Tell me you're not serious."

Owen smirked, letting him off the hook fast.

Just then, it didn't seem they had a lot of time to tease each other.

"If you find the treasure you could buy the lighthouse," Patrick suggested with a sincerity in his voice.

Owen turned back to the new lighthouse and watched the light pulse a few times before saying, "No, I think it's time to move on."

Owen thought he could feel his brother smile next to him, and when he turned, he saw that he was right.

"How about a song for the new light?" Owen asked, glancing down at the foghorns in front of them.

"I'm in," Patrick said with a smirk.

Owen pushed one of the buttons—there were six different-sized horns lined up in front of him. A low, loud, smooth but somehow growing roar blasted out over the water. Owen and Patrick laughed while the sound echoed into silence, bouncing off the rocks and into the cove and across the sea.

Ignoring a slight ringing in his ears, Owen chose another foghorn and let loose a higher-pitched wail—then another slightly lower and another and another, and he wasn't sure but ... it sounded like that old Gaelic song Ellen O'Malley sang to herself. He struggled to remember the name of it and stopped blowing the foghorns. Patrick smiled at him, looking as happy as Owen felt. "Lay Me Down," Owen remembered.

Then all was quiet.

"Again," Patrick chuckled.

And Owen stopped his thumb half an inch from one of the buttons. He tipped his head to one side and goosebumps sprinkled across his forearms.

"Listen ..." Owen whispered.

"I don't hear anything," Patrick replied, his voice a bit too loud.

Owen waved at him to be quiet with one hand and gripped the iron railing with the other.

No vibration. Just cold.

"Exactly ..." Owen said. He didn't hear anything either. "Come on."

Owen crawled back in through the narrow door into the lantern room and was down the curving stairs so fast he nearly tumbled to a stop at the bottom. He weaved through a few pieces of the lantern housing still cluttering the floor and was through the kitchen and out the back door like a shot.

He ignored a twinge of stiffness in his back as he crossed the moonlit courtyard and burst into the shed.

The stench of diesel fumes hit him the second he stepped into the little space.

"Shite," he gasped out, as much to himself as to Patrick, who he assumed had followed him down, "there must be a leak in the fuel line."

A dull yellow light flooded up out of the tunnel. Owen slid into the tunnel and scrambled down and around the dogleg and ground to a halt next to the drill mechanism.

The wooden trolley was soaked in diesel fuel and there was a big pool around the base of the motor, which sat silent and still. The fumes in the tunnel burned Owen's eyes, and he lifted his shirt up to cover his nose and mouth. The drill was still embedded in the lime-cement. Squinting, Owen leaned over to examine the generator. Patrick peered over his shoulder.

"Broken fuel line." Patrick asserted.

"Shite," Owen breathed as he stared at the fuel still dripping from it.

Patrick said, "You just had to bash it, didn't you?"

"It must have been …" Owen started. Then he pulled his shirt away from his mouth and said, "It must have been a faulty fit."

"You broke it," Patrick accused. "You'll have to refill the diesel."

Owen shook his head, put his shirt back up over his nose and mouth, and said, "That was the last of it."

"What?" Patrick huffed. "What's powering that?" He looked up and pointed at the dull yellow floodlight. "You must have a backup generator."

"This is the backup generator. That's my emergency floodlight. It runs on a battery," Owen replied indignantly.

Patrick sighed and looked around—at a loss.

Owen put his hands to his temples and closed his eyes. "There was plenty enough … shite! Quinn should be home. He'll have some." He started climbing out of the tunnel and barked at Patrick, "See if you can fix the fuel line."

Gasping and panting, Owen ran straight through the lighthouse and out to his truck, fumbled the keys out of his pocket, climbed in, and started it up—to a splutter and a clank, then nothing.

It was out of diesel.

Owen shouted out a string of curses—all aimed at himself—and banged the steering wheel with his right fist so hard he left a bruise on his hand. He pushed the door open, ran around to the truck bed, grabbed two jerry cans out of the back, and started off on foot.

• • •

Ellen had allowed herself to be slowly pushed through the densely packed room to be deposited safely at a table in the corner with her cousin Mary—who was having the *craic* with friends and neighbors, slipping in and out of her chair, pausing for a drink and a laugh before being pulled out to dance.

Ellen found the space itself to be a bit on the drab side, but it worked for what it was: a community center in which the Clare Islanders could gather and drink and trade tall tales.

And the islanders had made a real effort to cheer the place up by hanging bunting and handwritten banners. The biggest read "SEAFARERS' FESTIVAL"—this one having been professionally made, not handwritten. Frayed around the edges, the thing might have been twenty years old or older. But to Ellen that made it all the more endearing, and she realized how much she had missed being part of such a close-knit community.

Mary took a turn around the dance floor with her son Ryan, who bumped into a rosy-faced Derry, the younger of the two brothers already more than a little drunk. Quinn the church caretaker leaned across one of the little tables to make a point with the tip of his finger to Dougal, who laughed with a wide, gap-toothed grin.

The priest was there, ordering a drink from Darragh, and Mr. O'Connell from the council, who'd decided to stay on Clare for the celebration. He tried to make his way across the room but ended up being pushed this way and that by the vibrant crowd.

The music was up louder than usual, and with everybody seeming to be talking—shouting, really—all at the same time, Ellen wanted to put her hands over her ears.

She scanned the crowd for Owen, but he wasn't there. At first she thought maybe he was sitting down. There were very few chairs to go around, so almost everybody stood.

But he wasn't there.

She would have seen him by now.

She took a sip of warm, too-sweet white wine and sighed.

. . .

Owen had every intention of running but with two jerry cans and six and a half decades weighing him down, he had to settle for something like a stumbling, staggering, just-faster-than-normal walk.

A muscle in his lower back argued with his left hamstring over who was more inflamed, but Owen did his best to ignore the exchange and kept going.

The full moon lit his way across the uneven ground of the island, but he still managed to step in the occasional little hole, so soon enough his right ankle added to the chorus of complaints.

Without really being aware of getting the idea, Owen started humming a tune to himself, in some effort to force himself forward after a very long, very hard day's work. It was that Gaelic song of Ellen's again, and once again, he'd forgotten the name of it.

And then he was at Quinn's cottage and knocking, then pounding on the door.

No answer.

He pounded again and shouted Quinn's name.

Nothing.

Owen turned to the church—the priest wasn't going to let him in or help him, even if he wasn't at the Seafarer's.

He looked up at the steeple, painted silver in the

moonlight, with its missing spire making it seem somehow amputated, reluctant to reach for the sky.

Or just too tired after all these years.

• • •

Ellen had never seen the man before but at first glance she could tell this was the cleanest he'd been in months, if not years. His hair was too carefully put together, his suit obviously brand-new but still somehow rumpled. He pulled at his collar in a way that said, "I never wear a tie." He banged a glass on a table, startling the people sitting there, and shouted over the crowd—tried to, anyway. Ellen could see him shouting, but couldn't hear a word he said.

After a minute or so of that, the crowd, more or less the entire population of Clare Island, started to quiet down. A few people started yelling at the rest to quiet down, and a few people started yelling at those people to shut up themselves, and someone whistled really loudly, that actually hurt Ellen's ears, and the man in the suit banged the glass again.

With an undercurrent of murmuring voices still filling the cramped space, the man went to stand up on a chair. A younger man in a striped sports top tried to help him; then a woman in her late forties pulled the older man down by the other arm. Her shrill voice shot through the room: "What are ya tryin' to do, kill yerself?" But the suited man, determined to take the stand, brushed her off. "Let me be—I'll be fine."

A good-natured scuffle followed, during which Mary leaned across the table to Ellen, jabbing a thumb in the direction of the disturbance and said, "Our esteemed mayor."

The islanders at least thought of him as their mayor, but it wasn't an official title. He was more of an appointed community leader.

Ellen smiled and nodded, and the mayor, in a solid, booming voice roared out, "I'd like to thank you for coming to the festival tonight."

The crowd cheered, and Mary banged the table with her palms.

"I think in these difficult economic times," the mayor pressed on as the crowd settled, "we need to unite as a community more than ever."

Heads bobbed up and down, and a few people shouted out sounds of general agreement.

"Lobster stocks are down, and we've not seen as many tourists as we'd have liked this year," the mayor continued, jabbing his hands into the pockets of his suit jacket and looking down. The mood of the crowd palpably fell. Then the mayor looked up, pressed his lips tightly together, pulled a hand out of his pocket, and pointed across the room to one end of the bar. "Mr. O'Connell is here from the Mayo County Council to sell the lighthouse …"

O'Connell smiled and waved but looked a bit pale.

"... but I'm sure if you have any questions or concerns about community issues that he'll be more than happy to answer them ..."

Ellen looked back at O'Connell and laughed lightly to herself at the look of sheer terror on the man's face. He stepped back, bumped into a local, then brushed past and fetched up against the wall. He tipped his hat, and even from across the room, Ellen could see that his hand was shaking—regretting his decision not to take the ferry back to the mainland with the potential buyers.

"... now to tonight," the mayor went on. "The sea is our lifeblood." He paused and looked down, swallowed, and took a deep breath.

Someone hooted from the middle of the room, and a few people laughed. Someone said, "Quiet now, will you," rather loudly, and at last the crowd started to quiet.

"So," the mayor went on, his voice faltering ever so slightly, "this is our chance to offer up thanks to those that keep the community running." By the time he'd finished that sentence, he'd gotten a hold of himself and even managed to smile. "A special thank you to Ryan and Derry of the *Granuaile* for getting us all safely to and from the mainland."

Applause shook the room, and Ellen happily joined in.

She spotted Ryan and Derry in the crowd, beaming, waving then fending off pats on the backs, handshakes, fist bumps, and high fives. Then Ellen saw her cousin Mary beaming along with them, and she felt proud to be a part of their family and a tinge of sadness that she didn't have her own.

• • •

Crossing Dougal's yard in broad daylight could be a treacherous enough undertaking, but at night, even under the rising moon, it was downright terrifying.

Owen, panting, sweating, knees shaking, picked his way around piles of old rusted bits of this and that. In the dark it seemed to be a minefield of swarming snakes or piles of charred bones.

He eventually made his way to the door and dropped his jerry cans. He'd already made such a racket, breathing so hard and banging the empty cans against his knees as he ran. He fully expected Dougal to be waiting for him, but instead Owen was forced to pound on the door.

He called out for Dougal and barely waiting half a second for an answer, went to a window and looked in—all the lights were off, and no one was moving around inside.

He tried pounding on the door again, shouting out for Dougal a couple more times … but he wasn't home.

Owen rummaged almost blindly through piles of recycled parts until he found a sturdy enough steel bar. "I owe you a lock," he whispered to the absent Dougal and made his way to the shed.

He jammed the bar into the rusty padlock loop and pulled, but the bar just slipped free.

Owen swore, then put the steel bar into the lock again and pressed firmly, then pulled down with all his might but the bar hardly budged. Then it slipped out so fast Owen staggered back a few steps, knocked into an old rusty engine, and almost fell.

After a few more minutes of twisting and turning and pulling and prying, Owen tossed the steel bar aside. He went to the closest pile of scraps and started digging around until he came up with a length of plastic tubing … but it was too small. He sifted through some more, cut his hand on something, but kept looking, tossing parts aside, until he found another length of tube—one that was just long enough.

He took the length of tubing over to Dougal's van and twisted off the diesel cap. All this was done more by feel than by sight. Having siphoned off his fair share of diesel, Owen managed it easily enough, pulling the diesel into his mouth and spitting it out, gagging a little on it.

The fuel flowed—he could hear it pouring out on the ground. He struggled to get one of the jerry cans over and upright, then he kneeled on the ground, away from the spilled fuel, and listened as it drained into the empty jerry can.

"I owe you a tank of—" Owen started to promise the absent Dougal, looking up at the perigee full moon hanging almost straight above him now. But then the steady flow of diesel turned into a rapid series of drips, then just a drip here and there …

"Oh fer feck's sake!" Owen shouted at the moon.

Sweating, his knees aching, he pulled the tube out of the van, then out of the nearly half-full jerry can, and stood up. He looked this way and that, his mind racing through all sorts of impractical ideas to try to get that shed open and get to that diesel pump.

He staggered around the yard a bit, then finally bent over at the waist and rested his hands on his knees to catch his breath. The cool night wind dried the sweat on his forehead.

As he caught his breath, Owen looked up and realized he was facing the community center. Down the hill from Dougal's, he saw the lights of the building and the overflowing car park—every vehicle on the island seemed to have congregated there, like a herd of sheep huddled together for warmth.

CHAPTER 14

Owen avoided the front of the Clare Island Community Center, where some of the partygoers stood around smoking and chatting. He went around to the side instead, a field that served as a sort of overflow parking area. It was darker there, with no light posts, only the dull glow from windows hung with tatty old curtains.

The din of voices and too-loud music rolled out from the walls themselves, filling the dark car park with a sort of murmuring roar. They were applauding something in there, which was good enough for Owen. He banged one of the jerry cans—the one that was nearly half-full—on his knee for what felt like the thousandth time. And though he cursed under his breath at the pain, he was at least happy for the applause and music and voices, which covered the dull bang and his footsteps on the gravel.

Owen rambled along a line of vehicles, giving each a cursory inspection. He recognized many of the cars and trucks—there weren't all that many on the island. People had left various items in some of them—a jumper for later if it got cold, most of a case of cider in the backseat of another—and one even had the keys hanging from the ignition. And next in line from that, he found what he was really looking for: a diesel-powered truck.

Owen crouched next to it. He waited for a few seconds, eyes scanning this way and that, then quickly unscrewed the truck's diesel cap and pulled the length of tubing from where he'd stuck it through the back of his belt.

After another quick scan around the dark, empty car park, Owen fed the tube into the truck's fuel tank.

The applause and music died down under shouts for attention and before the noise fell away entirely, Owen quickly unscrewed the cap on the nearly half-full jerry can.

Then a familiar voice came from the window above him, shouting over the decreasing din, "… and to Owen for his loyal lighthouse duties and service to the community …"

Owen rolled his eyes when the crowd in the community center applauded that. He drew a great gulp of diesel up through the tube, then bit down on it and coughed out half a mouthful of the mouth-burning poison.

He swore quietly as the mayor went on, "… which

unfortunately has come to an end with the start of the new lighthouse today …"

The fuel fell back down the tube and into the truck again. Squinting from the sting of the diesel fumes, Owen spat on the gravel a few times and waited for more noise to cover his second attempt.

"… now I know that he likes to keep to himself, but as a thank you, we have bought him a fine hamper and a bottle of whiskey …"

The crowd burst into applause and catcalls, and Owen rolled his eyes again.

•••

Ellen managed to push her chair back just far enough so that she could stand up. With everybody—or, at least, almost everybody—turned toward the mayor now, it was hard to see everyone's face, but she scanned the room for Owen again. And she wasn't the only one. The mayor cast about himself, as did both Ryan and Derry. A couple of islanders, including Dougal, shouted Owen's name; then the mayor shrugged when Owen didn't present himself.

"… well, that's enough from me—please enjoy your night," the mayor finished, stepping down to a scattering of applause.

The music started up again before both the mayor's feet touched the floor.

The room didn't spare a second before getting on with drinking, talking, singing, and dancing, all at the same time.

Ellen stepped back to avoid bashing into a couple of her neighbors but was so packed into the place that she ended up being gently pushed back to sit at the table. Mary waved at her, and Ellen climbed up onto her knees on a chair and waved back.

Mary dragged the mayor along with her and some of the partygoers slapped the man on the back as he passed.

"I'd like you to meet my cousin, Ellen," Mary yelled into the mayor's ear.

Momentarily distracted by someone in the press of people, the mayor finally turned, and when he saw Ellen climbing down from her chair, his eyes lit up. She'd seen that look before and was getting just old enough to appreciate it.

"... delighted," the mayor said, seamlessly moving from one thought to the next and turning his back on Mary, who was already being dragged out of the crowd for a dance. "Could I get you a drink, Ellen?" he asked.

Then Dougal in his red shirt, his hair greased back—and in Dougal's case, Ellen worried it might be *literally* greased back—appeared behind the mayor and looked at her with the same twinkle, the same nervous half-smile, as the mayor.

"Hello Ellen," Dougal called, startling the mayor,

who was deftly pushed to the side. "You look grand this evening."

Ellen wondered if any of the men on Clare Island were married.

"Well," she said, "thank you."

"Now, I'm a bit out of practice," Dougal went on, and Ellen could see that his hands were shaking, "but I was wondering if—"

"You have something on your shirt there," Ellen interrupted, just as fast as she could.

Dougal shook his head, then looked down at one of half-a-dozen little grease stains on his shirt. As he worried at it with the side of his thumb, the mayor was greeted by glad-handing islanders and Mr. O'Connell appeared as if from thin air.

"Ellen," O'Connell said with a wide smile, hat in hand. "How lovely to see you. Could I get you a drink?"

The mayor turned back around and looked O'Connell up and down at that, and Dougal took a step toward him but didn't seem to know what to do after that.

Desperate for escape, Ellen scanned the room again—still no Owen. But when her eyes passed the window the mayor had been standing in front of, she saw a shadow bob up and down.

How could she be sure from what she saw in the blink of an eye that it was Owen? But Ellen was instantly sure of it.

Without taking her eyes off the window, she said, "Excuse me, gentlemen," and brushed past all three of them and into the crowd.

• • •

With the party apparently back on, Owen adjusted the tube in the truck's fuel pipe and put the end in his mouth.

He paused briefly to consider what the mayor had said. They'd bought him a gift. They at least thought about him for a minute.

Then Owen blinked at the truck he was stealing diesel fuel from and recognized it as the mayor's. When the mayor wasn't doing his few hours a month of civic duties, the rest of the time he was a farmer, and he used a heavy-duty diesel truck as his workhorse.

Owen drew in a gulp of the volatile liquid, then spat out the tube when Ellen called his name from right behind him. "Owen?"

He held the mouthful of diesel behind tightly pressed lips.

She edged closer to him, the light from the community center window illuminating enough of his burly frame to confirm it was him.

"About … earlier," she said. "I … it was all …"

The taste of the diesel wasn't just bad; his entire body wanted to reject it for the poison it clearly was.

"… a bit of a surprise."

Owen wanted her to talk faster or, better yet, go away. He didn't want to turn around but didn't want to keep his back to her, didn't want to be rude.

"Is everything okay?" Ellen asked.

Owen nodded and hoped she couldn't hear the fuel sloshing around in his mouth.

"The truth is," Ellen continued, and Owen could hear her take a step closer to him, "I've spent so long learning to be happy on my own that I just …"

The diesel started burning his gums. He could feel the outlines of his teeth.

Ellen took another step closer, then another.

"Ellen?" Father O'Brien said loudly, his voice screeching in the cold night air. Owen sagged, almost swallowed, but didn't. "Are you okay, my dear?" the Father asked her.

A scuffle of gravel told Owen that Ellen had turned around to talk to the priest. "Fine, thank you, Father," she said. "I'll be back inside in a few minutes."

More footsteps on the gravel, and the priest said, "Owen?" Then he must have turned to Ellen. "I'm sorry. I thought you were alone."

Owen spat the mouthful of diesel on the ground in front of himself, as quietly as he could, hoping the sound of footsteps on gravel and the music and voices from inside would cover it. He gagged, almost retched, and spat again. His tongue burned, and he wondered how long it would be before he'd be able to taste anything.

The priest wandered off, and Owen turned to Ellen, coughing.

"I know how much courage that must have taken …" she said, stepping closer still. Owen covered his mouth and coughed. He really needed to spit, but he didn't though he didn't want to swallow it either. "When you tried to kiss me, I mean. Look, what I'm trying to say is …" and she stepped closer still. "Kiss me again."

Owen coughed and turned to the side and spat. He really didn't want to, but had to. "Now," he said, his voice hissing in a tight throat, "is not a good time."

Ellen's eyes went narrow, and her brow furrowed. She squinted in the darkness and asked, "Is everything all right?"

Owen coughed and wiped his mouth with his sleeve. "I have to go," he said, not looking at her.

Owen backed up, and Ellen stepped closer, moving with him. Her nostrils flared as she caught the aroma of diesel fumes. He led her back and away from the jerry cans and the tube and the mayor's open fuel tank. Ellen seemed at a loss for words, and Owen was as grateful for that as he was for the trustworthy islander who'd left his keys in the car next to the truck.

He opened the door and got in the car—not as easy as he'd hoped. He wedged himself in behind the steering wheel rather ungracefully. The seat was set for someone much thinner, but rather than fumble about for the slider handle in the dark, Owen turned the key in the ignition.

And for a moment, he fully expected the car not to start. He thought for sure that he'd hear a coughing rattle, or a rattling cough, and yet another engine would goad him with an empty tank.

But the car started right up, its little engine making a whining hum. Owen put the car in reverse and pulled around to the other side of the mayor's truck, where he'd left the jerry cans and tube.

Ellen backed up a few steps. He couldn't see her face just then, but Owen knew she must have been looking at him as though he'd finally gone completely mad.

But he had things to do, so he put that out of his mind and hauled himself out of the car, squeezing between the steering wheel and seat. He opened the hatchback, grabbed the empty jerry can, and threw it into the boot. Then, racing the sound of Ellen's footsteps approaching on the gravel, he ripped the tube out of the mayor's truck, closed the nearly half-full jerry can, and shoved them both into the boot as well—not at all easy, but pressed for time and more worried about getting the hell out of there than securing them in some organized way, Owen mashed them in and slammed the hatchback shut just as Ellen's footsteps were coming around the truck.

He pushed himself back into the driver's seat, dropped the little car into gear, and sped off, leaving the crunch of gravel and a little puff of dust to mark his exit.

Owen spared a glance in the rear-view mirror to see Ellen painted in the red hue of his taillights, standing, hands on hips, in the car park, frustrated and bemused.

• • •

Owen didn't want to take any more time away from the drill, but he paused in the kitchen just long enough to rinse what was left of the diesel from his mouth with a few swigs of whiskey. His tongue and gums felt raw— he didn't want to look at them in the mirror—but at least it wasn't getting any worse.

He dragged the can down into the tunnel a little slower than he liked. The little pain in his back had turned into a nagging, knotting, pulsing thing, and his shoulders protested any attempt at movement.

Still, he managed to get the jerry can down to the generator that rested behind the drill on the sodden wooden trolley. He unscrewed the caps, of the can and the generator fuel tank, then propped himself against the wall of the tunnel, trying a few different positions before attempting to fill the little fuel tank. The can was heavy, and he'd spilled enough already—and hadn't brought back even a quarter of what he'd hoped for.

Finally, he managed to fill the tank with maybe a liter and a half that was left in the can. He screwed both caps closed tight, coughing from the fumes in the tight, already-dusty space …

With no time to waste, he pushed buttons and pulled levers to get the generator started, only to watch it splutter to a stop after barely a second's worth of life.

Wincing from more little jabs of random pain, Owen leaned forward and squinted in the dim light to examine Patrick's work on the fuel line.

There was no work on the fuel line. A drop of precious diesel hung from an inch-long gash.

"I was about to send out a search party," Patrick said from behind him, and Owen jumped, his heart skipping a beat.

With a huff Owen slouched back against the tunnel wall, almost tipping over the little toolbox he'd left in the tunnel so Patrick could at least try to fix the fuel line while he was out scouring the seemingly abandoned island for a few drops of diesel.

"You lazy …" Owen said with a grimace. "Couldn't you just do one thing?"

Patrick crouched in the tunnel, his arms folded. "There's no point fixing the leak. The motor is soaked in diesel, it'll need to be stripped down, dried out, and rebuilt."

Owen felt his fingers clench into a fist as he looked up at the tunnel ceiling, as though the secret to this man he called his brother might be etched in the cement.

Then Patrick uttered the words, "It's over."

And Owen growled. It came deep from the pit of his stomach, and it got louder and louder as his right fist unclenched and his fingers curled around the handle of the pickaxe on the floor next to him. He picked it up, raised up into a half kneel, half crouch and swung it back as far as his weary arms would carry it.

With all his might, he drove it as hard as he could into the wall with an almighty—*thwack!*

Then he yanked it out, swung it back, and surged forward, striking the wall again, even harder this time. As if he were talking to the end of his tunnel and not Patrick, he shouted, "Why did she leave me for you?"

Then he slammed the pickaxe against the wall again, so hard the handle vibrated and he almost dropped it.

"*Why?*" he yelled, insisting on an answer from Patrick, from the tunnel, from anyone or anything that might be able to offer one. "Tell me why!" he yelled again, now almost pleading.

"She didn't," Patrick said from behind him. His voice was calm, and though a part of Owen wanted it to sound condescending, demeaning, teasing—it was none of those things. "Your mind has twisted the facts."

230

That was worse than the wrong tone of voice. Owen hefted the pickaxe and swung. "That's—" and he hit it again, harder still—"*bullshite!*"

Owen saw the crack begin, but didn't fully register it. His vision was blurry. He wasn't sure what he was doing or seeing anymore.

"You'd already broken up," Patrick said. His voice was steady, still, almost devoid of emotion. It was as though he were reading the news on the radio. "You weren't right for each other. You said so yourself."

Owen wasn't sure how to reply to that—wasn't sure if that were true or not. All he could think to say was, "I trusted you!"

He hit the wall with the pickaxe again, and another crack appeared, splintering out from the deep hole the huge drill had bored into the cement.

Owen leaned forward on his knees. His back demanded that he stop, but he tried to stand up, using the pickaxe to steady himself.

"*I trusted you!*" Owen screamed at the cracking wall, or Patrick, or both.

And it was as if the wall heard him, even if his brother didn't.

It started to give way slowly, but then faster and faster, accelerating through its own destruction as though with every passing half a second it became more and more convinced that it was over, that it was time to just give way, to just give up.

Owen sank back to his knees and held the back of his right hand against his nose and mouth to deflect some of the dust.

He stared at a hole in front of him that opened out into a dark space.

Those words passed through Owen's mind one at a time: Hole. Space.

He'd broken through.

His back bedamned, Owen turned to look at his brother, who stood staring at the hole with a look on his face that made Owen think he was looking into a mirror.

Owen turned back to the hole and locked his eyes on it. *Was his mind playing tricks on him? No—there was a hole, there was definitely a hole.* He used the pickaxe to clear some debris from the edges. He made it a bit bigger, then used his hands to make it bigger still. Some of the cement was still sitting there by habit alone, and it was a simple matter to pull it apart.

Eventually Owen ended up with a hole just big enough that if he really tried, he could get through. The tunnel was as still and quiet as it was dark—the emergency floodlight, a casualty of his manic pickaxe swinging.

It was a dark so complete that Owen couldn't see his hand if he'd held it to the tip of his nose.

But this had happened before over the years—more than once—and if Owen knew anything at all, it was the inside of that tunnel.

He felt next to him for the toolbox and put his hand on a … it took him a second … screwdriver, then the claw hammer, and then the flashlight.

He clicked it on, and the shaft of light made the tunnel look bigger.

"Is it …?" Patrick whispered, and Owen turned the flashlight on the hole in the wall.

Within was a chamber of sorts formed from stone blocks. Just a little space, like some kind of basement crawlspace.

Dust swirled in the beam of light, disturbed by Owen's own panting breath.

He leaned in closer to the hole and put his arm in, the flashlight in front of him. He followed the flashlight with his head. Under some chunks of concrete and a thick layer of dust-dry soil, was a wooden chest with a slightly rounded lid.

Heavy, black iron hinges secured the back of it, and straps of the same black, pounded wrought iron banded the wood.

"It's …" Owen whispered.

"Owen?" Patrick queried quietly behind him.

Aside from a couple of warped, misshapen boards and a small split next to one of the hinges, the chest was well preserved; sat there for centuries under its blanket of dust, waiting …

"It's …" Owen whispered again, but he couldn't finish the sentence.

He placed the flashlight carefully down on the dusty floor within, then dragged himself through the hole.

"Owen …" Patrick said with obvious concern.

Owen ignored him and hauled himself into the little chamber, ignoring every jab of pain and protesting joint to curl up into the tight space. He picked up the flashlight and slid up against the back wall, and from there he could see the front of the chest, with its big, black iron lock and its empty keyhole …

He dragged the gold key out from under his shirt and held it for a few seconds.

The key glinted in response to the light from his flashlight.

Owen swallowed. He opened his mouth, closed it, then opened it again.

His hand was shaking—he could feel the chain tickling his neck. *Key and lock apart for over four hundred years*, he thought.

He unclipped his neck chain and slipped off the key. Then held it prone. He closed his eyes for a second and took two deep breaths, then opened them and slid the key into the lock.

A perfect fit.

Patrick's eyes lit up.

"What did I tell you?" Owen whispered—it seemed somehow improper to speak too loudly in the treasure vault of Grace O'Malley.

"Get it open," Patrick whispered. Then he glanced back over his shoulder as though afraid someone would sneak up behind them. "Come on!"

Owen stuck the flashlight under his arm, clenched his fist, raised it to his mouth, and blew a breath into it as if it might bring him luck. Then he took hold of the key. His hand wasn't shaking anymore.

He turned the key—gently—afraid it might simply snap in the lock.

Click.

Owen licked his lips.

Click.

Owen swallowed.

Click.

Owen closed his eyes.

Then slightly louder … *click*.

And the ancient mechanism surrendered to its long-lost key.

Owen set both hands on the sides of the lid and looked back at Patrick, who nodded once.

Then Owen opened it.

His eyes threatened to leave his head entirely to float up to the Heavens like helium balloons. Spots moved across his vision, and he blinked and coughed and swallowed.

"Owen …" Patrick whispered.

Owen stared into the chest for a few moments more, transfixed on the contents.

Patrick raised his eyebrows, waiting …

Then Owen heaved the chest around so that Patrick could see for himself.

No gold. No silver, just rocks! Cold, gray, worthless stone.

CHAPTER 15

Ellen sat on a bench and looked up at the full moon almost straight over her head and shivered even though it wasn't that cold. Something about the silvery-blue light just gave her a chill.

A bell clanged lazily from the harbor—maybe from Ryan and Derry's ferryboat tied up on the quayside. She tipped her head, surprised she could hear the bell with the dull rumble of music and voices coming through the walls of the community center.

Despite growing up on Clare, after spending most of her life in the city she hadn't quite gotten used to the way sound carried on the island or how it looked under the cold light of the moon, but at least it was starting to feel like home again. The rough terrain of the island seemed to have been smoothed out in the darkness. At that moment, with the sound of what may as well have been some tribal celebration behind her, the clang of sea bells and the calls of sea birds and the whisper of the sea itself in front of her, Ellen wouldn't have been surprised if a faerie or some pagan goddess suddenly materialized in front of her. Imagining that made her smile, but the smile didn't last long.

Despite the magical surroundings, something was missing.

"Is everything okay?" some pagan goddess asked from the darkness.

Ellen turned to see her cousin Mary and said, "I'm not sure ..."

Mary sat down on the bench next to her, rubbing her arms against the same full-moon chill.

"I just saw Owen," Ellen said. "He was acting strangely. Really strangely."

Mary sighed and bumped into Ellen playfully. "If you'd known him as long as I have, nothing would surprise you," she said, and without the slightest indication of a switch in gears asked, "You have a thing for him, don't you?"

Ellen looked up at the sky again and saw clouds in the distance—a storm rolling in, already revealing flashes of distant lightning. She sagged forward, holding her forehead in both hands and trying to work out whether to laugh or cry. Mary nudged her again.

"I came here to get over my marriage," Ellen said, neither laughing nor crying, her head still down, elbows biting into her knees. "It's the last place I expected to meet someone."

The two cousins sat there in silence for a long moment, and then at last Ellen sat up straight and looked at Mary. It may have been a trick of the moonlight, but Ellen thought she saw a trace of jealousy in Mary's face and heard a smaller trace in her voice when she said, "Well, you've made quite a hit. Since you've been back, I don't think there's a man on the island that isn't after you."

Mary had lived there her entire life, and Ellen had swept in and become the belle of the ball in a matter of a couple of days. But by the time she'd finished, that probably-imagined jealousy was gone, Mary's smile shining in the moonlight. Ellen sighed and swept mental images of the balding priest and the gap-toothed mechanic and the councilman from her mind the second she conjured them. Not much of a ball to be the belle of.

The bell rang again in the distance, and someone—a woman—laughed loudly from the community center.

Ellen spent half a second arguing with herself as to whether or not to say, "He tried to kiss me earlier, and I froze," then just said it anyway.

Mary whipped her head around to face her, eyes wide, and Ellen returned the look until they both collapsed in laughter.

"Well," Mary finally stopped laughing enough to say, "isn't he full of surprises."

As their giggles subsided, Mary asked, "Come back

inside for a drink?" Ellen could hear in her voice that she didn't think they were actually going to have that drink.

"No," Ellen replied, "I think I'll head home now."

But she didn't stand up, and neither did Mary. The bell rang again, twice.

"You'll break some hearts in there tonight," Mary said with a smile.

Ellen smiled back, said goodnight, and the cousins fell into a comfortable, slightly drunk hug.

• • •

Owen had been saving a bottle of twelve-year-old malt whiskey for when he found the treasure of Grace O'Malley.

He couldn't read the label in the darkness, but anyway, it was older than twelve now. He opened the bottle and almost put it to his lips but stopped. He leaned up against the chest-high wall of the courtyard and stared out to sea. The rocks rose in front of him like jagged fangs.

No, he thought then, not fangs.

Just rocks.

The rocks rose in front of him like rocks.

Dead, mindless stone jutting up out of the ocean because some plate pushed on another plate or some ancient earthquake shoved this bit of dirt against that bit of dirt and here he was, on a rock covered with weeds in the middle of a cold sea, overseen by an automatic blinking light on a steel pole that would still be blinking away when he and the rest of the islanders and every man and woman on Earth was as dead as those rocks.

He almost dropped the bottle over the edge of the cliff. Why not let it smash on the rocks?

All those years of back-breaking digging, the scars on his hands, lungs caked in dust … for a box of worthless rocks. "Feck it," he grumbled, then he did put it to his lips. It burned, and he didn't care. It was a fine drop, but he didn't care. He had already swallowed too much, but he didn't care.

And then the bottle was empty.

Owen closed his eyes and pressed his teeth together so hard he was afraid they might shatter in his head— and so what if they did?

He wanted to cough but held it in. He staggered back half a step. He needed to cough, but still held it in.

He'd coughed enough for any one lifetime.

Owen leaned forward against the wall again and opened his eyes, looking at the empty bottle in his hand. He didn't drop the bottle off the cliff, he threw it. And he threw it so hard he almost fell back, but steadied himself with his other hand on the wall. The bottle was swallowed up in the darkness, and he might have heard it shatter on the rocks below but might not have. What did it matter if it smashed on the rocks or floated away on the tide?

He belched and wiped his lips with the back of his hand, tasting sweat and cement dust.

He was SO sick of the taste of cement dust.

Then Patrick was standing next to him. Owen hadn't heard him coming but hadn't heard the bottle shatter, either. Sometimes you have to want to hear something in order to be able to hear it.

"Leave me alone," he said to his brother, who answered with a shake of his head and a look on his face that Owen turned away from rather than trying to figure out what his brother was thinking.

Owen staggered across the courtyard to the back door of his lighthouse—which on Monday morning would be someone else's lighthouse.

He staggered through the kitchen, into the living room, and straight to the bookcase without thinking, and then all he thought about was clearing the books off. They were dirty, covered in dust, and useless stacks of paper.

He tore them off half a dozen at a time and hurled them behind him; then another half dozen went right over his shoulder, and then he had only one in his hand, and he flung it like a boomerang. As he followed through with that motion, he spun, heard the book hit the wall—hard—then tried to stop spinning but only spun faster, and the lighthouse spun the opposite direction, and he thought maybe if he hit the floor hard enough it would finally just be still, so he lifted his foot to stomp on it, and he blinked and slammed down onto the floor.

But it didn't help—he was lying on his back, and the room went on spinning regardless.

"That's only half a poem," Patrick said, standing over him, arms crossed, and even though the room was spinning faster and faster and faster, Patrick didn't spin at all. He just stood there.

Owen closed his eyes, and there was Ellen and she was singing so loudly and he wanted to sing along, but all he got out through his throat was a whiskey-drenched croak. He gagged and stopped himself from throwing up on Grace O'Malley's tomb and didn't bother wondering how he'd gotten to the church. He read the poem on the tomb—or recited it from memory—roughly to the tune of Ellen's Gaelic song. Then he was running his finger across the rough stone relief of the O'Malley coat of arms, and there was another finger there, thin and delicate and belonging to Ellen, and she still sang but wanted him to see the ship riding the waves as the drawing of Gracie's coat of arms merged with the O'Malley coat of arms. And the ship fell from the waves and sank onto the sand.

She moved her lips in time with the song, but Owen heard, "Maybe she isn't buried there?" instead.

Owen shook his head and was sitting in Ellen's living room, on the couch. Cardboard boxes full of shining gold coins were strewn all over the room, some of the coins spilling out on the wooden floor. Owen bent to pick one up while Ellen said, "It's old … it's a bit of a family heirloom, I suppose."

Owen sat back, and in his hand was the Spanish spire from the church, but he was sure he'd picked up a coin, and anyway the spire seemed too light, as though made of cardboard.

"What's it called?" Owen said, then shouted it again over Ellen's singing. She was singing so loud.

And she didn't stop singing, just also at the same time said, "I think it translates as 'Lay Me Down.' "

And Owen took a deep breath, and the crescent-shaped spire was a gold coin, and then he was sitting on the floor, not the couch, and he was in the lighthouse living room, and the boxes of coins were books—his books.

And there was Patrick.

Owen blinked and breathed a few times slowly, in and out.

He put his right palm on the floor in front of him, and the wood was solid and real and not moving, and it stayed that way until he finished counting to twenty.

Owen looked up at his brother, who still stood over him with his arms crossed. As he pushed himself up from the floor, he said, "Paddy, come quick …"

. . .

Owen didn't notice that Patrick didn't seem to notice that they were in a "borrowed" car. But whatever got them there, Owen brought it to a stop in front of Ellen's cottage. He hadn't thought to look at his watch, even ignored the clock on the dashboard. It was night—late, too, but how late Owen didn't care.

"You wait here," he told Patrick as he crawled out from behind the wheel. He hadn't even paused to figure out how to move the seat back.

He stepped to the door, trying to walk off the rest of the bottle of whiskey. He'd been just able to drive—at least with no one else on the road. The whole island was still at the community center, but Owen didn't want to go back there—hoped that he'd find Ellen at home instead.

He knocked frantically—too loud, too many times—then stopped to listen with both hands on the doorframe. He shook his head, dizzy, but not as drunk as he thought he should have been. But still it was easier to lean than to stand.

There was no answer, so he knocked again, not quite as loudly.

"Who is it?" Ellen asked from behind the door. Her voice was low, sleepy.

Owen smiled and clung onto the doorframe.

"It's me?" he said, not intending to phrase it as a question.

The door creaked open, and there was Ellen in … Owen didn't know what to call it … some kind of night … thing, or underwear … thing.

Hot blood rushed to his cheeks, and he blinked and by sheer force of will, dragged his eyes up to hers. Her lips curled up in an effort to smile but then dropped back down, and she said, "What were you doing outside the community center?"

She looked him up and down and Owen wanted to step back from the door but couldn't. He still needed to hold himself up.

"And whose car is that?" she asked, nodding behind him.

Owen shook his head and tried to lean a bit to block the car and Patrick, waiting inside it, from her sight. "I need to ask you something," he said, then cleared his throat, afraid he sounded drunk.

Realizing that she wasn't going to get much sense out of him, she said, "It's late, Owen … let's talk tomorrow."

"No, we need to talk now …" Owen demanded, coming in just a few steps and leaning against the wall.

A little perturbed by his insistence, she said, "Well you had better come in then," stepping aside, "and I'll make some coffee."

"I need you to sing the song to me," Owen fired back.

She turned to him, eyebrows way up on the top of her forehead. "At this time of night?"

Owen nodded and motioned her toward him, wanting her to start singing now.

She moved away from him a little, unsettled, and crossed her arms, shifting all her weight to her right foot.

"I need you to sing the song for me," he repeated.

"Can't this wait till morning?"

Owen shook his head again, which made him even dizzier. "I've no time to explain …"

Ellen looked him up and down again, and Owen knew he must have been quite a sight—like some kind of mad homeless man covered in dust and sweat and stinking of booze and diesel.

"Come inside," she insisted.

She went into the kitchen, and Owen sagged against the wall. He didn't have time for coffee, or— "I need you to sing the song for me," he repeated again.

"Owen Kerrigan," she said, and Owen closed his eyes against her disapproval, "you suck the diesel out of the mayor's truck, drive off in someone else's car, then you burst into my house at this hour, stinking of whiskey, and tell me to sing a song." Her accent suddenly had more Irish than American, and Owen smiled a little. "I won't," she continued, "until you tell me what is going on."

"You won't believe me," he said, afraid to look her in the eye.

"Try me," she shot back.

Owen came off the wall and found he could walk just fine. He started pacing back and forth. Ellen came toward him.

"Trust me," she said, clearly frustrated. "I want to help you."

Owen shook his head and held up a hand to stop her from coming any closer. He needed another minute to think.

Crossing her arms, her weight all on one foot, Ellen stood there and gave him his minute.

"Grace O'Malley," he said finally, "buried the treasure of *El Gran Grin* somewhere on this island, and I think it's in her tomb."

Owen swallowed and took a breath.

"At least," he said, "I do now."

Ellen's brow crinkled, and her eyes narrowed.

"The location is in the song," Owen said. "The location of her tomb … her real tomb."

"Owen!" Ellen shouted at him. She moved over to close the door, "It's folklore, that's all."

"You said yourself that Gracie was hiding something," Owen retorted.

"Maybe she was," Ellen replied with a shrug, "but nothing worth getting yourself this worked up about." She stopped and looked at the floor, thinking, then said, "Is that why you're always covered in … dust and dirt … and whatever else all the time? Have you been digging up this island looking for buried treasure?"

Owen shook his head and withered a little from the look on her face. She really did think he was mad. "No," he said, then realized how ridiculous that sounded. "Not … all of the island."

He smiled at her and said, "I've told you my secret. Now will you sing the flamin' song for me, please?"

It was Ellen's turn to sag. Then she shook her head and reluctantly started to sing, *"Leag mé síos—"*

"No, no …" Owen interrupted. "In English."

"I've never sung it in English before," she said.

"Go on," Owen said, "you can do it."

Ellen closed her eyes to think for a moment, then began to sing, tentatively at first, then in that beautiful voice …

"Lay me down in this land I call home
Amongst my clan so I won't rest alone
When I wake from my slumber I wish it be night
So I may be bathed in the glow of the moon most bright
Lay me down in the crescent moon
And with me shall rest all that I own."

While she sang, Owen, listening intently, scribbled the words down onto a scrap of paper whilst he stumbled around the room, searching on the floor and in the scattered boxes. He found what he was looking for: Ellen's drawings of both Grace O'Malley's and the

249

O'Malley family's coats of arms. He picked them up, and his eyes darted from one to the other as she finished the song, then locked on Grace O'Malley's.

A shield.

A boar.

Three bows and arrows.

A ship resting at a slight angle on the sand.

"TERRA. MARIQUE. POTENS."

"O'MAILLE."

Owen smiled, and felt all of the frustration and disappointment of the last twenty-four hours slip away.

He couldn't help it and didn't try. He took Ellen up in his arms and squeezed her just about as tight as he could.

Then he kissed her full on the lips and she pulled back again, and by the look on her face, she was worried that he'd completely unraveled, but Owen smiled, knowing just the opposite was true.

He backed off and turned to avoid the look he didn't want to see on her face. He folded up both drawings and stuffed them into his fleece pockets along with the scribbled scrap of paper with the lyrics written on it.

"I need these drawings," Owen said. "I'll bring them back."

"Owen," Ellen said, stopping him as he moved for the door. "You're scaring me."

Owen went to the door and opened it without another word.

Ellen called after him, "Owen! Don't go … please. Owen!"

And with that, Owen was back behind the wheel of the car.

He slammed the car door and looked up just in time to see Ellen still stood in the doorway.

He touched the key, then realized he'd left the engine running.

"You should really find out whose car this is," Patrick said, sitting patiently, straight up and down, in the passenger seat.

Owen ignored him, put the car in reverse, and swung out onto the narrow road. "We should have seen it before," Owen said, jamming the car into gear and stomping on the accelerator. "It was right in front of our eyes."

Patrick looked over at him, one eyebrow raised, saying without actually speaking: "I told you so."

"It was in the song," Owen explained as he drove. "The family heirloom. It was Gracie's way of passing the secret down to her descendants. She must have buried the treasure with her." He pulled the lyrics from his pocket. " 'The moon most bright' is the full moon … the *perigee* moon."

"Isn't that tonight?" Patrick questioned.

"It is—and the crescent-shaped Spanish spire.

That's the crescent moon," Owen said. "That will show us where her tomb is."

Owen leaned forward as the car bumped along, and he looked up into the dark sky. More of the stars had been obscured by the storm rolling in, and the distant flashes of lightning were just a bit less distant. "We've no time to waste."

Patrick took a breath and continued, "Has it not escaped you that the spire is not only not on the steeple, but it's locked inside the church?"

Owen shrugged and said, "If Quinn can get it down, I can get it back up."

• • •

With a now-familiar crunch of gravel the car ground to a stop in front of Quinn's cottage. Owen opened the door and started to squeeze out of the car, then swore under his breath and felt around the bottom of the seat. He finally found the steel bar he knew was under there and pulled up on it to slide the seat back. It only gave Owen a couple more inches, but he could get in and out of the car at least two inches faster now.

Patrick was about to get out of the car.

"Wait here. Patch doesn't like you" he said to Patrick. "I'll get the key."

Patrick shrugged and folded his arms, and Owen got out of the car and charged up to the door of Quinn's cottage. He didn't bother to knock, he knew that Quinn was bound to still be down at the community center with the rest of the islanders. He tried the handle, found it unlocked, and stepped in.

On the off chance that Quinn had come back from the festival early, Owen whispered, "Quinn? Quinn?" into the dark room.

He was answered by a loud, rumbling snore that led him a few steps toward the sofa. Quinn had made it that far at least. A bottle of whiskey sat leaning in a loose grip in one hand, balancing on the floor and against his palm.

Quinn's old dog looked up at Owen from the floor, blinked at him a couple times, then rolled over onto his side and went back to sleep.

Owen stepped over the dog and retrieved the bottle, placing it on a side table next to the rusty iron key that he was looking for. Owen swapped the bottle for the key. On his way out, he spotted Quinn's flashlight on the table next to the door and instinctively dropped it into his pocket. Then he went outside, leaving Quinn and Patch to their rumbling sleep.

Pocketing the key, Owen went around behind the little cottage where the moonlight illuminated a tall extension ladder leaning against the back wall. Next to it was a shovel, and Owen took both.

The ladder was heavy and unwieldy. Owen dragged as much as carried it across the yard. As he came out from behind the cottage, Patrick joined him. Owen expected his brother to pick up the back of the ladder, maybe at least take the shovel from his other hand, but once again, the oh-so-delicate Patrick with his back problems just walked along, oblivious to Owen's struggles.

That didn't occupy Owen's thoughts for too long, though. Once he got the ladder to the church, he dropped the shovel and extended the ladder to its full extent. That made it even more difficult to maneuver on his own, but after a few grunting attempts, he got it upright against the side of the old church. The moonlight gave the whole affair a strange, unreal quality, made worse by the low rumble of faraway thunder. He swore he could hear Grace O'Malley calling to her charges …

• • •

There were no trees on Clare Island that tall.

And even had there been, they wouldn't have gyrated the way these did—staggering across the horizon, then seeming to leap up into the air only to fall lower than they'd started.

They were not trees but masts. From the height of them, it could only be the largest of vessels. Their sails tightly furled against the whipping wind, still the masts seemed to grab hold of the wind and pull against it.

"*Long!*" one of Grace O'Malley's kinsmen shouted over the wail of the storm. From their perch atop the watchtower, still they couldn't see the hull of the ship or *long* in Gaelic—whatever ship it was.

"*Spáinnis,*" Grace O'Malley said in an assured tone as lightning crashed into the sea, forward of the ship, illuminating the sails and flags flailing on its masts.

She stood majestic on her watchtower as the wind and rain lashed down, drenching her auburn locks. *For now it belongs to the storm,* she thought, *and when the storm has had its fill of her, the ship will belong to the rocks, and once the rocks have split her open, then it will be mine.*

"*Fiacla Dragain,*" she shouted into the wind as she pointed to the treacherous dragon's-teeth rocks that looked like an open-mouthed beast submerged under the sea, ready to devour its prey.

Some of the men might have cheered, but Grace couldn't hear it over the howling wind.

Then she led her men off the watchtower and down to the gift the sea and storm had offered up to them.

• • •

Owen fished the rusty iron key out of his pocket and unlocked the padlock. He swung the heavy church door open, the screech of the tired old iron hinges raising goosebumps.

"Keep an eye out," Owen said as Patrick turned to look back in the direction of the road.

Owen went in and dragged the heavy crescent-shaped spire out from it's resting place, then grunted and groaned, ignoring this little pain and that to swing the spire up over his shoulder. It bit into his collarbone, and Owen shifted the weight, almost dropped it, then found an at least slightly less painful way of holding it.

He tramped out to the foot of the ladder, and as he passed, Patrick whispered, "This is madness."

CHAPTER 16

Owen, the heavy spire still propped on his shoulder, started up the ladder without giving it a second thought—

—until he passed the top of the arched door, his feet maybe nine feet off the ground. His left hand gripped the ladder rail, the smooth aluminum chilling his rough palm. The spire sat heavily on his shoulder, held by his right hand. Owen leaned forward into the ladder, but his right elbow bumped the rail. The blood drained from his head at how much the ladder shook. He almost let go of the spire to hold on with his right hand but leaned forward again, pushing his right elbow out enough so that his chest rested against one of the ladder rungs.

He stood there for a long moment while the ladder slowly came to rest again, and the pulsating sensation of it made Owen weak at the knees.

"Owen ..." Patrick said from below, "Will you please get down from there before you kill yourself?"

Standing there, Owen wasn't quite sure how he'd made it this far, and he was only barely a third of the way up. Knowing he was in danger of thinking—about how dangerous this was, how insane this was, how obsessive this was, how much it would hurt when he hit the ground and the hefty spire fell on top of him— he took a deep breath, released his grip on the ladder ever so slightly, then put his right foot up on the next rung. He straightened his right leg, sliding his left hand up and gripping tighter when his right leg was straight; then he put his left foot on the same rung as his right; then straightened his left leg.

The ladder bowed a little but came back and was steady within a second or so.

The tide was rapidly going out, the storm was rapidly blowing in, and the spire wasn't getting any lighter.

Urging himself forward with a whispered, "Come on, man," Owen put his right foot up on the next rung, straightened his leg, then pulled up his left leg to join it, straightened it, and it was okay.

The metal was cold and felt slippery, and the soles of his shoes slipped on the rungs, and the whole ladder bowed under his weight and seemed to want to catapult him off into the night with every step, but with every step he also got closer to the top.

He'd remembered hearing that if you're nervous on a ladder or some other high place that you shouldn't look down, so he tried not to. He looked up to see how much farther he had to go, and his head spun and the ladder bowed and one foot slipped a little.

He paused again, tried to shift the weight of the spire on his right shoulder but stopped before he'd barely moved at all. The ladder twisted ever so slightly. Owen imagined all sorts of horrifying outcomes, the ladder twisting and collapsing, bending and collapsing, falling back off the side of the church … "Get a grip, man," he muttered to himself as he forced the images from his mind.

But looking up was just as bad as looking down, so he looked at the stones directly in front of him instead. As long as there were stones in front of him, he had to keep climbing. He tried to imagine the ancient masons who'd erected the church so long ago. They would have had to be up on a ladder—and one not quite as elaborately engineered as the one he'd borrowed from Quinn.

And Owen was reminded then of the fact that Quinn had climbed the same way, the same height, to bring the spire down even if not in the middle of the night and with a storm building.

And up a few more rungs, just when he thought his legs were going to give way, he emerged at the top.

He closed his eyes and breathed for a few seconds. Then the weight of the spire on his shoulder reminded him of why he'd climbed up there in the dead of night.

He leaned into the ladder, letting his body weight hold him against it while he used both hands to swing—ever so slowly—the spire off his right shoulder.

It was easy enough then to set the crescent-shaped spire into place.

Then Owen gave himself a couple of deep breaths to steady himself and started down.

His right shoulder hurt and so did his lower back, but he was afraid to stop and stretch while still on the ladder, so it was a long, painful climb back down, made worse now that the adrenaline of the climb had managed to counteract the whiskey on the way up. Even with the weight of the spire off his shoulder and the use of both hands, the descent was worse for Owen as he'd started to sober up. The ladder felt slippery, and thunder and lightning startled him more than once on the way down, and his weary legs were shaking like jelly. He clenched his teeth together so hard his jaw began to ache.

When his right foot landed on the grass, he staggered back and almost fell, as though his body was trying to launch itself off the hated ladder.

Owen bent forward, hands on knees, and took a few deep breaths again. He didn't remember being afraid of ladders, of heights … of anything in particular. But it was dark, the moon casting an eerie, magical silver light punctuated by the amber flash of lightning … and the *bean sí* howled, a blood curdling shriek like the scream of desperate sailors being torn apart on the dragon's teeth.

• • •

The treacherous sea seemed to work in concert with the brutal storm as the sailors were beaten about in the unforgiving water around the razor-sharp rocks. There seemed not even the tiniest sliver of hope that they would survive this night under the glow of the full moon.

But perhaps it was just that—hope, or the sight of the moon shining like an opulent orb cutting through a gap in the angry clouds above him—that made Don Pedro de Mendoza grasp whatever it was he'd tried to cling to in his cabin. Was it hope that drove his legs, spinning furiously? Could hope alone have driven his arms to claw and strike at the bone-chilling water as it tossed him this way and that?

Whatever drove him, it was in vain. Don Pedro was drowning.

And then something other than hope stepped in. Call it Providence, or a miracle, or good seamanship, but something caught him under his right arm. The fingers of his left hand tightened on the cold steel in their grip. In his confusion, Don Pedro didn't know left from right.

But a third force took him and dragged him up— and there was air, and he gasped a breath in and took some seawater but also some air, and he opened his eyes and saw that the cold steel that he had dragged from his sinking ship and that his left hand clung to was his morion helmet—flat brimmed with a ridge from front to back; it was a gift from his former captain, the once ornate red and white plumes sodden, listless.

Then he was under again, jaws clamped tight, so precious was that tiny gasp of air that he refused to cough out the seawater, however badly it burned his lungs.

And he was up again, and there was shouting—the language familiar, the voices indistinguishable. His right hand found rough wood, and he opened his eyes, and there was a boat, then only black water again.

Then up once more and a voice: "*¡Capitán!*"

And he was under again, fighting for consciousness, holding his helmet in his left hand, a life-saving oar in the other.

He prayed, begging the Lord to lift him up.

And he was lifted up.

Then there was nothing until he awoke coughing and gagging, spilling seawater and bile onto the cold, wet rocks of this deadly foreign shore. He lifted his face enough to see another man doing the same as he, then another sitting up and either laughing or crying—Don Pedro couldn't tell but felt like doing both himself. Lightning revealed more men, some alive, some dead, many somewhere in between, strewn on the rocks of the cove.

And so they had come to Ireland.

...

"Come on," Owen said to his brother, grabbing the shovel off the ground and tramping into the cemetery.

The stones stood in black silhouette against the moonlit sky, and once Owen stopped walking, there wasn't a sound to be heard. Then the faraway hiss of the waves floated in together with the rumble of thunder.

Owen looked up at the spire, carefully moving sideways through the graveyard, steadying himself from time to time on one of the stones or using the shovel as a sort of cane.

Just a few more steps this way and that and the moon had now dropped a few inches on the horizon and was behind the church steeple. Owen squinted as he visually lined up the spire so that the crescent took a bite out of the brilliant perigee full moon—even now being chewed slowly away by the gathering storm.

"This is it," Owen whispered.

He looked down and pushed the shovel into the ground at his feet. He pulled up a shovelful of grass and dirt, then another and another. His back protested, and so did his right shoulder. Owen ignored the pain—there was no time. It was now or never, and he'd already come face to face with "never" once that day—and once was enough.

It was down there, just under his feet, and nothing could stop him digging.

Thunder crashed and a cool wind blew up as if in answer.

"Hurry up, will you?" Patrick stage-whispered as if he had somewhere else he needed to be.

Owen didn't bother telling him to find a shovel and help if he wanted the damn hole dug faster. Patrick wouldn't do it, and Owen really didn't want him to; this was Owen's work. It was for Owen to finish.

"Can you not just let her rest in peace?" Patrick said. He'd moved off some, watching from several yards away, closer to the church to raise the alarm if he spotted someone.

Owen shrugged and kept digging. He couldn't stop. He'd dedicated the best part of his life to this. He had to get to the bottom of it. To whatever Gracie was concealing in her tomb …

"Digging up the dead …" Patrick snapped, his voice carrying on the wind. "Is this what you've become?"

"I've spent more time underground than some of these corpses," Owen growled as he rammed the shovel deeper and deeper into the ground, then *clang*.

He stopped and lifted the shovel a few inches and tapped it down again—not too hard, but it came again: the distinctive clang of steel on stone.

It began to rain.

Owen dropped to his knees, tossing the shovel aside, and started clawing at the soft earth.

His hands ached, but he took out great clumps of dirt, loose rocks, and roots to clear off a horizontal slab of rough stone. He dug at it with his fingernails, pulling out thick mud from carved lines in the stone. He knew what it was just by the feel of it. Patrick stood, arms crossed, looking down into the blackness of the newly dug hole. The rain seemed to be getting a little harder with every cold drop.

Owen pulled Quinn's flashlight from his pocket and turned it on to reveal precisely what he'd hoped to see. Engraved on the stone slab was a coat of arms. Owen dug at more pressed-in mud and grinned at what was revealed.

• • •

Don Pedro managed to take a few steps at a time, but was mostly dragged by two of his men. They weren't particularly strong men, just average sized, tired and exhausted, but they hauled their captain all the same.

Surely El Gran Grin *wasn't the first ship to break apart on this island's fanglike rocks*, Don Pedro thought as he drifted in and out of consciousness. His eyes flitted open to see that he was being hauled into a cave.

He tried to speak but just coughed, tried to get to his feet again but stumbled and was dragged.

Don Pedro swung his head around, and when he saw the treasure chest behind him, the strength he'd struggled to regain drained away, and he sagged between the two men on either side of him.

"¡Capitán!" one of his men shouted from behind. "Estamos vivos," the sailor said more with an air of disbelief than jubilation.

Don Pedro was gently lowered onto a rough stone floor, loose stones biting into his knees. He was dragged and propped up against the treasure chest, which his brave men had somehow salvaged from the sinking ship. He stared into the eyes of the few survivors. They were completely devastated by their last few hours in the ocean.

• • •

"Look!" Owen said to Patrick, shining the light on the crudely carved ship that rested on the sand. "Gracie's coat of arms. It must be under here."

Leaving the flashlight on the grass next to him, Owen grabbed the shovel and struggled to his feet. He placed the shovel carefully at the edge of the slab and gingerly dug around to make sure he'd found the true edge. Then he pushed with all his weight, foot on the shovel-head, and wedged it under the slab. It took his full weight and the occasional pause to clear dirt from around the edges, but finally he pried the stone slab up, expecting it to cover some vault in the earth, but under it was more mud and loose rocks.

"What …?" Owen breathed. "It's not a grave, it's just …"

"Lift it out so I can see," Patrick urged.

Owen crouched and grabbed one side with both hands.

"Straighten your back and bend your knees," Patrick advised.

Owen grunted at the weight and at his brother. "I know, damn it!"

He got it up on one edge, then walked back and braced it as best he could so that when it fell over on its face, it didn't fall too hard or from too high.

Then he grabbed the flashlight and shined it first on the hole—there was definitely nothing underneath it, no vault, no …

Then he played the flashlight over the underside of the stone slab itself, and there was … something there …

He placed the flashlight carefully on the slab and used his fingers—aided by the rain still falling harder and harder—to dig at the mud caked to the back of it. After a few minutes of this muddy, occasionally painful work, he managed to reveal another carving.

When he'd cleared away the mud, he stood up, panting, almost gasping for breath, and shined the flashlight down through streaks of raindrops on an engraving that Patrick began to read aloud:

"Lions of the black-browed sea
Tamed by the light of the moon
A passage opened by the waves' retreat
Wrecked the ships by wind and mighty crest
Will wash the thorn from the hog's foot
A king's ransom for the return of the lions
Upon a cliff, beneath it sanctum wailed
A tower to watch over the beautiful bounty."

Owen stood next to the hole, following along as his brother read. His breath slowly eased to almost normal. His head spun, his mouth was dry, and his knees shook so badly Owen worried he might collapse.

But through all that, the words embedded themselves in his mind, a transmission from a forgotten age.

"See?" Patrick said. "You only had half a poem."

"It's not a poem. It's a riddle," Owen barked back as he took the drawings from his pocket and unfolded them. He made sure he was looking at the right ones: Gracie's coat of arms and not the O'Malleys'.

"On the O'Malley family crest," Owen said, "the ship at the bottom is riding the waves. On Gracie's, the ship at the bottom is settled on the sand."

" 'Lions of the black-browed sea, tamed by the light of the moon,' " Patrick read.

Owen nodded and continued, "*El Gran Grin* sank on

the night of the perigee moon, it must have been wrecked on the rocks exposed by the especially low tide."

" 'A passage opened by the waves' retreat'?" Patrick asked.

Owen shook his head and replied, "There must be a cave that only becomes uncovered when the water level drops below a certain level."

" 'Will wash the thorn from the hog's foot,' " Patrick continued with a nod.

" 'The hog's foot' is Clare Island," Owen clarified.

He ran a filthy fingertip across the drawing of Gracie's coat of arms. "Look at the bow and arrows on Gracie's coat of arms. That one points to a different part of the hog than on the O'Malley coat of arms."

"The 'king's ransom' is the gold," Owen continued without taking a breath.

" 'Upon a cliff, beneath it sanctum wailed,' " Patrick went on. " 'A tower to watch over the beautiful bounty'?"

Owen nodded and said, "The treasure isn't under the watchtower that my light was built on. The watchtower was looking over it. Look … the arrow must be the 'thorn.' " He pointed to the drawing again, but Patrick was still looking down at the graven stone. "It's the cove!" Owen exclaimed. "The Spaniards must have made it to the cove with the treasure and found refuge in a cave. That's the sanctum."

Patrick took a deep breath and rested his chin in his hand.

···

Don Pedro slumped up against the treasure chest with his men huddled around him, when torchlight drew all of their eyes to the passageway that led from the entrance of the little chamber into which they'd been crowded.

He saw her in silhouette first, and marked her by her hair, wild and unkempt. With the torchlight behind her, her auburn locks glowed fiery red. Some of Don Pedro's men stirred a little, and she drew her swords as fast as any swordsman Don Pedro had ever seen—one in each hand, the polished blades glimmered in the torchlight.

Just a few paces behind her, her loyal kinsmen shuffled around her to form an impenetrable barrier.

The Spaniards grabbed what they could to protect themselves. Some had managed to escape the wreck with their swords, but most grabbed lumps of rock from the cave floor or the sodden pieces of wood that had helped them to safety.

Don Pedro forced himself to his feet with as much dignity as he could muster. He still couldn't see her eyes but could feel them follow his every move as he steadied himself with a hand against the damp stone wall.

The light came around to reveal Grace O'Malley's face, and the sight of it took the words from Don

Pedro's tongue. As rough as her dress was, she was a handsome woman and a sight to behold for a man who had been so long at sea.

"Do you speak English?" she asked.

Don Pedro nodded and replied "A little. I am *Don Pedro de Mendoza el Capitán* of *El Gran Grin*—"

She did not offer up her name. But it was obvious to him that she was in charge of the island clan. The swords hung in her hands so easily, Don Pedro knew she could dice him to ribbons, should he say the wrong thing. But then the thought came clearly to his mind: *She will kill me anyway.*

Don Pedro cleared his throat and made her the only offer he had to make. Picking up a handful of gold doubloons that had seeped from a split in the treasure chest, he uttered *"Oro—"* then the English word suddenly came to him. "Gold ... gold."

The gold glinted in the glow of the torchlight as he tossed the coins at the woman's feet and then stretched his arm out, pointing at his men. *"Libertad?"*

A coldness descended quickly and thoroughly across her face, and that freezing gaze roamed his entire form, from the tips of his ears to the tips of his toes.

"Freedom?" she said.

Don Pedro gave an overenthusiastic nod in response as he turned and attempted to drag the heavy chest toward her, but it wouldn't budge.

Instead the stretching motion pulled at a wound in his chest, and he let out a pained groan. He grabbed at it, and when he took his hand away, there was blood. A few of his men gasped and one moved to help him, but Grace O'Malley stopped him with the tip of her sword.

"I already have your gold. If I give you freedom, the English will come for us," she said.

Don Pedro's heart sank. It would surely only be a matter of moments before he felt the cold steel of her sword in his chest. Although many of his men could not understand what she had said, their captain's face told them all that they needed to know.

The woman pushed one of her swords to Don Pedro de Mendoza's neck.

Wincing with pain, Don Pedro closed his eyes as he waited for the inevitable.

Then, with a swift flick of her blade, she cut the heavy gold key from around his neck.

She leaned over to grab it as it fell and clasped it in her hand, her blade then shooting back to the same spot on Don Pedro's neck.

• • •

"It's the perfect hiding place," Owen said. It's only accessible for one night every thirteen months. They must have carried the stone-filled chest up to the watchtower so that everyone watched them and passed the story on. The watchtower was a red herring all along—it was never under my light."

Owen, still breathing heavily, stared down at the stone slab.

"You don't say ..." Patrick said.

Owen ignored the condescension, and the two brothers stood there for a moment in silence. Then Patrick asked, "What time does the tide turn?"

Owen rubbed his beard whilst his mind sifted through the last few days of tidal calculations. "It'll start coming in at twelve forty-five ..." Owen replied. Then he shined the flashlight on his watch: 01:02 a.m.

"It's already turned," Owen gasped. Thunder crashed, and he winced, squinting against the rain. "Quick ... we've no time to waste."

• • •

Ellen pulled her coat around her against a sudden chill and now pouring rain. Still, she knew it wasn't as cold outside as she felt. Her knuckles stung a little when she knocked on her cousin's door. Maybe the cold wasn't entirely in her head.

There was no answer, and no lights on inside.

Ellen wasn't even sure what time it was—she hadn't bothered putting on a watch when she dragged on a pair of jeans and a t-shirt and paced her living room for some unknown length of time, trying to decide what—if anything—to do.

She knocked again, louder.

A light came on somewhere in the house, a dull glow coming to the little window in the door.

"Mary?" she called out, her voice taken away by the wind and the rain. "Mary ... it's Ellen."

She heard footsteps approach, and then the door swung open slowly to reveal Mary—squinting, confused, her hair a mess—in her nightgown.

"What time is it?" Mary asked, her voice croaking.

Even before Ellen could answer, Mary had rubbed the sleep out of her eyes and must have seen the worry on her face. Mary reflected that look right back at her. She reached out and took Ellen by the arm.

"I'm really worried about Owen," Ellen said, her voice starting to break. Tears warmed her eyes. "Will you come with me?"

Nodding, Mary tugged on her arm to bring her into the house and said, "I'll get dressed. Come inside."

Ellen followed her in, her mind racing, trying to work out what to tell Mary—trying to understand herself what she was thinking and what she thought Owen might be doing, or trying to do. It wasn't a conversation to be had on the phone. She didn't want to tell her cousin that Owen was drunk and babbling about buried treasure, that he might even have stolen a car … and she didn't want to tell herself that it really wasn't any of her business anyway.

And right in that moment, standing in the darkened living room of her cousin's house in the middle of the night, Ellen realized that she DID want it to be her business, that she DID care, and that she DID want to understand what this loony old lighthouse keeper was doing.

And it had nothing to do with gold coins or Grace O'Malley.

• • •

The little car skidded out onto the road in the direction of the cove.

"How will we find this cave?" Patrick asked.

"Quinn's lobster boat is tied up in the cove," Owen answered, coming to that conclusion even as the words passed his lips.

"I'm not getting into a floating coffin," Patrick scoffed.

Owen shrugged, pulling the little car a bit to the right, then quickly correcting on the rain-slicked gravel. "I can't do it on my own. We can pull the boat along on the ropes, and it has an engine on the back if we have any bother."

Two figures appeared in the little car's dim headlights, and Owen swerved gently around them.

Lightning flashed and the face of Grace O'Malley spun around to look at him, blazing in the combined light of the headlights and the lightning. Owen gasped and jerked the wheel enough to fishtail—but he corrected quickly, and the face of Grace O'Malley became Ellen … and her cousin Mary. They squinted at him, and Ellen waved her arms in an attempt to get him to pull over, but much as he may have liked to, Owen didn't stop. He didn't even slow down.

Patrick sighed heavily as they left the two women behind them. "Shouldn't we pick them up? They'll get soaked to the skin in this weather." But Owen ignored him, just focusing intently on the rain-soaked road ahead and the rhythmic thrumming of the wipers.

They drove the rest of the way—not far—in silence. Despite the wind-driven rain and nearly continuous flashes of lightning, Owen's mind eventually calmed, and his eyelids started to feel heavy. He squeezed the steering wheel more tightly, and though he should have asked Patrick to watch him, make sure he didn't fall asleep, he didn't say anything. He realized he probably should just pull over and let Patrick drive— should have let him drive all along—but he didn't pull over; he was far too stubborn for that. He blinked the heaviness out of his eyelids and shifted his weight in the tight little seat, doing what he could to get some blood moving.

It had been a long day, and it wasn't over yet.

There was still a treasure to claim.

At last they came to the turnoff and went from the road to a muddy dirt track that led down to the cove. Even with the tide coming back in, every second precious, Owen slowed the little car along the cliffside. It wouldn't do to kill himself and his brother with maybe a hundred yards more to go.

The car slipped a little to the left, and Owen gritted his teeth, bumping up out of a rut. His mucky boot weighed down on the accelerator pedal, then let up on it. He was reluctant to use the brakes for fear of getting stuck in the mud.

Owen felt almost as nervous as Patrick looked as they bumped and slipped their way down to a level patch of boggy ground near the stone jetty running along the south side of the cove.

They both sighed with relief when Owen brought the car to a jolting stop just a few feet from the walkway.

Owen got out of the car, leaving the lights on and ignoring some crack from Patrick about running down his poor vehicle donor's battery.

"This is certain death," Patrick sighed as Owen slipped and tripped his way down to the water's edge. The tide coming in, further driven by the storm, sent waves rolling into the cove to burst against the jetty's rock wall. Cold saltwater spray mixed with the near-horizontal rain attempted to form a liquid wall to cut off their path as if summoned up by some angry pagan sea god. Owen's foot slipped out from under him at nearly every third step, but he managed not to fall.

Quinn's little lobster boat was cradled between its three ropes but with the incoming tide washing over toward the jetty on the south side, the rope that stretched from the north of the cove was almost taut; the one on the west of the cove near the waterfall and the one attached to the jetty were both drooping in the water. As a result the boat was tossing about a few feet away from the ladder that Ellen used to get in and out of the water for her daily swim.

Owen turned the flashlight on as he pulled it from his pocket. Once it was wedged under his arm, he went to work on the drenched knot that secured the lobster boat to the south siding. But untying the soaked rope was tough going.

The waves rose and pulled back, rose and pulled back, each a bit more intense than the last.

Patrick stepped back when a wave washed up over the jetty, threatening to swamp the little boat that Owen was still struggling to untie.

"Stand back," Owen teased, "I wouldn't want you to get your feet wet."

Finally, Owen managed to undo the rope and drag the boat closer to the rock wall, every yank of the rope a tug-of-war with the waves that threatened to pull him into the water and then push the boat out on top of him. And with every tug, the other two ropes that attached the boat to the cove pulled taut.

Owen, the rope now wrapped around his right hand, turned to tell Patrick to climb into the boat, when the rope jerked violently. Owen went down on one knee, and when he pulled against the waves, his back twisted again, and his jaw clenched against the pain.

Owen leaned back, putting all his weight into it; then a wave helped him, and he dropped to his backside.

"Okay," Owen grunted. "I'll hold it. You jump in."

Patrick stepped away and tipped his head. Owen rolled his eyes in response.

The two bothers stared at each other while Owen continued to struggle with the boat, and finally, without showing any sign that he was ever going to move, Patrick stepped forward. Owen tipped his head in the direction of the ladder, and the lobster boat's gunwale banged up against it.

Patrick stood at the top of the ladder and paused, looking Owen in the eye again.

Owen nodded once, and Patrick started slowly, carefully … reluctantly climbing down.

Owen gritted his teeth against the pull of the waves.

Patrick made it into the skiff and half sat, half fell onto one of the seats, which were just wooden benches that ran between the gunwales. Then Owen started on his way down the ladder himself, pausing to toss the flashlight to Patrick. Patrick seemed to be ready for it, but more intent on staying in the boat himself, he didn't even try to catch it. Luckily it fell into the bottom of the boat and not overboard—and it didn't break, either. The shaft of light rolling around gave the boat an even more dangerous cast.

Still holding the rope, though, Owen climbed down the rusty ladder—it was the second scariest encounter with a ladder he'd had that night.

When Owen landed onto the aft seat, he bashed into the rusty little outboard engine, and the boat dipped under his weight and water washed in. Owen grabbed the flashlight before it was swamped and shot Patrick, who sat much higher in the bow, an irritated look.

"It's going to sink!" Patrick shouted over the roar of the wind and waves echoing back and forth in the dark confines of the cove.

"We'll make it!" Owen shouted back. Squinting in the rain, Owen struggled with Quinn's two remaining ropes attached to the sides of the cove to drag the boat along. Tugging and yanking on the ropes slick with dangling strings of seaweed, Owen eventually figured out how to pull them along, moving the boat deeper into the cove. As each wave came in, the little boat was lifted and pushed forward, then fell and was pushed back—two boat-lengths forward, one boat-length back, but at least they were moving a step forward each time.

"Use the engine," Patrick shouted against the wind.

"The current is too strong, the ropes are our best bet," Owen shouted back.

Patrick gripped the bow so tightly his knuckles glowed white in the moonlight as he begged Owen, "Let's go back! There's nothing here."

"It's here!" Owen yelled, resolutely shaking his head. "Keep looking."

A wave crashed against the wall of the cove, dousing Owen's face with salty spray. He shivered and wiped his eyes with his sleeve. The little flashlight was of scant help, as Owen scoured the interior of the cove that was black as pitch. Still, the serrated silhouette of a shorn rock rose in front of them, a wave carrying them fast and hard in its direction.

"OWEN!" Patrick screamed, "THE ROCKS!"

Owen let the ropes unwind from his hand, and the wave took them not just a little farther back but a little farther out into the middle of the cove—something Owen had hoped to avoid—but at least they didn't smash against the rocks.

Not like *El Gran Grin*.

Owen played the flashlight against the west rock face of the cove as a wave rolled them in toward the waterfall, and when they rose up on the swell, the moonlight flooded in and at least provided some contrast.

There was a small patch of deeper black at the base of the waterfall.

"They're not ropes down the side of Gracie's coat of arms. It's falling water. It's been under our noses the whole time!" Owen shouted, pointing almost straight ahead at the waterfall. "That must be it!"

As Owen yanked on the rope attached to the west rock face nearest the waterfall with a mighty tug, the boat skimmed along the waves toward the patch of black. When Owen was sure they had enough momentum to ride the wave in, he quickly untied the two ropes from the boat that he'd used as pulleys in case they snagged on the cave entrance, leaving just the one in the boat that he'd freed from the south siding.

And the waterfall cascaded down onto them …

CHAPTER 17

The pain in Don Pedro's chest flared with each step, and his breathing became harder with each breath. His mind was racing. Why did she not kill them there and then? Why drag it out? Did she intend to cast them back into the treacherous sea? He and his exhausted, half-drowned crew were at the mercy of Grace O'Malley and her clan. So once again he surrendered himself to hope.

They came out into a chamber lit by the torches of a scattering of kinsmen and onto a ledge overlooking a flooded cave through which Don Pedro could make out the occasional flash of lightning through the waterfall covering the entrance, most likely the way they had come in, but Don Pedro had been in and out of consciousness then.

"*Libertad,*" Grace O'Malley said, and her eyes flicked to Don Pedro's wound, which bled freely.

Blinking and holding his breath with the effort to stand and look her in the eyes, Don Pedro met her gaze, and her glare went through him, making the pain briefly subside—briefly. *"Libertad?"* Don Pedro asked. He could barely believe that she had said the words.

Grace O'Malley was a tempestuous woman, but also one of compassion. Whether it was a whim or something more, no one would ever know her reason, not even her loyalist kinsmen—and they knew better than to ask and risk provoking her. Her decision was always final.

And in that moment when Don Pedro stared into her piercing eyes, he realized that her words were true. He told his men to put him down and made the best attempt at a bow that he could, as the excruciating pain ripped through his chest and he collapsed to the ground.

His men gathered him up as the O'Malley kinsmen herded them to the water's edge. The clans' boats were tied up inside the cave just a few feet from the waterfall that guarded the narrow entrance. As the Spaniards began climbing into them, Don Pedro hesitated. One of his men had succumbed to his wounds and collapsed against the rocks by the ledge. Don Pedro pulled off his morion helmet and gently placed it into the dead sailor's hands before allowing himself to be eased into one of the boats.

As Grace O'Malley walked back up into the catacombs—alone.

• • •

The crash of the waves seemed dull and distant, as though the sound was swallowed up by the oppressive darkness of the cave. The air was heavy with salt and fish and moldering seaweed, the rocks smooth and slippery. The dark was impenetrable, the only light coming from the thin shaft of the little flashlight. Owen saw the interior of the cave in circles a meter or less in diameter.

Inside, the water was still choppy but nothing like the swell in the cove.

The entrance itself was barely big enough, and Owen nearly decapitated himself when the boat surged through, but then it widened out almost immediately into a roughly circular chamber bored into the black rock by centuries of wind and wave.

Owen played the flashlight beam across the ceiling and thought it might be thirty feet above the waterline. The boat hit the wall gently enough, and Owen grabbed for the rock. It was cold and slimy, but still he managed to find—blindly, at random—a good enough series of handholds that he was able to get the little lobster boat under a semblance of control. He pushed it along the wall, nudging against the rock, once almost running aground on a submerged boulder or maybe just a shallower part of the cave.

Pushing the boat along with his left hand, he held the flashlight in his right, scanning the beam around the cave and finally settling on a naturally formed ledge that ran along the side of it.

"Looks high enough that it probably stays above the waterline," Owen said.

At one point, not far away at all, Owen spied a lower portion of the ledge, a collection of tumbled rocks, really.

"I'll put the boat aground there," he said.

Patrick sat in silence in the pitch blackness behind Owen's flashlight beam.

Owen pushed the boat against the wall of the ledge.

"Climb up," he said to his brother. "I'll steady the boat."

He didn't hear Patrick moving, so he shined the flashlight at the front of the boat so his brother could see what he was doing.

Patrick scrambled up onto the ledge, crawling on the rock and swearing under his breath. Owen looked up—and it was an easier climb for him. With a smile and a determined set to his brow, he reached up and set the flashlight on the ledge, then hoisted himself up after it. He had the rope in his hand, and when he was on the ledge, he pulled the skiff up, hearing it scrape against the rocks. Then he used the flashlight to check that he'd run it aground successfully, and for good measure he looked for a place to tie it up.

Moving the flashlight beam slowly along the wall,

Owen thought maybe he could find a loose rock heavy enough to hold the rope down—and then he was looking into a dead, empty eye socket in a grim, cracked yellow skull.

His heart jumped in his chest.

Owen scrambled back—almost fell into the water.

"What the...?" he gasped, his voice pinging off the closed-in walls of the cave.

"Would you look at that," Patrick murmured.

Owen closed his eyes and took a deep breath.

The skeleton sat up against the wall looking like nothing less than a prop from some pirate movie. Owen shined the flashlight on it and slid closer, still holding the rope.

The man had been dead for hundreds of years— and then the flashlight beam found the helmet that rested in his hands.

"That's a morion helmet," Owen said in hushed tones, a funeral voice. "That must be one of the Spaniards."

Patrick had gotten to his feet and carefully made his way over in the darkness. Crouching in front of the skeleton with its twisted grimace, Patrick sighed heavily and said, "What a way to go."

Lightning illuminated the water a pure emerald green, and thunder crashed outside—for the first time loud enough to be heard over the crashing of the waves.

Owen shined the flashlight on the rock floor in

front of Patrick so it reflected up to reveal his face without blinding him. "Is there a good way?" he asked.

"In my own bed—" Patrick started.

But Owen pulled the light away and said, "Come on."

Owen shined the light against the back wall of the ledge, to its deepest point. He climbed to his feet and looked around—nothing really to secure the rope onto. He looked back at the skeleton and wound the rope around the morion helmet, which looked like it had slowly fused to the skeleton's hands over the centuries.

Patrick expressed his disapproval with a raised eyebrow and a swift head shake.

"He might as well make himself useful," Owen responded, "Come on now."

Owen let the rope drop on the ledge and gave it a quick tug to make sure his newly recruited assistant had a firm hold and then with slow, shuffling steps so as not to trip in the darkness, moved to the tunnel entrance at the back of the cave with his brother still muttering his dissension a few paces behind him.

They walked into the low-ceilinged tunnel and catacombs beyond to be immersed in pure darkness.

"Do you think it might be haunted in here?" Patrick said in a low voice.

Owen put the flashlight beam under his bearded chin and, with a teasing smile, replied, "You'll be the first to know."

Patrick shook his head at his brother's antics.

Owen chuckled to himself as he shined the flashlight deep into the tunnel and found that it snaked into the cliff face, gently sloping upward a little, then taking a sharp turn to the right.

He ducked and pushed his way into the tunnel, and as he edged farther from the sea cave, he realized it was actually wider than he thought. He had plenty of room to walk. The footing was easy enough. He knew the tide didn't get up as high as the skeleton or it would have been washed away years ago, so with the cave going slightly up, he felt safe pressing on, even with the tide coming in.

It occurred to him that the Spaniards or Grace O'Malley's kinsmen might have left some sign of their passage, and he played the flashlight slowly around the walls and the floor—and THERE …

Something heavy had been scraped along the floor.

On stiff, tired legs, Owen kneeled, wincing, to get a closer look. He couldn't tell which direction the thing was dragged, but could it have been a chest full of gold?

He climbed back to his feet and made a right turn, only to be immediately confronted by a fork in the tunnel.

"Which way?" Patrick whispered from behind him.

Owen shrugged, shook his head, and chose the right fork simply at random. But after only one step, he paused and shined the flashlight back on the floor—and found no sign of the drag marks.

"No," he said over his shoulder, "back up."

Patrick gave way, and Owen followed the drag marks into the left fork. He was so intent on following the trail that his forehead banged on rock when the ceiling was all of a sudden just a little lower. He swore in a harsh whisper and paused only long enough to make sure he wasn't bleeding—and he wasn't.

It was only a few more steps, and he came into a small, claustrophobic chamber.

"It's a dead end," Patrick said.

Patrick then gestured to another entrance in the little cave, and Owen realized the two forked tunnels came to the same place.

And the place they came to was empty.

"Nothing here," Patrick confirmed, and Owen scowled at him.

Then he shined the flashlight on the floor and tried to read the language of the scrape marks.

"The chest was in here," he said, then paused to think. "Then someone dragged it back out …"

"And buried it where you found it?" Patrick prompted.

"But without the gold," Owen fired back.

Owen crouched to look closer at the scrape marks. He reached out to touch them, running the tip of a calloused finger along its depth into the shadows until it drove into something—damp, withered animal skin. He grasped it and pulled it into the flashlight beam where he stared at the remains of a leather sack that he now held in his hand. His face glimmered in the flashlight as he scrunched his eyes closed.

• • •

Grace O'Malley stared down into the chest of gold and willed herself to breathe. She'd never thought there could be so many gold coins in one place. Hesitantly, her hands uncharacteristically shaking, she plunged her fingers into the doubloons and felt their cool weight. The voices of her men prodding the Spanish sailors into the boats in the sea cave echoed back to her through the narrow confines of the tunnel.

She knew that such a vast treasure came with a price. The Spanish would surely want it back. If the English got wind of it, they would come looking for it themselves. And then there were her men. These were trusted kinsmen—family by any other name—but could she trust them with this? They hadn't opened it—only she had the key and had waited to use it until she was alone in the little cave—but they had seen the handful of doubloons that Don Pedro had tossed at Grace O'Malley's feet; it was fair to assume that the chest held many hundreds if not thousands more. And though most didn't understand the words spoken with the Spanish captain, they were smart enough to know a deal had been struck, a deal for the key that opened that chest, and Grace O'Malley thought it worth the lives of the sailors and the risk of both Spanish and English attention paid to little Clare Island.

Little Clare Island, she thought. *An island off the shore of an island off the shore of an island. And in all the wide world, this treasure had come here.*

And here it will stay.

She closed the lid, then quickly strode back to the sea cave, where three of her men were still on the ledge, lowering the last of the Spaniards into the boats.

"Bhur málaí," she demanded of her men. Without hesitation they handed over their bags to her right away. Then with a wave of her hand, the three men sheepishly followed their foreign charges into the water.

Alone in the sea cave with a single torch, she emptied the contents of the leather sacks and took them into the chamber deep inside the catacombs where the chest now resided. It took some time for her to fill them up with the gold—all of the gold—as evenly distributed as she could. One of them split, scattering doubloons across the floor. So she discarded it and stuffed all that she could into the other two sacks. The few coins that remained on the floor she tucked into her pockets. She would have liked to have counted it all, but despite the long climb, a march with the prisoners, then a still-treacherous circuit with the boat in the passing storm … she wouldn't be alone long enough for that before her kinsmen returned.

The cave yielded enough loose rocks to fill the chest and give a rough approximation of its original weight. Then she carefully locked it. As far as anyone in the world but her knew, that locked box still held the ransom of the Spanish Armada.

Strong as Grace O'Malley was, she couldn't manage more than one sack at a time, and when she had both out into the sea cave, she was already breathing hard.

It had been a long night.

With her hands on her hips, she caught her breath, staring up into the back of the sea cave, reaching out with her torchlight. High above the waterline was a sort of hollow in the cave wall, a roughly oblong hole the torch's light wouldn't penetrate.

First Grace found a place to wedge the torch. It would be dark even a few steps from it, but it would have to do. Then she threw one of the heavy sacks of Spanish gold over her right shoulder and started to climb.

Grace knew that climbing by feel, with her right arm also bearing the considerable weight of the gold, would require patience as much as strength.

Her foot slipped, and the sack shifted on her shoulder. She pressed herself against the wall and held on tight, holding her breath, too. After a few heartbeats, she reached up with her left hand and felt for a handhold—she found one that was good enough, but still took a few more heartbeats to find a better one.

And in this way—a toe slipping here, fingers protesting there—she made her way about twice her own height up the wall of the cave and out to her right so that by the time her left hand found the lip of the little alcove, there was nothing beneath her but churning black water.

Not bothering to look inside the hole, Grace braced herself with the toes of both feet and her left forearm on the lip of the hole and unceremoniously dumped the leather sack up and over. She gave it a little shove, but as heavy as it was, it hardly moved. Looking up in the weak torchlight, she tried to make out any part of the sack leaning over the edge, but there was nothing to see. It was as well hidden as she could make it.

Rather than waste any more time and strength climbing back down, Grace let go and splashed into the cold water. Popping quickly up to the surface, she smiled and treaded water for a while, resting. Then she dragged herself up onto the ledge, hoisted the second bag, and hoped she remembered where all the best hand and footholds were.

"She hid it in here," Owen said as he opened his eyes.

He then paced down the tunnel, grasping the remains of the leather sack, using the flashlight beam to pry into all of the dark niches on his way back to the sea cave. Patrick followed him.

"And you've determined this how, precisely?" Patrick asked.

Once in the sea cave, Owen stepped forward to examine the cave wall while he answered, "We know she took the gold out of the chest and filled it with rocks, then locked it again and had it dragged out of here. She must have put it into leather sacks. We just need to find a hiding place that's big enough to hold a king's ransom in gold."

Not bothering to look back for Patrick's reaction, Owen dropped the withered sack to the floor and started scanning the walls of the sea cave with the flashlight.

"That is the only hole in this cave that's big enough," he said as he waggled the flashlight beam on the hollow in the cave wall high above the waterline that opened into an oblong hole.

He set down the flashlight on the stone floor of the ledge, on its end so the light shone up to reflect off the ceiling, which was wet with the sea spray splashing against it. The light gave the already eerie cave a preternatural aura that brought gooseflesh to Owen's arms and neck.

"And how are you going to even get up there?" Patrick probed.

Ignoring him, Owen started to climb.

"You have got to be kidding me," Patrick scoffed.

Owen, holding on for dear life, his fingers, toes, ankles, wrists, arms, back, and legs already loudly complaining, growled, "Any better ideas?"

He moved his right hand over to find an indentation or outcropping in the rock to hold onto. He could barely see in the flashlight's weak illumination, so he ended up closing his eyes and feeling for something. He grew increasingly impatient, his whole body starting to shake, until he found something he hoped he could grasp—hoped, but didn't really think he could.

But his fingers held long enough for him to move his right foot to a little nook in the wall that would bring him out over the water and a good ten inches up. His toes felt solid—and he recalled the ladder and the church spire and tried to tell himself he could do anything tonight …

Even while he was falling …

Into the roaring water he went to the sound of his brother shouting his name; then he was under. The water was cold and flooded his sinuses, and he wanted to scream out a curse at it but kept his mouth shut until he'd managed to get his head above water.

A wave came rolling in and lifted him as though he were a newborn infant—only to slam him up against a rock covered in a slick of algae, which took the sting out of the impact but made it impossible for him to get a handhold—and he slipped back under again.

He didn't have time to wonder if he was going to drown when he was this close—so close—before his head came up out of the water again. Between waves, he managed to doggy-paddle his way to the ledge and find a relatively slime-free patch that he held onto for dear life while another wave pressed him up against the rock wall hard enough to drive most of the air from his lungs.

Using the tied-up boat as a hand-hold, Owen dragged himself half out of the water, entirely unconcerned over how undignified he must have looked, until he looked across at the skeleton holding the boat's rope. Owen was sure he was smirking at him.

He turned his attention back to the ledge and was almost onto it when an idea struck him and he carefully slid down into the boat.

With the dim glow of the flashlight partially blocked by the ledge itself, Owen had to untie the rope by feel alone, first from the morion helmet and then from the boat, and though it took him longer than he'd hoped—having to pause three times while the building waves threatened to wash Quinn's lobster boat off the rocks and take him down once again—he eventually got the rope off, tossed it up onto the ledge, and then climbed up after it.

Owen didn't let himself think about what might happen if they needed that rope to get out of the cave and back to the jetty in the cove; the two other ropes were still attached to the cove—they would have to suffice.

He tied it into a sort of lasso while Patrick added in the occasional snide comment. When he was as done as he thought he could be, Owen staggered to his feet and took a couple of deep breaths to steady himself before going to the side of the ledge closest to the oblong hole high up in the cave wall.

It took him three tries hurling the rope at the rocky outcrops next to the oblong hole until it finally found something to hold onto, and for that Owen was infinitely grateful. He gave it a little tug, reluctant to pull too hard, and it held.

But as Owen finished tightly securing the rope to the rocky outcrop, the tide brought another wave in and it splashed onto Owen—more water, stronger than before.

Gritting his teeth, Owen grabbed the rope with both hands and reached out with his foot until he found the foothold that had held him before. The rope slipped a little, and Owen and Patrick gasped in concert—but it held his weight.

He went hand over hand—doing well the first few changes of grip, largely out of panic-fueled courage. His foot slipped once, severely testing the grip of his makeshift lasso on its precarious support, but he set more weight on his left foot and quickly found another foothold. He didn't look down. Just as he'd learned the hard way at the church, he kept his eyes on the rock wall in front of him, glowing with the diffuse light of the flashlight.

"You can do it," Patrick urged. Those were the first words of encouragement that Owen could remember hearing from his brother in a long time. And they helped.

Up he went a little more, and the rope slipped a little but he held on.

His toes found a hold, but then slipped, then found another one, and he was another foot up.

Then another.

And then he could get his left forearm up over the edge of the hole. This took most of his weight, so he could ease up a little on the rope, his toes wedged into a hole just barely big enough for that purpose.

Another wave rolled in, and Owen was sure he could feel it on the soles of his shoes, but that couldn't be. Patrick was completely silent, somewhere in the dark, down on the ledge by the water's edge.

Owen hauled himself up with his right hand, and his eyes crested the lip of the hole, but there was nothing to see but a dead black space—a sort of primordial darkness that Owen was reluctant to reach into.

But reach in he did, and his hand came to rest on something … Owen didn't know what, but it wasn't rock. He pressed his fingers into it, and it gave a little—some kind of rough cloth—but that was about all his numb fingertips could determine.

He dragged it out, and it was heavy—dead weight. It crossed his mind that it could be a dead body, and his skin crawled until he remembered that anyone who might have crawled into the hole in Grace O'Malley's day would have been a skeleton, just like the Spaniard below him.

Heavy as it was, Owen moved the thing onto his shoulder, and he could smell old leather—it was a sack, just like the withered empty one he had found earlier. But this sack was full of something heavy …

He took a breath and closed his eyes, understanding in that moment that he'd found it.

But he still had to get it back down.

With the heavy sack resting on his right shoulder, still sore from the church spire, the added weight tested the rope to its limits. He knew he wouldn't make it down with the extra weight. There was nothing else for it. He closed his eyes and tossed the sack with all his might onto the ledge below. He watched it fall, regretting his decision the moment he made it. Then it landed with a metallic crunch. He braced himself for the bag to split and spray his precious coins into the water … but barely a handful of doubloons fell from a small tear. Owen let out a deep sigh of relief as he felt inside the hole and his fingers found the second bag.

Well, it worked last time, he thought, as he tossed the second leather sack onto the ledge beneath him to hit the same spot. It landed half on the other sack and half on the ledge and survived the fall without a blemish.

He pushed his weary hand as far into the hole as he could and groped around in search of more bags, but content that he had emptied the hoard, he turned his attention to getting back to the ledge below.

His descent back down the rope was rapid. All the pain from his body was replaced with one thought: *Gold!*

• • •

"Well," Patrick whispered in awe, "would you look at that."

Owen's mouth opened slowly, his jaw almost locking agape. He drew in a breath so slowly and for so long, he started to get dizzy as he knelt down and picked up one of the gleaming gold doubloons that had seeped from the small hole in the first sack. The memory of the hundreds of pictures he had spent hours staring at in books came to life in glorious three-dimensions in his hand.

He frantically worked on the knot that kept the leather bag cinched tightly closed. It took him a dozen slow, laborious breaths but the knot finally slipped open, and as Owen reached one hand into the sack his fingers closed around pieces of hard, cold metal. Lots of it!

Then a fistful of coins was out of the bag and in his hand and in the light of his flashlight, and it was pure, perfect gold and they were heavy, even just a handful out of … how many? Two sackfuls.

"Hundreds of them …" he whispered.

Owen stood up, and his legs started moving all on their own. He was bouncing. He hadn't bounced in over fifty years, but he was bouncing. He was grinning. Tears blurred the already blurry light, and Patrick was bouncing, too, and then they were just bounding up and down like … well, like they'd just found buried treasure—a king's ransom in Spanish gold.

Patrick stopped and shot a look at the cave entrance.

His smile was gone in the blink of an eye, and then so was Owen's as the flashlight shined at the cave entrance and it was smaller … much smaller than when they'd ridden the waves in. It was disappearing, in fact—with every new wave washing in, getting smaller and smaller.

"We need to get out of here," Patrick said, "*now!*"

Owen looked at his brother and saw his own fear reflected back at him. Then they both looked back at the leather sacks on the ledge. Owen bent and started to drag the bags to the lip of the ledge and the lobster boat beneath them.

"Leave them," Patrick hissed. "Let's get out of here. We'll be trapped if the entrance gets cut off."

"Not on your life," Owen shot back even before Patrick had finished speaking. "Get into the boat. I'll pass them down."

Patrick, shaking his head, got on his knees and scrambled down the ledge into the boat.

Owen grabbed the first sack and shined his light down. The boat was coming up off the rocks—even with Patrick's weight in it.

Owen reached down with the bag. It was so heavy it threatened to dislocate his elbow. His shoulder burned at the exertion as well, but the boat was coming up to meet him, and, eyes closed, jaw clenched, Owen let the sack drop into the boat. The sack had survived a fall from a far greater height, he reassured himself as it dropped …

Then it hit the bottom of the boat and burst open with the sound of cascading gold medallions.

Then the boat lifted up as a wave filled the cave. Owen's ears stung with the sound of it—the wave, thunder, or both.

"We have to leave *now!*" Patrick exclaimed.

Owen let out a growl as he stared at the loose coins, but with no time to waste he tossed the second sack in, expecting the same fate to befall it. Instead, it hit the wood with a dull, uneventful thud. He looked down and played the flashlight beam over it, and it was just fine.

"But it isn't ours," Patrick protested. Owen looked over at the skeleton of the Spaniard, the light causing shadows to move slowly across its features.

It was as though its face—its skull—had come to life and was speaking with Patrick's voice. "It belongs to the O'Malleys."

"This isn't the time, Paddy," Owen said as a wave washed over the side of the lobster boat and the sacks turned black where they got wet, as the coins from the split bag sloshed about in the bottom. Owen scrambled over the side of the gunwale in an ungainly but effective manner. He pushed off from the wall before putting all of his weight in the boat, and it came up off the rocks and away from the ledge as a wave receded back out into the cove.

Then another wave crashed in—higher, stronger, more violent than before. It looked black-green in the light of the flashlight.

Owen lay flat over the sacks and coins in the middle of the boat, using his body to hold them in the skiff while at the same time getting as much of himself under the gunwales as possible.

There was precious little space between the water

and the top of the cave entrance, but with the next big wave, the boat scrapped through the hole and rode out into the cove.

Owen sat up as fast as he could, at the same time pushing the still-intact sack closer to the bow of the boat to balance it. Even though Patrick sat up there, wide-eyed, and shimmering in the moonlight, his weight alone wasn't nearly enough.

The boat was tossed back at the cave by the next oncoming wave, and Owen fended off the back wall of the cove with both hands. The wave washed across the boat, but it stayed upright and didn't break against the rock wall. Blinding flashes of lightning came like fireworks, and the roar of almost continuous thunder harmonized with the crashing waves to mask any other sound that dared try to make itself known.

And there was water in the bottom of the boat now—only a few inches, but a few inches with each wave would sink them in a matter of minutes. The bags and coins were half submerged when the next wave rolled over the bow.

Owen pushed off the rock face as hard as he could as he scrabbled for Quinn's rope that was attached to the west wall by the waterfall.

With the boat filling with seawater, Owen managed to dig his fingers into the sodden rope, but as he tried to get a grip on it, the boat was lifted by a wave and it slipped from his hand.

As the wave receded, it dragged them farther from the rock face, deeper into the cove. A succession of receding waves followed, pushing them farther and farther into open water—no rope to pull on, no wall to push against.

"The engine!" Patrick shouted from the bow. "Start the engine!"

Owen spun and lunged for the little outboard. He was vaguely aware of having lost Quinn's flashlight.

He found the pull cord and yanked it. The whir of the starter motor was lost in the crashing of the waves, and Patrick yelled something he couldn't quite hear.

He pulled again and nothing.

Again, and nothing.

Owen's blood went cold, and his hand dropped over the fuel cap.

He unscrewed it while Patrick yelled at him from the bow, "Don't tell me … you siphoned that off last week!"

Owen stared into the hole to see about half a tank's worth of fuel sloshing around in it. He glared back at Patrick as he screwed the cap back on and ripped the cord so hard it almost came off in his hand. The aging engine coughed, coughed again, then kicked into life.

The smile that rose up on Patrick's face was short-lived as a wave slammed into the skiff and almost capsized them, but Owen grabbed both sides of the boat and used his own weight, his own strength, to keep it upright—upright, but nearly filled with water.

Owen smacked down onto the wooden seat and twisted the engine throttle as far as it would go, contorting his wrist into a shape he'd never seen it make before.

But Owen was right in his initial verdict on the engine. It didn't stand a chance against the fierce current and the mighty swell. Quinn would never take his boat out in these conditions, and that was just with the weight of a man and some fresh lobster. Laden with gold all the propeller did was churn up the water behind them.

Another big wave receded and dragged them farther out into the cove, and when the next one came, it was just a gentle swell under the boat. The crash of the wave came from behind them; then the wave came back and slid them past the entrance of the cove and out to sea.

Owen kneeled in the bottom of the boat, and the water was past mid-thigh.

"Useless feckin' thing!" Owen screamed at the engine as he pulled open the two clamps holding it to the stern of the boat and tossed it into the angry sea, the propeller still churning as it disappeared under a wave. *The reduction in weight was more likely to save them than the puny power of the motor*—Owen thought.

"This boat is going to sink," Patrick screamed.

The tone of his voice sent ice water through Owen's veins—cold as he was, drenched in rain and seawater already. He tried bailing the water out with his hands, getting maybe a third of a liter out with each attempt—while three times that washed in over the gunwale or pounded in from the storm. He shivered, and his teeth chattered. Owen was stiffening up, feeling as though he was turning to stone—but when another wave almost swamped them, he stopped trying to scoop water out of the boat; it was pointless, and he knew it. The weight of the gold alone would sink them.

He fell back into the skiff on his backside, his elbows touching the still-intact sack, and grabbed a handful of coins. The moonlight cascaded over the brilliant gold medallions. He stared at them, mesmerized.

"I'm not going to see Ciara again, am I?" Patrick asked, and his voice sounded close as the *bean sí* whipped around Owen's neck and sent a shiver down his spine. Still staring at the gold, at the treasure of *El Gran Grin*, at the vindication of years and years of lonely labor, Owen said, "Out of my way."

And he tossed the handful of doubloons over the side. Then he grabbed some more. Using his cupped hands like a simple shovel, he scooped up the coins and poured them over the edge. But still the boat sank.

"The sack," Patrick cried.

"All right—I know. I know!" Owen screamed back at him in the howling storm.

308

Rolling onto his side he dragged the undamaged sack to the side of the boat.

The boat rolled to that side, and Owen tried as best he could to balance that out with his own weight.

He grunted and groaned and pushed his feet against the side of the boat and heaved the sack to the gunwale, pulled open the cord, and tipped the coins into the raging black water. Reflecting in the moonlight, it looked like a trail of liquid gold pouring from the skiff.

Owen's face twisted up, and he felt as though his head was going to burst. His hands and knees shook—and not just from the cold. Tears mixed with the rain and seawater on his face as he tossed the empty leather sack to the waves. Patrick shouted something. Owen fell forward, then to his left when the boat rocked back his way, shed of the weight of the sack of gold.

Owen hit something—someone. Patrick was over the side.

Owen grabbed at him, but all he got was a handful of seaweed that slipped through his fingers. He cast about in the boat for anything—and found a wooden pole with a hook on the end used for grabbing lobster pots tucked under one of the gunwales. He stood in the boat, holding the pole as close to the end as possible to give him the greatest reach.

Owen felt something tug on the other end, and he

yanked with every last bit of strength he had—strength borne of desperation.

Then another wave and it felt as though the boat was lifted up and the pole was pulled down.

Then the boat dropped back down, and Owen wrenched his back, screaming from the pain. He yanked the pole with a mighty heave, and Patrick flopped into the boat like a big game fish, along with a huge clump of seaweed.

Owen slumped down against the gunwale and gasped, "Paddy ..." getting a mouthful of seawater for his trouble. "I've missed you."

"Can you forgive me for what happened?" Patrick pleaded, his voice somehow carrying over the cacophony of wind and wave and thunder, and it was a calm voice, not one of a panicked man who moments ago had been close to drowning.

"I've been a damn fool," Owen said. His eyes burned and blurred, and in the moonlight Patrick had become a shape—black against the deep gray of the boat. "You did nothing wrong ... just taken me this long to realize. I have a nephew I've never met."

Owen coughed out seawater and blinked. He hadn't thought of his nephew until then, until ...

"You'll meet him," Patrick promised, his voice clearer, louder against the crashing waves and the water sloshing in the boat.

"I'd like that," Owen replied, and maybe his

voice was too low to be heard just then, but it didn't matter.

Patrick looked over to the side of the boat at the waves crashing against the rocks all around them. "I'd always imagined this moment with a pint and a log fire …" he said, his voice catching in the end.

Owen started to laugh. He couldn't help it. Patrick joined him, then lunged forward by the force of a wave, and Owen took his brother up in his arms, and Patrick returned the embrace.

And the wave coming back out dropped one side of the boat, and another wave came over them, too fast on the heels of the last. Then everything was just a rushing of cold water and impenetrable darkness as the perigee moon was swallowed up.

EPILOGUE

White.

Owen awoke to all white, and bright sunlight, and blurred figures.

He couldn't be in Heaven. These couldn't be angels.

Someone said his name.

He blinked and was looking up at a plain, white suspended ceiling tile. Something beeped in his left ear.

Someone said his name again—who was that?

"Where am I?" he said. His mouth was bone dry and tasted of saltwater.

Another voice, also familiar, male this time, said, "Mayo General Hospital."

Hospital? Owen thought.

Not Heaven, then.

He blinked again and turned his head, trying to sit up. Someone gently pushed him back down—it was Ellen.

Mary stood behind her. The male voice he recognized was Father O'Brien's. Owen blinked again and saw Ryan and Derry standing in the corner, shoulder to shoulder, looking at him as though he might shatter.

"What happened?" Owen asked, trying to think of the last thing he remembered. He was climbing a ladder … had he fallen off a ladder? Why was he climbing a ladder at night?

"Me and Mary came looking for you," Ellen said. She sat gently on the bed next to him and folded her hands around his. Her skin was soft and warm. Owen remembered digging a hole, too. Digging for treasure? "We saw you get into Quinn's lobster boat in the cove." And an image of him and Paddy climbing into Quinn's boat in the cove flashed into his mind. "Mary sent the lads after you in the *Granuaile*."

"You are one crazy old goat, I'll give you that, Mr. Kerrigan," Ryan cut in, leaning forward with a concerned smile. "This man pulled you out."

Ryan patted his brother on the back, and Derry smiled as he bathed in his moment of glory. Then Ryan's arm went around Derry's shoulder, and the two brothers hugged … and it all came crashing back to Owen like the wave that had capsized the lobster boat.

The cove, the cave, the skeleton, the treasure … the treasure lost again.

Owen sat upright fast, the little pain in his back arguing against it. "Where's Paddy?" he asked.

The five people in the room all looked at him. As Owen tried to read their expressions, Ryan shrugged and Ellen's eyebrows crowded together.

"My brother," Owen explained, confused as to why he had to explain that fact. "He was in the boat with me."

Ellen looked at Mary, who shook her head and shrugged.

"You were the only one that we found in the cove," Ryan said. He looked at his mother, who gave him a reassuring nod. Then he continued, "You're lucky to be alive."

"No," Owen breathed, shaking his head—and wincing at the pain behind his eyes. "He was there with me. Call the Coast Guard."

"You were the only one who went out into the cove in Quinn's boat," Ellen said, patting his hand. "We watched you ourselves." Mary nodded behind her.

"No …" Owen insisted. "We were together when we capsized."

"Owen," Mary piped in, looking at him as though he were a child having just awakened from a nightmare, convinced there was a monster under his bed, "I ran down to the cove with Ellen to stop you. You were on your own. What on earth were you doing getting into that boat at that time of night and in that storm?"

Owen shook his head. "Ryan … Derry … you brought Paddy over on the *Granuaile* on Tuesday night."

The two boys looked at each other, and Ryan said, "The Dolan brothers were the only two passengers on Tuesday night."

Owen protested, "But he was with us in the lighthouse when we built the drill."

Derry gave Ryan a confused glance. "There was no one else there, Mr. Kerrigan. Just the three of us," Ryan insisted. Then he realized that their mother's eyes were burning through them. Mary would surely need answers about "the drill," but it would have to wait.

"Ellen," Owen tried, growing increasingly desperate, "he ran out of the church behind me … remember?"

That got a bigger reaction from Father O'Brien … surprise, though, not recognition.

Ellen shook her head and looked at each of the others as though taking a poll. Then she said to them, "Could I have a minute with Owen alone, please?"

Mary ushered her sons out.

Father O'Brien reluctantly loitered in the doorway, saying, "I'll be outside if you need me."

Owen realized the priest was probably waiting for an explanation as to why the spire on his church had been put back up late last night … and why someone seemed to have dug up a grave. But Ellen dismissed the priest with a smile, and when the door closed behind him, Ellen came back to sit on the bed next to Owen.

She took his hands in hers again, and he let her.

"Paddy's been staying with me for the last week," he said, not waiting for her to tell him he was crazy. "Remember? I told you."

Ellen sighed and didn't look at him as though he was crazy … she felt sorry for him.

A tear formed in her eye.

Owen couldn't look at her anymore. His chest felt tight, his throat tighter.

He looked down at himself, sitting up in a hospital bed, looking like a fool in a flimsy gown. He wasn't wearing his watch. He looked around the room … where were his clothes? His fleece jacket, still damp, hung on a hook next to the window.

"The letter," Owen said, realizing he'd been carrying it around with him for … how long? "It's in the pocket. Get it for me."

Ellen stood and took his fleece down from the hook. She patted it a few times, then shrugged.

"The baggy one," he said, now terrified that no one else would be able to see the letter either.

But she finally pulled the crumpled plastic pouch containing the envelope from his fleece and handed it to Owen. As he ripped open the plastic pouch and then carefully opened the envelope, he was surprised that the paper inside wasn't as soaked as he'd expected. The plastic pouch had saved it. Ellen sat on the bed next to him once more.

He peeled the envelope away from the letter inside

and unfolded it slowly, then squinted at the small, tightly controlled handwriting,

He reached out to Ellen with the letter and asked, "I don't have my reading glasses. Read it to me would you?"

Ellen didn't take the letter itself. Instead, she picked up the envelope and read that aloud: "Mr. Owen Kerrigan. The Lighthouse. Clare Island, Ireland." Then she flipped it over and read, "Ciara Kerrigan … Boston?"

Ellen shook her head. "No. It's for you to read."

Owen pushed the letter at her and said, "Please."

She sat there for what seemed like hours, staring at him, trying to read him, and Owen waited, the letter shaking in his hand.

"Please," he whispered.

She knew then that even if he had his reading glasses, he wouldn't be able to read it. With a sigh, she took the letter gently from his hand and held it a moment before she began to read aloud. " 'Dear Owen … I regret to inform you that Paddy has …' " She stopped and swallowed. Owen closed his eyes. " '… that Paddy has passed away.' " Owen put a hand over his eyes. His head hurt so much. " 'He died of a heart attack last week at home, with me by his side.' "

Ellen stopped to take a few deep breaths. Owen opened his eyes, leaving his hand resting on the side of his face. He saw a tear roll down her cheek. He tried to think of something to say but couldn't.

Then she began reading again. " 'I have only now been able to write what I wanted to say. His wish was always to …' " Her voice broke a little, but she cleared her throat and pressed on. " 'His wish was always to reconcile with you, but he never had the courage to face up to you.' "

Courage? Owen thought. *Courage.*

" 'I hope that you can find it in your heart to forgive him and me for what happened, what seems so long ago now.' "

Ellen stopped reading and looked at Owen. She put a hand on top of his and he nodded for her to keep going.

She took her hand away to support the cold, damp paper and read, " 'I hope that some consolation will come from knowing that he made me very happy, and that you were in his thoughts every day until his …' " Ellen paused to clear her throat again. " '… until his last. We were blessed with a wonderful son called Liam, who himself now has a family. He has always said how much he would love to meet you after hearing Paddy talk about your childhood adventures together.' " That made Ellen smile, and though Owen tried to smile, too, he couldn't. " 'I hope that you are well and that you have found your happiness.' " Her voice broke again when she said the word "happiness." Then she said quietly, "And it's signed, 'Love, Ciara.' "

A tear rolled down Ellen's cheek, and she wiped

it away with the back of her hand. Then she carefully placed the letter down on the table next to Owen's bed.

Owen put both hands over his eyes and just sat there, trying to breathe.

• • •

Grace O'Malley stood on the cliff above the waterfall that streamed into the cove. She had no idea how many men *El Gran Grin* had aboard her when she ran aground the night before, but all that were left alive fit snugly into two small fishing boats, bound for the mainland and with a letter and enough of their own coins that Grace had plucked from her pockets to buy them passage home on whatever European vessel might have found its way to port on the west coast of Ireland. Of course, whether any of them actually made it home at all was of no concern to Grace O'Malley. Her bargain with Don Pedro was duly fulfilled, and she was at ease with her decision to spare them.

The locked, stone-filled treasure chest was paraded before her clan and buried under the watchtower in case anyone should ever come looking for her bounty.

She looked down into the cove and tossed the ornate gold key into the calm waters, returning it to the sea from whence it came.

...

Owen lay on his back, suspended by the saltwater.

It was cold, but he didn't care. Sunlight bathed his face. Years of dust and dirt felt like they were at long last washing away, his body finally cleansed.

The brown and black rocks of the cove framed the perfect blue sky. The water was a deep blue beneath him.

Gravity had slipped away.

A warm hand touched him, soft skin, then her body, more soft skin, and Ellen wrapped her naked body around him in the water.

He smiled when his face dipped below the surface, and she gently nudged him back up. She giggled softly in his ear. Their eyes met and then their lips.

And just out of the cove, on the open water, a line ran down from a little homemade buoy to a lobster pot. Nothing had crawled into it, but the pot had come to rest on a leather sack, already dissolving in the seawater.

In the trap, the glint of gold.

Then a cloud of sediment and the pot was pulled up by the line, and Derry hauled it into their lobster boat.

It was heavy, and Derry was sure they'd hit the mother lode of lobsters. He called to his brother for help, and Ryan stood up from where he manned the little outboard. He helped his brother pull the trap up, and there were no lobsters, but it was heavy. There was something in it, something heavy, something … gold!

Derry let go of the line, so surprised by what he saw, and Ryan almost lost his grip and let the lobster pot slip back underwater. Then Derry grabbed the line again and they had the pot, and the treasure of *El Gran Grin*, up and spilled out over the floor of their boat.

They stared at the gold, then each other, then the gold. Back and forth as if their heads were on synchronized springs. And then it finally hit them. This was actually happening. They fell into the pile of gold coins, whooping and asking the wind and the sea where this treasure had come from. They hugged and laughed.

The priceless treasure returned to the O'Malleys once more.

Ellen embraced Owen as he laid on his back, looking up into the clear blue sky. The laughter of the brothers ringing in his ears, he turned his head and looked up at the spot on the hill. His spot, where he'd imagined swimming in the cove with Ellen but never believed it would come true. And there was Patrick sitting there, still dressed in the same immaculate clothes. He smiled at Owen. A warm, loving, sincere smile that only siblings can share. Owen returned the smile, and Patrick got up from his resting place, turned, and walked down the hill to disappear over the horizon.

Lightning Source UK Ltd.
Milton Keynes UK
UKHW040959261119
354268UK00002B/476/P